I REMEMBER YOU

*Louise Brindley titles available from
Severn House Large Print*

Death on the Heath
A Presence in Her Life
Time Remembered
View From a Balcony

I REMEMBER YOU

Louise Brindley

Severn House Large Print
London & New York

This first large print edition published in Great Britain 2005 by
SEVERN HOUSE LARGE PRINT BOOKS LTD of
9-15 High Street, Sutton, Surrey, SM1 1DF.
First world regular print edition published 2004 by
Severn House Publishers, London and New York.
This first large print edition published in the USA 2005 by
SEVERN HOUSE PUBLISHERS INC., of
595 Madison Avenue, New York, NY 10022.

British Library Cataloguing in Publication Data

Brindley, Louise
  I remember you - Large print ed.
  1. England, Northern - Social life and customs - Fiction
  2. Large type books
  I. Title
  823.9'14 [F]

ISBN 0-7278-7409-8

Printed and bound in Great Britain by
MPG Books Ltd, Bodmin, Cornwall.

In memory of my friend
and mentor, the late,
great, James Herriot.

Prologue

It had been a long tiring day, but rewarding, inasmuch as she had seen her husband safely ensconced in the sanatorium where he'd be spending the next six weeks undergoing treatment to clear up what he light-heartedly referred to as 'a damp patch' on his chest.

The children had been brilliant, Frances thought, helpful and supportive – making her feel old. But then she *was* old. Not ancient as yet, but getting that way. She smiled inwardly, wondering if she should hang a 'handle with care' sign round her neck.

Driving her home from the sanatorium, seeing her into the house, mending the drawing-room fire and refuelling the kitchen Aga, her son Bill said gruffly, 'Look, Mum, either Polly or I will stay with you tonight. You look all in.'

'Thanks, but you'll do no such thing. I'll be perfectly fine on my own. Besides, I have things to do, a meal to cook, a letter to write to your father.'

'But, Mum,' Polly protested, 'it's almost nine o'clock! Shouldn't you be thinking about bed? Having an early night?'

'What, and waste a perfectly good fire and a

fresh fillet of plaice? No, love. I have no intention of having an early night. I'll probably be pottering about till midnight. And I really must write a letter to your father. I promised to write to him every day, and today is not yet over.'

Polly said. 'But, darling, you've spent practically the whole day together, what will you find to say to him in a letter?'

'I'll think of something,' Frances replied, taking off her outdoor things and smoothing her hair. Then, looking in the fridge, 'I do think that fish should be eaten the day it is caught, don't you? I'll have this grilled, with a squeeze of lemon and some brown bread and butter.'

'In other words, why don't I mind my own business?' Polly sighed, then laughed. 'All right, you win! Of all the stubborn women!'

Frances kissed her offspring goodnight, waved them goodbye as the car sped away, and then, alone but not lonely, she stood for a while on the doorstep to breathe in the fresh, clean air of an early summer evening, noticing the burgeoning buds of the lilacs she had planted many years ago, in what she now thought of as the summertime of her life, when she had married the father of her children. The one and only man in the world for her.

Now the children were married, with children of their own to care for – the reason she had refused their offers to stay overnight with her, not wanting to become a burden

8

to them.

Turning away from the doorstep and closing her front door firmly behind her, going through to the kitchen to grill her fillet of plaice, she thought that possibly Polly was right in her assessment of her as stubborn. She always had been, would ever remain so, if stubborness denoted independence, a part and parcel of who she was that had stood her in good stead throughout the many and varied aspects of her life so far, and which, pray God, would stand her in good stead for whatever time was left to her.

Her supper prepared and eaten, she went through to the drawing room to write the letter to her husband. The house was very still, very quiet. The drawing-room fire cast flickering shadows on the walls and ceiling. Switching on a table lamp next to her husband's favourite high-backed chair near the fireplace, pen in hand, notepaper poised on her lap, she wrote: 'My dearest dear D'

Tears blurred her vision momentarily; hastily she brushed them aside, knowing the last thing he would want from her was a downbeat letter. Theirs had been such a joyous relationship, so deep that each knew instinctively what the other was thinking and feeling. Laughter had been their lodestar: laughter and love, so no need to tell him what he already knew.

At the onset of his illness, he had held her close to his heart and told her not to worry unduly, that his return to health and strength

9

was merely a matter of time if he did as he was told, cut down on his normal workload, gave up smoking, and submitted to medical attention in a sanatorium specializing in the treatment of tuberculosis. Thankfully, his symptoms had been spotted early on. 'And so, my darling,' he'd said in that light-hearted way of his, 'I'm not about to end up like Mimi in the third act of *La Bohème*.'

'Huh, I should hope not, indeed,' she'd replied prissily, joining in the game of pretence for his sake. 'Who's Mimi by the way? An old girlfriend of yours?'

'Oh God,' he said, pseudo-dramatically, 'don't tell me you've found out about Mimi and me? How long have you known?'

'Ever since you took me to Covent Garden to see *La Bohème*,' Frances reminded him, tongue in cheek. 'Don't tell me you've forgotten. I'd never seen an opera before. I couldn't make head or tail of it to begin with, just as I couldn't make head or tail of Shakespeare until I saw the film version of Henry the Fifth.'

'Darling wife of mine,' her husband said quietly, 'I've never forgotten anything about you, and I never shall. That charming air of innocence about you, the way you wear your hair – that ridiculous floppy bun of yours, which I adore.'

'So *that's* what was on your mind, and there was I thinking you admired my culinary skill, not to mention my slender figure and floury hands, and my kind heart. Huh, I see it all

10

now! You weren't interested in me at all! Not my clothes, my face, my nose, my lips, my eyebrows, only my innocence! Well, had I known that at the time, I would never have consented to marry you, and that's that!'

Nestling into his arms she confessed, 'But I'm so glad that I did, that I took a chance on love. You see, my darling, I'd been in love with you for a long time, and I could scarcely believe my luck when you told me that you loved me too. I've never been able to figure out quite why.'

'Then let me remind you – as if you need reminding. Because I recognized in you a kindred spirit...'

Deep in thought, continuing her letter to her husband, Frances wrote:

Sitting here in your favourite chair, by fireglow and lamplight, I'm remembering so many facets of my old life. My first day at school, for instance, when, placed aboard a rocking horse, I pulled out the poor creature's mane and tail in a fit of desperation at being left alone in a strange place, without my mother's comforting presence to rely on.

When my mother died, there was no one to rely on except myself. We were terribly poor. I remember that Mother paid a shilling a week into a clothing club to ensure that my brothers and I had decent shoes on our feet. I've never told you this before. I can't think why not except that I felt ashamed to admit to anyone, even you, the grinding poverty of

11

our lives following the death of my father, and to describe my brothers' cavalier treatment of my mother.

Then, when war came, I joined the Women's Royal Naval Service. I've told you about the girl I met then. How long ago it all seems now, and how futile. So many hopeful beginnings leading to so many sad, inconclusive endings, until I met you.

I remember feeling that life had passed me by, that no matter how hard I tried to create a new life for myself, to drag myself from the morass of my past and my ignorance of art, music, literature, history, geography, politics, world events. Well, you name it. Then suddenly, miraculously, there was *you*, my darling, there was *you*!

Now, whatever else escapes me in this uncertain world of today, though I may well forget to pay the milkman, the butcher, the grocer, rest assured, my darling, that I'll never forget you!

In the words of a wartime song, 'When the angels ask me to recall the thrill of them all, then I shall tell them – I remember you'.

Part One

One

She had never really been aware of stars before, until the blackout. Hitherto, gas lamps had sprung to life when darkness fell, and she'd been too anxious to get home from work to look up at the sky.

Losing her mother so suddenly had come as a shock to an eighteen-year-old girl of limited experience, faced with the responsibility of housekeeping: washing, cooking and cleaning, ironing her brothers' laundry; making the necessary funeral arrangements; organizing a buffet lunch for the mourners after the church service, all of which had been left to her by her unhelpful siblings, who appeared not to care in the least that their mother was dead, so long as they had clean, well-ironed shirts to wear at the committal of Mary Abbot's coffin to the ground, next to that of their father, and plenty of food and drink to go at afterwards.

Later that evening, standing alone in the back garden, mourning her mother, Frances had looked up at the stars, sparkling like diamonds in the blue velvet of the sky; had, for the first time ever, glimpsed a world far above and beyond the misery of the human race. And to think that she had never noticed the stars before.

Next day she had lain down the law, in no uncertain terms, to her feckless siblings. 'From now on,' she'd decreed, 'you'd best cook your own suppers when you come home from work! See to your own washing and ironing! I'm your sister, remember, not your slave! Mum thought the sun shone out of you, but *I* don't! I see you for what you really are, a couple of lazy layabouts who took advantage of our mother all the days of her life. Well, you'll not take advantage of *me*, and that's a promise!'

When her brothers had received their call-up papers, and when she had gone to live, temporarily, with her Aunt Dorothy, Frances had regretted parting with them on bad terms. Alan and Ernest were, after all, her own flesh and blood, and yet, as hard as she tried, she could not entirely forgive them their treatment of their patient, hardworking mother during her lifetime. The way they had teased her and made fun of her best-end-of-neck mutton stews, grumbled at the thickness of her pastry, forever hinting at the kind of grub their workmates' mothers provided for their families, forgetful of Mary's straitened financial circumstances since the death of their father and her all too apparent weariness and ill-health in her uphill struggle to keep a roof over their heads, let alone afford the kind of food they hinted at. Pork, chicken and steak and kidney indeed!

'Wait till you're in the army. You'll eat what you're given and like it,' Frances had told them heatedly, sick and tired of the pair of them. 'You're as much use as those pot dogs on the mantelpiece!'

She had been at work when her brothers had left. Returning to an empty house, tired, hungry and forlorn, she had burst into tears, struck by the realization that an old familiar way of life was over and done with for ever. Next week would bring the removal of her parents' belongings to a saleroom, the handing over of the house keys to the landlord and her own removal to her Aunt Dorothy's cheerless Victorian villa on the far side of town, a daunting prospect which she dreaded. But, as her mother had so often reminded her, beggars could not be choosers.

Aunt Dorothy, she knew, would not welcome her with open arms. She'd be given a cold, linoleumed room on the top floor and be expected to help with the housework and cooking and stump up her meagre wages to pay for her room and board – apart from five shillings pocket money per week to spend on bus fares, shoe repairs and what her aunt termed 'women's necessities'. This had been made abundantly clear to her beforehand. Aunt Dorothy regarded visits to the pictures as a waste of time and money; cinemas were dens of vice to be avoided at all cost. But Frances loved cinema-going as a means of escape from the boredom of everyday life, and had no intention of giving up that source of entertainment to please anyone – especially not a bigoted old woman such as her Aunt Dorothy.

Beggars could not be choosers? Well, here was one beggar who would choose her own path through life. And so, during one lunch break from work, Frances had gone downtown to the Labour Exchange to apply for admission to the Women's Royal Naval Service, in whatever capacity, as a cook or a steward, she didn't care which just as long as she could be shot of her aunt, free to live her own life.

And so, in the fullness of time, Frances had received a travel warrant to a Wren training centre near the east coast of Scotland in a town called Dunfermline, adjacent to the shipyards at Rosyth – to her aunt's shocked disbelief that a niece of hers had actually gone behind her back and left her in the lurch.

'What ever would your mother have thought?' had been her cri de coeur. 'After all I've done for you? Taking you into my home the way I have done. Well, no good will come of it in my opinion, young lady! The trouble with you, you don't know when you're well off! But then I daresay you take after your father, a chancer if ever there was one! I begged Mary not to marry him, but would she listen to me? Oh no! And look what came of it! My poor sister left penniless with four mouths to feed. Now *this*!'

18

'I'm sorry you feel that way, Aunt Dorothy,' Frances replied, 'but please don't denigrate my father. He didn't ask to die and leave my mother alone to bring up their children. That she managed to do so redounds to her credit, don't you think? As to all you've done for me, what does that amount to? A draughty attic room, as cold as Christmas; allowing me five shillings a week from my wages and keeping the rest for yourself, denying me the right to go to the pictures once in a while; using me as a servant. What ever would my mother have thought of *that*, I wonder? Not much, I daresay. Think about it, Aunt Dorothy. Think about love and charity, so sadly lacking in your own life that you dare to question the love of my parents for one another!

'I'll be leaving here early tomorrow morning. Won't you at least wish me luck?' she concluded.

She might have known what her aunt's reaction would be: a refusal to even bid her goodnight, much less to wish her good luck for the future.

And so, Frances had left the house early next morning, alone and unsung, to catch her train to Scotland and the unpredictable future awaiting her in a 'foreign' land, far from home.

Alighting from the train at Edinburgh's Waverley Station, following a seemingly endless journey to the back of beyond, she'd been met at the barrier by a young sailor, a

19

transport driver detailed to escort her to the WRNS training centre near Dunfermline.

'My name's Joe Fisk,' he told her. 'And you are Frances Abbot from Middleton in Yorkshire. I can spot a trainee Wren a mile off, despite the civilian clothing. It's the worried look that gives 'em away, that an' the gas mask cases.' He grinned amiably. 'Just hop aboard the transport and we'll be on our way.'

Half an hour later Fisk had nosed the bonnet of the transport vehicle into a compound of low buildings, mainly Nissen huts, bounded by barbed-wire fencing hung with warning notices emblazoned with the words: MOD PROPERTY. ALL PASSES MUST BE SHOWN. GUARD DOGS ON PATROL. There was a guard house at the entrance gates, from which stepped a fearsome-looking man in naval uniform to establish their identities.

Frances's heart had sunk to her shoes. The last thing she'd expected was a kind of concentration camp at her journey's end. Worse was to come: a narrow, barracks-style dormitory lined with iron bedsteads to accommodate twenty girls or more. Frances, who had never shared a bedroom in her life, shuddered at the lack of privacy. Allocated an end bed, near the door, having stowed away her gear in a green locker under the watchful eyes of a stout Wren chief petty officer, she was taken to the ward room to have her papers checked by a first officer, from thence to a refectory to be fed, of all things, best end of neck mutton stew, followed by rhubarb crumble and custard. Above all things – well nearly – Frances abhorred rhubarb and custard.

'You're new here, aren't you?' the pretty, fair-haired girl seated next to her asked quietly. 'Not to worry, you'll soon get used to it. I'm fairly new myself, but the girls are a decent bunch on the whole. My name's Cathy Crawford, by the way. What's yours?'

'Frances Abbot, Fran.'

'Feeling homesick, are you? Missing your family, I daresay.' Cathy sighed deeply. 'So am I. So are we all, come to think of it, but we're all in the same boat, so we'd best make the best of a bad job.'

She paused, than said, 'You can ring home, after supper, and there's a writing room, a bit of a library, picture shows two nights a week, and a Saturday night hop. We're also allowed out one evening a week to go to a proper cinema or dance, so it isn't all doom and gloom. Oh, and there's cocoa or tea and biscuits at nine o'clock, and a canteen where we can buy sweets and ciggies, and a common room with a record player, only it's too noisy in there, so I give it a miss. I prefer peace and quiet myself. How about you? I'll show you round, if you like, when you've finished your supper.'

'I have finished, thank you.'

'But you've scarcely eaten a bite,' Cathy said doubtfully, eyeing Fran's plate, 'and you'll need to keep your strength up. It's pretty hot down in the kitchens, then there's

21

lectures and squad drill practice, which seems a bit daft really since we're still in civvies. But there'll be a passing-out parade when we've got our uniforms, and we've been warned what will happen to us if we put a foot wrong.'

'Squad drill?' Fran's heart plummeted. 'You mean standing in line? But I can't! I mean I couldn't!' The thought of it filled her with dread. She'd faint, as she had done once at school during choir practice, standing in line with the other kids, needing something to hang on to. But there hadn't been anything to hang on to, and so she had fallen down in a dead faint. Never would she forget the horror of that moment of blackness: coming round to the dreadful realization that she had wet her knickers. She'd been ten years old at the time, what her mother called 'highly strung', lacking in self- confidence.

'Don't worry, you'll soon get the hang of it,' Cathy assured her kindly. 'Now I'd best show you where the phones are. You'll feel tons better when you've talked to your mum and dad.'

Seldom before or since had Frances felt so lonely, so isolated and bereft as she had done then, with no one to turn to for love and understanding. And so, venturing outdoors for a moment or two to gulp in breaths of fresh air, she had looked up at the stars.

Suddenly she had known, in her contemplation of the night sky, that the only way to conquer fear was to face it head on. She had at least escaped from the chilling confines of her Aunt Dorothy's abode to begin a new life of her own choosing. Now it was up to her to screw up her courage and emerge from the constraints of the past not as a cipher, but as an individual.

A few weeks later she left Dunfermline with a sense of relief at being rid of the cookery lectures, the hot food smells wafting from the ovens and having to wear overalls, and aprons when it came to scouring pots and pans and the flat metal trays in which the pork and mutton chops were cooked.

No sooner was one meal cooked and served than preparations for the next were under way. Sick and tired of the sight and smell of food, Fran had looked forward to her posting to a signals station on the outskirts of London as the Israelites must have looked forward to a land flowing with milk and honey.

On the eve of her departure to fresh fields and pastures new she had written to her Aunt Dorothy and her brothers, informing them of her promotion and giving them her new address should they need to get in touch with her. Not that she had received word from any of them since leaving Middleton. Alan and Ernest might well have been posted abroad, and Aunt Dorothy had not even bothered to send her a Christmas card last December.

Well, so be it. At least she'd received cards from her fellow Wrens. Moreover, the interiors of the grim Nissen huts in the compound had been festooned with balloons and sprigs of holly and there had been a candlelit Christmas tree in the refectory and a Christmas Eve carol service in the small chapel adjoining the main buildings. This had brought tears to her eyes, recalling her mother's efforts to make Christmas a joyous occasion for herself and her brothers, providing chicken for Christmas dinner and giving them the best presents she could afford from her meagre income: socks and hankies for her sons, a bottle of scent for her daughter, usually a small watch-shaped bottle of 4711 eau de cologne.

Nothing, of course, had ever been good enough for her brothers. A hard burden for Mum to bear. She'd said little, but Fran could see the pain in her eyes at her son's jeering remarks about the grub. 'Not bloody chicken again?' from Alan. 'The trouble with you, Ma, you've got no imagination. What? No stuffing? No sausages? Just onions, taters, sprouts and bloody parsnips? An' I'll bet any money there'll be damn-all fruit in the Christmas pudd'n'!'

'Please, son, you know I don't like hearing you swear.'

'The grub in this house would make a saint swear.' This from Ernest, who always followed his brother's lead. 'Why can't we have turkey an' all the trimmings, like other fellas?'

Fran had bitten back many an angry rejoinder for her mother's sake. Only after her death had she felt it expedient to tell her brothers what she really thought of them, when angry words couldn't harm their mother any longer. Poor, patient Mary Abbot who had died of heart failure. A broken heart, more likely, in Fran's opinion.

All over and done with now, she thought, climbing aboard the transport to Waverley Station, where, on a cold February morning, proudly aware of her smart Wren greatcoat and newly acquired pillbox hat, she had awaited the arrival of the train that would carry her from Scotland to ... *London*.

Two

Tanglewood Signals Station, near Wimbledon Common, seen through snow flurries on the winter afternoon of Fran's arrival, bore similar characteristics to the training centre at Dunfermline inasmuch as KEEP OUT warnings were posted on the perimeter fencing and barbed-wire entanglements, and yet she could not supress a feeling of elation that she had, by her own application and hard work, escaped from a future spent slaving over a hot stove.

Soon she discovered that slaving over a 'hot' teleprinter was no easy option. At least the work she was engaged in was far more rewarding than peeling vegetables and beating Yorkshire pudding batter. Moreover, the sleeping accommodation was more to her liking. Now she shared a room, known as a cabin, with five girls, not twenty, all of whom were on the same watch as herself. Their names were Delia, Daphne, Anna, Mamie and Pearl – quiet, well-educated girls, the crème de la crème of the Women's Royal Naval Service, all of whom had been friendly towards her, especially Pearl, a charming girl who had given no indication that she was, in fact, the daughter of a hereditary baronet. In short, the Honourable Pearl Galsworthy was the offspring of Sir Henry Galsworthy, a member of the Wartime Cabinet, and a personal friend of Winston Churchill.

To think that there she was, Frances Abbot, a bit of a jumped-up nobody from Middleton, rubbing shoulders with the aristocracy. A lass who had left school at fourteen and gone to work in a grocer's shop!

Realizing that Fran had discovered her identity, Pearl had taken her aside one evening after supper and explained the function of the the Wren uniform, or any other, come to think of it, as a levelling influence, ensuring that no one person, unless they had risen through the ranks, would be deemed better than the rank and file. 'All promotion proves,' she'd said sagely, 'is that some women are more ambitious than others. Nothing wrong with that. Some are born to lead, others to serve. How does the sonnet

26

go? "They also serve, who only stand and wait"? What I'm trying to say is this, as far as I'm concerned, there isn't a ha'porth of difference between the pair of us. You're a Wren, so am I, and we have our uniforms to prove it! OK?'

'Yes. Thanks, Pearl. But you're clever, well educated, well off, too, I daresay, with a posh house, servants, doting parents. Well, my parents are dead, and I haven't got a home.'

'Perhaps not, but you've got a brain in your head, free will, independence, a great future ahead of you if you'll stop feeling sorry for yourself and start looking forward. There'll always be people better off than yourself, much worse off, too.' She paused, then, 'What is it you want from life? Money? A posh house? Servants? Well, I can tell you right here and now that the only thing that matters a damn is integrity, being proud not ashamed of who and what you are deep down, setting yourself standards and living up to them come hell or high water.'

Shivering slightly, she added, 'Sorry, Fran, I didn't mean to give you a lecture, just a friendly word of two of advice. For what it's worth, you're wrong about me. My parents are far from doting, they are both too busy to give a damn about me. The reason why I joined up was to get away from the pair of them. So now you know!'

Early next morning, on her way to the tele-printer room to begin her five-hour-long watch, Fran bumped into a young sailor on his way from the wireless room along the corridor, bearing a sheaf of messages that scattered like leaves in a high wind as a result of their brief bodily impact.

'I'm sorry, miss,' he apologized, bending down to pick up the signals, 'I wasn't looking where I was going. You're not hurt, are you?'

'No. I wasn't looking where I was going, either. Here, let me give you a hand.'

When the messages had been retrieved, he asked, 'Are you new here? I haven't seen you before.'

'I came in February,' Fran said, 'about a month ago.' He had a nice face, she noticed, not handsome, but pleasant, with keen blue eyes and a generous mouth. His hair was light brown in colour, and he was tall and thin with a prominent Adam's apple. He looked vulnerable somehow, young, eager and expectant. Smiling up at him, she said, 'Well, I'd best be getting along now. The night watch girls will be be ready for breakfast. I know how they'll be feeling: dog tired and hungry.'

Turning away, she hurried to the teleprinter room. At the same moment, the other girls of her watch appeared at the end of the corridor, laughing and talking. Following in Fran's wake, the young sailor delivered his messages to the chief Wren, with whom he exchanged pleasantries before returning to the wireless room, smiling at Fran en passant.

The note had come as a surprise, written on a scrap of paper and handed to her surreptitiously by the young sailor when he came into the TP room to deliver another sheaf of messages an hour later.

Daphne Fairclough, seated at the next teleprinter, hissed urgently. 'Put that note in your money belt! For heaven's sake don't let Chief see it. You'll both be in hot water if she does. You *and* Eddie!' The chief petty officer in charge of No. 4 Watch was an eagle-eyed woman currently engaged in sorting through the new messages prior to handing them out to the five operators sitting at their various softly clacking machines.

Immediately, albeit furtively, Fran slipped the note into the money belt strapped about her waist, not wanting to cause trouble for Eddie, let alone herself, at the same time wondering what kind of message his note contained. Above all, what had prompted him to write to her in the first place? She'd never received a 'billet doux' before.

In essence, when she read the note later in the privacy of her cabin, she realized that the young sailor she had bumped into earlier that day had simply written a note of apology for his clumsiness in the corridor, ending with the words: 'If you are free this evening, perhaps we could meet at, say, eight o'clock, for a coffee and a chinwag. In the forces' canteen in the Methodist Church Hall basement near the War Memorial? Yours truly, Eddie Musgrove.'

The forces canteen was full to overflowing

with off-duty army, naval and air force personnel. It was dimly lit, noisy and fuggy with cigarette smoke. There were chairs and tables surrounding a small dance area, a snooker table, a stage with drawn curtains at the far end of the room and a counter with a tea urn; above which hung a list of the hot food items available.

Fran entered the room to the sound of 'We'll Meet Again', sung by Vera Lynn, a recording played on a wind-up gramophone, the click of snooker balls, gusts of laughter and the buzz of conversation. Rising quickly to his feet, Eddie came towards her, smiling. 'I'm so glad you came,' he said. 'I've saved you a seat, and I've managed to find a table for two near the platform. That's it, over yonder. Best hurry, before someone else nabs it. You go ahead, I'll bring the coffee – unless you'd prefer tea.'

'No. Coffee will be fine. No sugar.' Slightly nervous and ill at ease in unfamiliar surroundings, Fran wended her way to the vacant table, wondering if she had done the right thing in accepting an invitation from a comparative stranger. Still, a Methodist church hall seemed an innocuous meeting place. Had Eddie Musgrove suggested a drink in a bar parlour, warning bells would have rung in her mind, and she would have torn up his note and stayed in quarters to read a book. Or would she? Hadn't she felt flattered, intrigued, to be asked out by a seemingly decent, honourable young man?

Of course she had. Now he was coming towards her with the coffee.

He said, 'I had the feeling you might have decided not to come. I mean, it was cheeky of me, sending you that note. It's just that I kinda liked the way you helped me to pick up those signals. Most girls wouldn't have taken the trouble. I just figured that you'd be a nice person to talk to, quiet and understanding, like. Maybe in need of a bit of company, being a newcomer an' all.' He paused, then, 'Have you been here before?'

'No, I haven't been anywhere much,' she admitted. 'There hasn't been time, what with one thing and another: getting used to new surroundings, a new job. I've just changed categories, you see. I started out as a trainee cook. Now I'm a teleprinter operator, and, well, I have to concentrate hard on what I'm doing for fear of making mistakes.'

'Yeah, I know what you mean,' Eddie replied. 'There's so much at stake, isn't there? Other people's lives. It's the same with me. I was a painter and decorator in civvy street. Now I'm a wireless operator. Doesn't make much sense, does it? Doing one thing one minute, another thing the next? A few weeks' training then suddenly, wham, you're in at the deep end, wondering if you're up to it. Being responsible for other men's lives, I mean.'

Fran's heart warmed to him at that moment, and she thought that here was a man as decent and honourable as she had

31

imagined him to be.

'I come here quite often, myself,' he continued. 'The coffee's not much cop, neither is the grub, but I like the atmosphere, meeting up with blokes in the same boat as me, enjoying the odd game of snooker. listening to that Vera Lynn record over an' over again.' He grinned amiably. 'Frankly, I wish they'd give it a rest once in a while, that an' The Ink Spots singing "Whispering Grass". I'm into classical music myself. But I don't suppose anyone here would want to listen to the Moonlight Sonata or a Chopin nocturne. Would *you*?'

'I don't know much about music. I was in the school choir when I was ten, but all I remember is having to practice "Nymphs and Shepherds", which I hated, though I did listen to "The Chocolate Soldier" on the wireless, and I enjoyed that,' Fran explained self-consciously.

Eddie pulled a wry face. ' "Nymphs and Shepherds". Ugh! Enough to give any kid the hump! Tell you what, they have classical concerts upstairs in the church once in a while. I could get a couple of tickets if you like. What do you say? Would you like to come with me? I'm sure you'd enjoy it, and it isn't all highbrow music.'

Not wanting to dampen his enthusiasm, Fran said, 'Yes, that's fine by me,' wondering what she was letting herself in for; what, if anything, all this was leading up to. Was it remotely possible that Eddie found her physically attractive? Had his sights set on her as his girlfriend – in present-day parlance? If so, she'd best beware. She liked him well enough, but she knew next to nothing about him. He might be married, for all she knew. There were far better looking girls than herself, with far more sex appeal and personality. So why choose her?

He continued engagingly, 'Tell me more about yourself. What did *you* do in civvy street?'

'Oh, *that*? I worked in a grocer's shop when I left school at fourteen.' She spoke proudly, defiantly, defensively. 'I wasn't very bright. Besides, my mum was poorly at the time, and she needed the money. Not that my wages amounted to much, but she was glad of them just the same to help keep a roof over our heads, Dad having died young and her being left alone to feed and clothe my two brothers and me. Not that she cared much about herself. All she really cared about was her family, paying the rent, the gas bills, the food bills and so on. That was the reason why she died young, I suppose – it became too much for her to bear.'

Eddie said quietly, 'I'm so sorry. I didn't mean to pry. Please forgive me, miss— I'm sorry, I don't know your name.'

'You *don't*?' She regarded him thoughtfully across the table, ashamed of her misgivings concerning his motives. A man who didn't even know her name could not possibly have made enquiries about her beforehand, as a deceiver intent on seduction would surely have done. 'My name is Frances Abbot. Fran for short.'

'Pleased to meet you, I'm sure, Fran,' he responded warmly. 'Another coffee? Or would you rather I walked you back to the Wrennery? I just have a hunch you're out of your element here, am I right?'

Fran nodded. 'Yes, sorry. I'm not used to crowds. Sure you don't mind?'

'Not in the least.' Helping her into her greatcoat, he promised, 'We'll go somewhere quieter next time. There's a nice little caff a bus stop away, with quiet background music, lamp lights and proper tablecloths. I'd have asked you to meet me there tonight, except...'

'Except what?'

'Well, *you* know! I figured you might turn me down flat if you thought I was rushing things, trying to get fresh with you, or whatever, in a hurry, which I'm not, I assure you.'

Stepping outdoors into the cold air of a blustery March night, beneath a star-littered sky, closing the door on the noise, heat and confusion of the basement canteen, Eddie confessed, 'The truth is, I need someone to talk to right now. Someone kind and sympathetic, such as yourself. You see, I have a problem to solve, and I don't know what to do about it.'

Walking towards the signals station, Fran asked, 'What kind of problem? uncertain of her ground as a female Father Confessor, not

34

quite knowing how to respond to the fact that she had been singled out by Eddie not because he fancied her – a slap in the face for any woman – but because he needed a friendly shoulder to cry on. 'How can I advise you until I know what's bothering you? In any case, what makes you think I can help sort out your problem?'

'It's my fiancée,' Eddie blurted. 'Her name's Elsie. We were childhood sweethearts, so called. We lived next door to one another, went to the same school. Well, to cut a long story short, we got engaged on her eighteenth birthday, and that was that. Now she's pestering me to get married. She's got everything planned down to the last detail. Her mother's even started hoarding currants for the cake.'

'I see. So what's the problem?' Fran frowned.

'The problem is, I don't want to marry her.' Eddie sighed deeply. 'I know now that I'm not in love with her, and never was. I always thought of her as a sister, not a wife.'

'Then why did you ask her to marry you?'

'That's just it. I didn't. When I asked her what she wanted for her birthday, she said she'd seen a ring she fancied in a jeweller's shop window, so I bought it for her. Next thing I knew she'd slipped it on her engagement finger, started crying, saying how happy I'd made her, and wanted to know how soon we'd be getting married.

'Later on, at her birthday party, she

announced to all and sundry, friends, neighbours, her parents and mine, that we were engaged to be married, and there I was being congratulated, with Elsie clinging to me like a leech telling everyone that I'd made her the happiest girl in the world. So what the hell was I supposed to do? Tell her it was all a mistake?

'As luck had it, I was due for call-up the following Monday. I'd dreaded the thought of joining up, till then. But when the time came I couldn't wait to get away from Elsie. Cowardly of me, I know. I should have told her at the station, when she came to say goodbye, that there wasn't going to be a wedding. But how could I? She was in floods of tears, begging me to write to her every day, telling me how much she loved me, making me promise we'd get married on my first leave.

'Well, I'm due leave in a fortnight from now. But I can't face going home, I really can't! It'll be embarkation leave this time, you see.'

'*This* time?' Fran frowned perplexedly. 'You mean you've been on leave before and not gone home? Not told anyone? So where did you go? What did you do?'

'The first leave,' he admitted, 'I spent in London, sightseeing, staying in bed and breakfast accommodation near King's Cross Station. The second leave I spent in Wales at a youth hostel near Caernarvon; walking the hills, breathing in fresh air, trying to come to terms with the future. Not succeeding very well, I'm afraid.' He smiled grimly. 'Well, now you know me for what I am. A spineless fool of a man, about to make the greatest mistake of his life. So what do you think? What would you advise me to do about it?'

'The only thing you *can* do about it,' Fran said. 'Go home and marry the girl. It's the only decent option in my opinion. Who knows, you might even be in love with her, deep down, if you take the trouble to find out. You've known her long enough, for heaven's sake, so you must have a lot in common, otherwise you'd have given her the brush-off ages ago.'

'There's more to it than that,' he said quietly. 'You see, Fran, I think I'm in love with someone else. I think I'm in love with you.'

Staring at him, aghast, Fran exclaimed, 'Are you out of your mind? Do you think I was born yesterday? Oh, take that silly look off your face and talk sense!'

Anger boiled up in her. 'In love with *me*? For heaven's sake, man, we only met this morning. You'll be telling me next it was love at first sight!'

'It *was*,' Eddie uttered dejectedly, unprepared for Fran's outburst of indignation against him. 'The minute I saw you, I knew that you were the only girl in the world for me.'

'Huh! A likely story! Know what *I* think? That you saw me as an escape route. What you're after is an excuse not to marry Elsie. It would ease your conscience, wouldn't it, to write her a letter telling her you'd met someone else? Asking her to release you from your engagement. Far easier than admitting you'd been stringing her along with no valid reason for not wanting to go ahead with the wedding. Well, it won't wash! If you really don't want to marry the girl, at least have the moral fibre to tell her so, face to face. Don't drag me into it!'

Reaching the gates of Tanglewood, feeling sick at heart, searching in her shoulder bag for her identity card to show to the security guard, she had one thought in mind: to get back to the Wrennery as quickly as possible. Turning her back to Eddie, she said, 'This is as far as I'm prepared to go with you, now or at any time in the future. Understood?'

The security guard chuckled. He said, 'That's right, miss, you tell him! Made a pass at you, did he?' to which question Fran made no reply. How could she? She was far too angry and upset to do anything save wish that she had never set eyes on Eddie Musgrove in the first place.

A few days later, she received a letter from him. Opening it, she read:

Dear Fran,
    Just to let you know that I meant what I said when I told you of my feelings towards you. Thanking you for your advice concerning my future, I've decided to go ahead with my marriage to Elsie.

38

Just one favour I'd like to ask of you: there's a concert in the Methodist church, next Friday night. Please find enclosed a ticket. We won't be able to sit together. My seat is at the back of the platform, yours in the auditorium facing the platform. The guest artiste is the world renowned pianist Pouishnoff, and it would mean a great deal to me if you were there. If you do come, I'll take it as a sign that I'm forgiven for my bad behaviour. I hope you'll enjoy the concert and not think too badly of,

   Yours truly,
   Eddie

Fingering the ticket, Fran saw that the concert was due to begin at seven thirty p.m., which meant she had no valid excuse not to go, Friday being a rest day prior to the dreaded and aptly named 'Waterloo': morning watch preceding a week of night watches.

Digesting the contents of the letter, she wondered if she had been too harsh, too dogmatic in advising Eddie to go ahead with the wedding? What if she had condemned him to a lifetime of regret with a girl he wasn't in love with? Had she mistaken his motives in believing him capable of using her as a scapegoat to call off the wedding?

If only he hadn't told her he loved her. Now she thought that she could have scarcely reacted more violently had he told her he hated her. Why hadn't she listened to what he had to say, instead of flying off the handle the way she had done, in much the same way that she had flown off the handle with her brothers when, after the death of their mother, she had told them, in no uncertain terms, exactly what she thought of them? To what purpose? For all she knew she may never set eyes on them again. Just as, after the Pouishnoff concert, she might not set eyes on Eddie Musgrove ever again.

He had spoken of embarkation leave, which meant he would soon be leaving Tanglewood to serve aboard ship or, less perilously, somewhere in the Middle East. Wherever, his life would be at risk, especially at sea, on convoy duty. At this stage of the war, Allied shipping was under constant attack from enemy submarines: losses had been astronomical. Fran's heart sank at the thought of Eddie, a decent, ordinary young man, like so many others, caught up in a war the purpose of which they scarcely understood, their lives in jeopardy from enemy torpedoes.

The least she could do, Fran thought, setting off to attend the concert, was to assure Eddie, by her appearance in the church, that he was forgiven – if there was anything to forgive him for.

Finding her seat, she thought how this war had changed her from the quiet, compliant person she used to be into someone entirely different. Had standing on her own feet been responsible for alienating those nearest to her, her brothers, Aunt Dorothy, now Eddie?

Not that she had regarded him as anything more than an acquaintance, but she had been attracted by his decency, for want of a better word – his looks, his manners – so why had she dismissed him?

The church was packed to capacity. Glancing about her, Fran noticed the blacked-out windows, the platform with its solitary grand piano and an edging of early spring flowers, behind which rose the church organ and the choir stalls. Looking up, Fran saw Eddie sitting there, shoulders bent forward, head lowered as if in prayer, a forlorn figure. Then, suddenly straightening his shoulders, sitting upright, smiling faintly, his eyes met hers and she smiled back at him.

Seconds later, the figure of the maestro appeared on the stairs leading to the platform. An elderly man with a mane of white hair, the peerless pianist Pouishnoff ignored the burst of applause from the audience, sat down at the piano, ran his fingers over the keyboard and began playing the opening chords of Liszt's 'Liebestraum'.

One might have heard a pin drop, so quiet, so intense was the silence apart from the music, those crystal clear notes falling like cleansing rain into the lives of a generation of people, young and old, in need of spiritual refreshment from a war-torn world.

Listening to the music, Fran understood that Eddie had sent her a ticket to the concert so that she might share his love of classical music, draw solace from it as he had done.

Should she wait for him after the concert to wish him well? To apologize to him for her brusqueness? No, better not, she decided. She had proved to him, by her presence here tonight, that she was sorry for her actions. So what was there left to say?

Towards the end of the concert, edging her way to an exit, Fran paused momentarily to catch a final glimpse of Eddie's face, before stepping outdoors into the cold night air of a never-to-be-forgotten evening during which she had discovered not just the joy of classical music, but something even more important: her own shortcomings as a human being.

Three

Presumably Eddie had begun his embarkation leave. Fran had not seen him since the night of the concert. A fatiguing week of night watches during which signals had flooded into the TP room, followed by shallow daytime sleep in a blacked-out cabin invaded by the sounds of everyday life – the whirring of vacuum cleaners, the ringing of telephone bells in the duty office on the floor below, the chatter of conversation in the corridor outside the cabin, despite the 'Girls Sleeping' notice tacked up on the cabin door – had caused her to toss and turn restlessly in her narrow bed.

In the early hours of one morning, midway through their spell of night watches, sitting down on her bed in her dressing gown, Pearl Galsworthy asked anxiously, 'What's bothering you, Fran? Are you ill? If so, why not have a word with the MO? Report sick? That way you'll be relieved from duty and spared the remainder of our night watches. Think about it, Fran. Promise me you'll think about it?'

'Thanks, Pearl, but I'm not ill, just tired.' Fran attempted a smile. 'Well, I'm not the only one, am I? How do you think I'd feel reporting sick when I'm not? I have something on my mind, at the moment. Something I can't come to terms with right now.'

'Fair enough,' Pearl conceded, liking the girl enormously for her honesty. 'Right then, think about this. In case you'd forgotten, we, that is you and I and the rest of the girls of Number Four Watch, are due a long weekend's leave come Friday. So how would you like to spend it with me at my home in Gloucestershire?' Chuckling softly, she added, 'No sleeping problems there, I assure you. You'll probably die of boredom – all those rolling acres of land and not a damn thing to do except eat and sleep.'

'But I couldn't,' Fran demurred.

'Why not?'

'Because – well, you know why not. I don't belong in your kind of world. I wouldn't know what to say to your parents.'

'No need to worry about that. Daddy won't

43

be there. He has a bolt hole near the Foreign Office. Chances are that Mummy will be there too, doing what she sees as her duty, organizing various fundraising events in aid of the war effort, in her own inimitable way.' Pearl sighed deeply. 'My mother loves playing Lady Bountiful, you see. Chairing committees, delegating responsibility – more specifically, keeping an eagle eye on my father, who has been known to stray from the straight and narrow occasionally with some bright-eyed, bushy-tailed secretary or other. So what do you say? Will you come home with me?'

It was a big, rambling house with broad stairs, mullioned landing windows and a complexity of corridors and narrower staircases leading to what had been the servants' quarters in years gone by, when The Grange had engaged a small army of domestics to light fires, cook and clean, wait at table, tend the children, polish silver, wash and iron clothes and see to the garden.

The massive front door, beneath a pillared portico, had been opened by an imposingly tall and well-built woman with short, iron-grey hair, dressed pompadour fashion, who Pearl had introduced as Mrs Bates, the housekeeper, and to whom she had in turn introduced Fran as 'A chum of mine, Frances Abbot,' adding, 'So where are you putting us? Any old corner will do. We've just finished a week of night watches, so all we need is a good kip till we've come to our senses.'

'I made up your bed when I knew you were coming,' Mrs Bates replied equably, 'and I've made up a bed for Miss Abbot in your dressing room. A good kip, indeed! Knowing you, young lady, you'll be awake half the night gassing!'

'How well you know me, Batesie,' Pearl laughed. 'No pulling the wool over your eyes.' Obviously a deep bond of friendship existed between the two women, Fran realized.

'So I should, the time I've known you,' 'Batesie' responded chirpily, leading the way upstairs to a bedroom on the first landing, a front room with windows overlooking the garden – the most beautiful room Fran had ever seen, with a tester bed, walnut furniture, pink-shaded lamps and fitted wardrobes with full-length mirrors. A door led through to the dressing room, in which a single bed with a puffy rose-coloured eiderdown and matching sheets and pillowcases had been prepared for her.

'The bathroom's through that door yonder,' Pearl said airily. 'You go first. There's bound to be lashings of hot water.'

'Yes, but only five inches each,' Mrs Bates reminded them. 'There's a war on, remember?'

'Oh, so there is! So that's why we're in uniform.' Pearl laughed. 'Any chance of a cuppa when we've abluted and put on our dressing gowns?'

'I'll put the kettle on to boil,' Batesie said, heading towards the landing, 'and start the supper.'

'Don't tell me you've killed the fatted calf,' Pearl quipped.

'Huh, chance'd be a fine thing. There ain't no fatted calves to kill nowadays,' Batesie grumbled. 'Not that I've ever fancied veal myself, so you'll have to make do with shepherd's pie. Thankfully, Bates,' referring to her husband, 'has kept the kitchen garden going, so there's always plenty of vegetables to go at, especially potatoes. I've taken to calling him "Potato Pete" lately, after that "Dig for Victory" character Lord Woolton's always on about.' She added, over her shoulder, 'Come down to the kitchen when you're ready. Have you brought your ration cards with you, by the way?'

Stepping into her five inches of water after ridding herself of her uniform, Fran marvelled at the bathroom fittings: the shell pink bathroom suite with gold-plated taps, the bottles of bath essences and skin perfume in the bath rack and the pile of fluffy pink bath towels arrayed on a Victorian towel holder. A far cry from her old environment in Middleton with its plain white bathroom suite and the glass shelf above the wash basin filled to overflowing with her brothers' shaving gear – damp shaving brushes and hastily discarded razors – left there for their mother to clear up after them, along with the thin, damp towels littering the floor.

Never before had she been aware so acutely,

so painfully, of the differences between the haves and have nots of this world: between gracious living and dire poverty. Yet here she was, a guest in a rich man's home, revelling in luxury, remembering her mother's valiant attempts to create a loving home for herself and her siblings, despite the constant spectre of poverty overshadowing all their lives.

After a cup of tea in the kitchen, Pearl showed Fran the downstairs rooms of The Grange. 'This used to be the dining room before the war,' she explained, opening the door to reveal a long polished Regency table surrounded by richly brocaded dining chairs beneath a crystal chandelier. 'Mummy and Daddy used to entertain lavishly here in the old days. Of course, we had servants then to serve the food and pour the wine. All in the past now. The male servants disappeared, one by one, to join the army, navy or air force, and the maids went into munitions' factories, the ATS or the WAAF, which effectively put paid to the so-called good old days.

'Can't say I'm sorry to see the back of them! I simply loathed all that spurious pomp and ceremony, being waited on and called "miss" by girls of my own age, subservient because their livelihood, their very existence depended on their servility, their willingness to kowtow to folk better off than themselves.

'Here's another relic of the past,' she continued deprecatingly. 'The drawing room. Note the grand piano, silver-framed photographs, oil paintings, marble fireplace, velvet curtains, deep settees and the armchairs. Imagine my parents, in full evening regalia, holding court here following a blow-out dinner in the dining room, being waited on, hand and foot, by their paid employees.'

'Please, Pearl,' Fran said quietly, 'I get the picture. You must miss your parents dreadfully, just as I miss mine.'

'Who said I missed them?' Pearl asked, and Fran thought to herself that she never would be able to fathom the complexities of family relationships.

They ate supper at the kitchen table. Mrs Bates had made the shepherd's pie in a deep earthenware dish, accompanied by tureens of home-grown vegetables – carrots, parsnips and boiled potatoes – and followed by a home-baked apple pie and thick dairy cream.

Enchanted by the informality of the occasion, the warmth of the kitchen and the presence of Mr Bates, a thickset countryman with a weather-beaten complexion and a flourishing moustache, wearing his working clothes, Fran overcame her initial shyness and her habitual lack of appetite to enjoy the food set before her. Not that she ate much, but no one pressed her to eat more than she wanted, and what she did eat was delicious.

Awake early next morning after a good night's sleep, staring up at the ceiling, Fran thought about Eddie, wondering where he was and what he was doing, where he and

Elsie were spending their honeymoon. Not that it was any of her business, but even so she couldn't help speculating.

Emerging from her bedroom, yawning and stretching, Pearl said, 'Oh good, you're awake! So how about a walk before breakfast? It's a glorious morning. We could nip down to the farm to fetch the milk. The fresh air will do us a power of good and, if we're lucky, we may well lay hands on a few fresh eggs and a slab of butter.'

And so, half an hour later, wearing civilian clothing, Fran and Pearl set off together down a narrow farm track leading to a sprawling, stone-built farmhouse with smoking chimneys and the tantalizing odour of fried bacon issuing from the kitchen, where a plump woman, Mrs Ives, the farmer's wife, was forking rashers in an iron frying pan.

Turning at the sound of Pearl's voice, Mrs Ives said delightedly, 'Well I never. I heard tell you was comin' but I never thought to see you so early on in the day. Come in and sit you down, my dears. There's tea in the pot, just help yourselves while I finish cooking Ives's breakfast. He'll be in directly from the dairy.' So saying, she cracked a couple of eggs into the pan. 'You'll have come down for the milk, I daresay.'

The tea was hot and strong. The girls drank appreciatively. There was a loaf of bread on the table, Fran noticed, a butter dish, a pot of honey, and a bunch of cowslips in a jam jar. Unlike The Grange kitchen this room was

49

untidy, with old coats pegged up behind the door, Wellington boots in a corner near the massive stone fireplace, baskets of logs on the hearth, and a kitchen dresser on the shelves of which were arrayed an assortment of plates, cups and saucers, toby jugs, brass ornaments and a pipe rack.

'Ah, here's my man now!' Mrs Ives exclaimed, removing the eggs and bacon from the pan on to a plate in readiness for the tall figure who entered the room at that moment, smiling, not one whit perturbed by the presence of visitors as he sat down to enjoy his breakfast. 'Morning, Miss Pearl,' he said. 'I saw you an' the other young lady coming down the lane a while ago, reckoned you'd come for the milk an' mebbe a few fresh eggs. So how are you keeping? How long are you staying? I could do with a bit of extra help in the dairy, if you've nowt better to do.'

Pearl laughed. 'You know as well as I do that I can't tell one end of a cow from the udder! In any case, it's only a weekend leave. We have to report back on duty first thing Tuesday morning.'

'That's a pity,' Ives mused, cutting into a rasher of bacon, 'but there's summat you could do, if you've a mind to. Young John Skipton joined up last week, an' there's no one to play the organ on Sunday, an' it won't seem like a proper service without music.'

'Of course I'll play for you,' Pearl said gaily, 'and Fran here can sing in the choir.'

'Sing in the choir? But I can't sing for

50

toffee,' Fran demurred.

'You won't be singing for toffee,' Pearl reminded her. 'You'll be singing for the Lord.'

On their way back to The Grange with the milk cans and eggs, Pearl asked, 'Do you like music?'

'I don't know much about it,' Fran replied, 'though I went to a concert in the Methodist church a little while ago, and I enjoyed that.'

'You mean the Pouishnoff concert?'

'Yes. Why, were you there?'

'No, though one of the sailors offered me a ticket. When I turned down the invitation, he said he'd pass it on to someone else.' Pearl shrugged dismissively. 'We couldn't have sat together anyway. An incentive, come to think of it. The poor guy had domestic problems and, frankly, I didn't want to know. Selfish of me, I guess, but I had problems of my own to worry about and I'd already advised Eddie to go home and sort things out with his wife. He was due embarkation leave anyway – an ideal time for "making up" wouldn't you say, especially with an infant on the way.'

Fran's face had turned deathly pale. So Eddie had fed her a tissue of lies from start to finish? He'd been married to Elsie all along? Thank God she hadn't believed him when he told her he loved her. Thank God she had left before the concert ended.

'Are you all right, Fran?' Pearl asked concernedly. 'You look as if you're seen a ghost.' She paused. 'If it's the church choir you're worried about, forget it.'

51

'No, it isn't that. I'll be happy to sing in the choir, if you really want me to,' she said, remembering Pearl's advice to forget about the past and look to the future. The sooner she forgot about her brief encounter with Eddie Musgrove, the better. All she really regretted was the time wasted so far in thinking about him at all.

That Saturday afternoon, Pearl had taken her to the village, a mile or so from the Ives farm, explaining that she needed a few personal items from the chemist. There were bottle-pane windows, blue and gold apothecary jars, glass-knobbed drawers behind the high mahogany counter, brass scales, and a curtained-off dispensary from which a thin, grey-haired lady appeared, peering owlishly over pince-nez spectacles.

Fran felt that she had been whisked back in time to a different dimension, as if the war had ceased to exist in this remote village with its pretty cottage gardens, thatched roofs and village green. Gazing about her at the budding trees and the early spring flowers in the churchyard, she experienced a feeling of belonging, a sense of security hitherto unknown, far removed from her old life in Middleton, and thanked her lucky star that she had accepted Pearl's invitation to spend her weekend leave at The Grange.

They had afternoon tea in the Bluebird Café, run by two sisters struggling to make ends meet despite the shortage of fat, sugar and currants necessary to their home-made scones and cakes. Not to mention tea for their willow pattern china cups and teapots. Pearl, Fran noticed, received a warm welcome wherever she went. Not, Fran realized, because she was the daughter of Sir Henry and Lady Galsworthy, but a loving, kind-hearted person in her own right, possessing no airs or graces, just a way of speaking to people on their own terms – as she had spoken to her, Fran remembered.

That evening, after supper in the kitchen, when the washing-up was done and the dishes put away, Batesie said wheedlingly, 'Why not give us a tune on the drawing-room piano? Something nice and soothing. Bates an' me'll listen from the kitchen. Play the Moonlight Sonata.'

'Oh, come off it, Batesie! I haven't touched a piano in ages. Besides, what about the blackout?'

'Bates'll see to the blackout! Any road, if you're about to play the church organ tomorrow, happen you'll need a bit of practice.'

'Oh, very well then. Anything for a quiet life! But why the Moonlight Sonata? Why not "Guide Me, Oh Thou Great Redeemer" or "All Things Bright and Beautiful"?'

'Cos hymns are best played on a clapped-out church organ, not a Steinway Grand,' Batesie decreed sharply. 'In any case, I can't stand "All Things Bright and Beautiful". Singin' the same refrain over an' over again

53

seems like a waste of time to me!'

And so, seating herself at the Steinway Grand, Pearl had played Beethoven's hauntingly lovely Moonlight Sonata in a blacked-out, candlelit drawing room, a faraway look in her eyes, the torchière of candles near the piano glinting on the fair, naturally wavy hair framing her piquant heart-shaped face, highlighting her cheekbones and tenderly smiling lips.

Seated in a dark corner of the room, gazing in fascination at Pearl's slim, unerring fingers on the keyboard, Fran knew that she would remember this night, this enchantment, for the rest of her life, as surely as she would always remember Pearl Galsworthy.

Next morning Pearl entered Fran's bedroom at eight o'clock. 'Well, today's the day,' she said brightly. 'So what do you think we should wear at the church service?'

Fran said unhesitatingly, 'I think we should wear our Wren uniforms – as a mark of respect to the community. What I mean is, so many of them have relatives, both men and women, in the armed forces, and I'd like them to feel that we were somehow representative of our king and country.'

Pearl smiled mysteriously. 'My own sentiments precisely,' she said approvingly. 'So let's get ready to show the flag, shall we?' She laughed. 'Buttons and eyeballs polished, hair neat and tidy, titfers tilted at the right angle, ties correctly knotted. Let's march into church side by side shall we? Eyes front. Ready, steady – march!'

'Oh yes, let's,' Fran replied ecstatically, proud of her uniform, the crossed flags on the sleeve of her jacket that she had worked so hard to obtain, despite all the odds against her at the outset of her entry into the Women's Royal Naval Service.

She had never felt so proud in all her life as that breathless moment when she and Pearl entered the village church together as uniformed members of the senior service, to the obvious delight of the congregation already gathered there, and the two young women parted company smartly, Pearl to take her place at the organ, Fran to take hers in the choir stalls.

A fluttery, elderly parson, the Reverend Josiah Peabody felt it incumbent upon himself to announce the first hymn not as 'All Things Bright and Beautiful' but 'Onward, Christian Soldiers'. The only hymn that Fran knew really well from her school days, and which she sang beautifully in a clear, steady soprano, reaching effortlessly the high notes, without thinking, to her own surprise – and Pearl's, who, drawing Fran aside after the service, said tautly, 'Ye gods, girl, where on earth did you learn to sing like that?'

'I was in my school choir, but so were all the other girls in my class,' Fran explained. 'Trouble was, I couldn't bear standing in line with nothing to hold on to, so the music teacher had a word with the headmistress and

I was given sums to do, instead.'

Pearl regarded Fran thoughtfully, thinking how little she knew about her background. She said breezily, 'Well, not to worry, you sang beautifully this morning. Now we'd best be getting back to The Grange for' – about to say 'luncheon' deciding not to, she substituted the word 'dinner'.

Deeply aware that Fran had not been brought up in the lap of luxury, that snobbish, rarified atmosphere in which dinner meant a meal to be eaten not at midday, but at eight o'clock in the evening, and being the kind of girl she was, she had no intention of making Fran feel awkward or inferior to herself in any way whatsoever.

'Hope you're feeling hungry, I know *I* am,' she continued light-heartedly. 'And just to think we have a whole long afternoon ahead of us after dinner. So how would you like to spend it?'

'I'd like to talk to you, if you don't mind,' Fran said quietly. 'There are things I need to explain; something I'm rather ashamed of. Could we go into the garden? It's such a lovely day, and we'll be leaving here tomorrow, going back to London. Back to the war.' She shuddered slightly at the thought of returning to the soulless atmosphere of Tanglewood.

'But of course,' Pearl replied. 'There's a little gazebo in the garden. Let's change back into civvies first, shall we? Then we can talk to our heart's content.'

As Fran's story of her involvement with Eddie unfolded, Pearl listened, and when it was told she said sympathetically, 'You must not blame yourself. We were all taken in by him to some extent, myself included. He was so plausible, so seemingly honest and above board. The kindest thing to do is remember his good points – his kindly nature, his good manners, his love of music – and forget about the rest. Can you bring yourself to do that, Fran?'

'I guess so,' Fran said softly.

'You weren't in love with him, by any chance?'

'No. I scarcely knew him, but I *was* attracted to him: flattered by his attention, to be honest, though I didn't believe him for one moment when he said he loved me. I mean, how could he have fallen in love with me?'

'Quite easily, I'd say,' Pearl assured her, realizing that Fran really had no idea of her own potential, her youthful prettiness and appealing shyness of manner – a bit like Wordsworth's Lucy: 'A violet by a mossy stone, half hidden from the eye! Fair as a star when only one is shining in the sky'.

Arms linked, the two girls wandered back to The Grange for afternoon tea in the diminishing sunshine of a springtime afternoon. Twilight was fast approaching, heralding nightfall, with the deepening of shadows over the garden and the fields beyond and the rising of a new moon amid a constellation of stars.

Four

Fran's weekend at The Grange was destined to have lasting repercussions on her future. She returned to Tanglewood feeling valued for the first time in her life, remembering the warmth of Mrs Bates's arms about her when they'd said goodbye, and her words: it's been a real pleasure having you here, Miss Fran. I hope we'll meet again soon.'

Back on duty, Fran remembered the highlights of her weekend break; that picturesque village seemingly far removed from the exigencies of a war-torn world; that magical evening when Pearl had played Beethoven's Moonlight Sonata in a candlelit drawing room; Pearl's quiet understanding of her dilemma concerning Eddie Musgrove when they had talked together in the gazebo and she had encouraged her to forgive and forget about Eddie's trespasses, to remember only the good, decent things about him, as she, Pearl herself, had done.

In other words, 'Forgive us our trespasses, as we forgive those who trespass against us.'

Had she been too unforgiving of her brothers' and her Aunt Dorothy's trespasses against her? Fran wondered, hammering out code messages on her teleprinter keyboard. If so, she must try again to heal the breach between herself, her siblings and her mother's sister.

So, desperate to make amends, Fran wrote a long letter to her Aunt Dorothy, saying she was sorry for the misunderstandings between them, caused by her own foolishness and pride in joining the WRNS without telling her beforehand that she was intending to do so, and begging her forgiveness for leaving her in the lurch.

Meanwhile, the war dragged on interminably. The London Blitz had begun towards the end of 1941, claiming the lives of ordinary citizens as buildings collapsed into heaps of rubble from the high-explosive enemy bombs raining down indiscriminately, night after night, on young and old, rich and poor alike. Even Buckingham Palace had been hit, but Queen Elizabeth had stood firm, announcing bravely that the King would never leave London and that she would never leave the King.

At Tanglewood, the pressure of work was unremitting. Signals poured into the TP room by day and night, leaving little or no time for relaxation or respite from the heavy burden of responsibility on the shoulders of Wrens and sailors alike as they struggled to cope with the volume of messages flooding into the WT station. Grim faced, close to exhaustion, they battled on, faced with the realization that this was a battle for survival against Nazi domination.

It scarcely mattered any longer to Fran that she had received no word from her Aunt Dorothy in reply to her letter of apology, written over six months earlier, until suddenly, out of the blue, she had received a letter from a Middleton firm of solicitors regretting to inform her of the death of her aunt, in Middleton General Hospital, in the second week of January.

The letter went on to explain that, according to the late client's instructions, her funeral had been a simple, private affair, arranged by themselves, which included a service in the Middleton cemetery chapel prior to Miss Hunter's interment in the family plot, as she had requested.

Sick at heart, Fran read on through tear-dimmed eyes...

Later Pearl asked her warily what was wrong. 'Not bad news, I hope?'

'My Aunt Dorothy is dead,' Fran replied bleakly. 'Dead and buried. Oh, Pearl, if only I'd known she was ill, I'd have moved heaven and earth to be with her when she died. And yet that letter I wrote her must have made a difference. You see, Pearl, according to this letter I am her sole beneficiary. She has left me everything she owned, her house and its contents, her life's savings and her insurance policies, along with her love and her deep regrets for any pain she caused me during her lifetime.

'Oh, Pearl, and to think she didn't tell me sooner! Why didn't she? *Why? Why not?*'

'A matter of pride, perhaps.' Pearl suggested quietly. 'Old people are like that, in my experience, never wanting to admit to their own shortcomings.' She continued sympathetically, 'Take my advice, Fran, request a fortnight's compassionate leave, return to Middleton to sort out your inheritance with your aunt's firm of solicitors.' She added, referring to the Wren station commander, 'First Officer Langtree is a very humane, understanding person, and I should know since she happens to be an aunt of mine by marriage.'

And so Fran returned to Middleton to visit first her aunt's firm of solicitors, Franks and Bessacre, to learn the extent of her inheritance and decide what to do about the house and its contents. She visited her aunt's grave, where she laid bunches of budding daffodils, accompanied by Mr Charles Bessacre, an honourable grey-haired gentleman, who had strongly advised her to sell her aunt's house and its contents to the highest bidder and reinvest her capital in government bonds, stocks and shares. Advice which Fran chose to ignore for the time being at least, her idea being to let the house and its contents for the duration of the war and to make up her own mind what to do about it in the fullness of time, when the war was over.

'But,' Charles Bessacre demurred, 'what if we lose this war?'

'Then it will scarcely matter one way or the

other what happens to a Victorian villa in Middleton,' Fran replied fatalistically. 'But we are *not* going to lose the war.'

Leaving the cemetery, Fran and Charles Bessacre went to the Middleton Railway Hotel for afternoon tea, the weather being chilly despite straggling rays of sunshine from a pale, watercolour sky. 'What puzzles me,' Fran said, pouring the tea into thick white cups, 'is why no mention of my brothers appeared in my aunt's will, why she left everything to me.'

'It had to do with a letter she received from you some little time ago,' Bessacre said, holding the cup to warm his hands. 'Forgive my saying so, but Miss Hunter was a strongwilled, unpredictable old lady, and you were the only member of the family who had kept in touch with her.'

'I see. And have my brothers been informed of her death?'

'Certainly letters was sent to them, addressed to the War Office. Whether or not they received those letters I can't say for certain. Miss Hunter seemed to think they had been sent overseas – to the Middle East – but they had left no forwarding address, so we were all in the dark, so to speak.'

The tea was weak, but hot and refreshing. Asked where she intended to stay during her leave she replied that she might just as well stay at her aunt's house, forgetting that it was now *her* house.

Mr Bessacre said doubtfully, 'But your bed

will need airing. And what about food? Also, I regret to say that the property is in dire need of cleaning. Miss Hunter had rather ... let things go. Understandably so, the poor lady. A series of slight strokes had rendered her more or less immobile. Finally came the massive stroke that killed her.'

Fran said as brightly as possible, 'No need to worry about me, Mr Bessacre, I'll put hot water bottles in my bed. As for food, I have a temporary ration card with me, and I'm used to housework. I'll enjoy giving the house a spring clean.' She added, less brightly, 'I'm sorry if you think I'm acting unwisely in wanting to keep the property for the time being, rather than sell it and invest the money, as you suggested. Letting the house would provide me with a weekly income pro tem, and the property would still be mine to sell after the war, or whenever. I'll visit a reliable estate agent tomorrow to set the ball rolling. Meanwhile, I'll give the house a good old going over, see to my aunt's personal effects, her clothing and so on, and hand them over to the Salvation Army to dispose of as they see fit.'

Charles Bessacre smiled at Fran, admiring her youth and vitality, her unquenchable spirit of independence. Rising from the tea table, he said warmly, 'Well, good luck, young lady. By the way, you'll be needing these, the keys of your kingdom. We'll be meeting again quite soon, I daresay. There'll be certain documents requiring your signature to conclude the matter in hand.' Laying down the keys of the house on the table, he added, 'Please don't hesitate to contact me, or my business partner, Lionel Franks, should you need further help or advice and, of course, to sign the aforementioned documents.'

'I promise I'll be there,' Fran assured him. 'And thank you for being with me at the cemetery. I don't think I could have borne to go there alone.'

First, Fran went shopping for bread, milk and porridge oats at a corner shop near her aunt's house – for she still regarded it as such. Somehow, she could not bring herself to believe that she had lain flowers on the woman's grave earlier that day.

Opening the front door, entering the narrow hallway with its steep, haircorded staircase and the familiar smell of boiled cabbage pervading the atmosphere, she half expected to see the gaunt figure of her aunt coming towards her from the kitchen, wanting to know why she was late home from work, filling her ears with complaints about her tardiness and lack of gratitude at having a roof over her head. 'The trouble with you, Frances,' she'd complain bitterly, 'is you're bone idle, just like your father before you!'

But Aunt Dorothy was dead and gone now, and this was her own house she was entering, Fran thought bleakly, walking towards the kitchen to place her meagre groceries on the table, shuddering slightly as she did so. The house was so cold. Deathly cold – and empty.

Mr Bessacre was right, the house had been neglected, but Fran would soon put it to rights. Hot soapy water and soda crystals, wash leathers and sweeping brushes would soon make a difference; so would a cane carpet-beater and a bucket and mop for the linoleum.

The most depressing job was clearing her aunt's clothing from drawers and wardrobes and packing it in readiness for the Salvation Army to collect. Dorothy's most prized possessions, a few ornaments, pictures and photograph albums, she wrapped carefully in newspapers and placed in cardboard boxes, which she took with her to the solicitors' office when she went there to sign the documents Mr Bessacre had mentioned, in the hope that storage space could be found for them.

'But of course, my dear,' Bessacre beamed, taking charge of the two small boxes. 'They'll be quite safe in our basement storeroom. 'Now, how are you getting along with the spring cleaning? More importantly, are you getting enough to eat?' And, 'Oh good,' he nodded, when Fran told him she went daily to the Railway Hotel for a midday meal. 'It doesn't do to neglect the inner man, or woman, as the case may be. Now, how are you off for money? We are in a position to advance you some ready cash now the documents have been signed. Say twenty-five pounds? Then you must let me know if you would prefer the balance of your legacy paid into a bank or a Post Office account.'

Twenty-five pounds seemed like a fortune to Fran, not to mention the sum of £714.10s 4d which she intended to deposit in a Post Office account. If only her mother had had access to more money during her lifetime, what a difference it would have made to her peace of mind. There might have been turkey, not chicken, at Christmas.

Returning to Tanglewood when her leave expired, Fran experienced a deep feeling of satisfaction at having wound up her affairs so successfully. The estate agent had envisaged no difficulty in letting the house to reliable tenants at thirty shillings a week. Indeed, he already had in mind a decent middle-aged couple employed by the town council, who would take pride in the property.

'You've done well.' Pearl said admiringly. Then shyly, 'Now I have news for you. I've met someone, you see. Someone rather special. His name is Peter Drysdale. He's a flight lieutenant. Oh, Fran, I've never been in love before, but I am now.'

One look at Pearl's glowing face and shining eyes convinced Fran of that. She said, 'It must have happened very quickly. Has he asked you to marry him?'

'Oh yes, and we intend to get married as soon as possible. After all, why wait?' Her glow diminished somewhat as she confessed to not having told her parents about her engagement. 'They'd kick up a fearful fuss,' she admitted ruefuly, 'try to talk me out of it, advise me to wait till after the war. That's why Pete and I have decided upon a quiet register office wedding in ten days from now. Please say you'll be my bridesmaid.'

'Of course I will,' Fran assured her, caught up in the romance of her friend's love affair, thinking how wise it was of her not to have told her parents, recognizing the urgency of Pearl's desire to marry the man she loved.

They had met at a cocktail party at Ringrose Aerodrome, situated fifteen miles north of Tanglewood. Mess parties were still a feature of the social activities between the airfield and the WT station as morale boosters. Sailors, Wrens, air crews and Waafs alike enjoyed one another's company in those brief respites from the arduous duties the war imposed on them.

It was easy to see why Pearl had fallen in love with Flight Lieutenant Drysdale, who possessed all the attributes of young English manhood. He was tall, athletic, good looking, strong minded but not aggressively so, with a charm and tenderness about him well suited to Pearl's warm, loving personality.

Theirs was a simple marriage service attended by the girls of Number Four Watch and members of Peter's flight crew, First Officer Langtree, the bride's matron of honour, and Group Captain Alex Condermine, Peter's best man.

The wedding reception was held in a private room at a nearby hotel; a room in which a buffet luncheon, including a wedding cake, took pride of place. The food was simple but delicious; there was cold poached salmon, cucumber and egg and cress sand-wiches, a sherry-soaked trifle and, more im-portantly as far as the guests were concerned, two magnums of vintage champagne, cour-tesy of Group Captain Condermine, to drink to the health and happiness of the bride and groom as they cut the wedding cake.

Afterwards, the newlyweds, granted a week-end's compassionate leave for their honey-moon, had quitted the reception for a desti-nation unknown. Smiling, blissfully happy, they had run down the hotel steps together, hand in hand, to Peter's two-seater sports car parked near the kerb. Turning the corner, they had waved back at their guests, two deliriously happy young people in love with life and one another, anticipating their honeymoon: forty-eight precious hours alone together.

An inevitable feeling of anti-climax follow-ed the departure of the bride and groom, at which juncture Group Captain Condermine had invited the wedding party to dine with him that evening at his hotel in Wimbledon.

Obviously a man of substance and panache, capable of string pulling when necessary, he rumbled jovially, 'No reason why the fun should end here. We owe it to the newlyweds to end the celebration of their union on a high note, don't you agree?'

Everyone had agreed wholeheartedly. 'Good, that's settled then.' Alex nodded his approval. 'Leave everything to me, transport and so on. We'll meet in the hotel bar at, say, seven o'clock, shall we? Dine at seven thirty? Dress optional, of course. Uniform not de rigeur, I assure you. I daresay you gals will enjoy wearing civvies for a change, am I right?'

Not in her case, Fran thought despondently; her civilian clothing consisted of ancient tweed skirts, hand-knitted jumpers and flat-heeled shoes. She'd far rather wear her wren uniform any day of the week. Then she suddenly remembered the balance of that twenty-five pounds advanced to her by Charles Bessacre, which meant she could afford to go shopping, that afternoon, to purchase a dress, perhaps, and even a pair of high-heeled shoes. A wicked waste of money, in her view, but necessary on this special occasion in her life.

Thank God, she thought later, joining her fellow Wrens in the bar parlour of the Wimbledon Hotel, that the soft blue woollen dress she had bought that afternoon fitted her to perfection, though she could scarcely hobble in her new high-heeled shoes. But what the hell? All that really mattered was that Pearl should feel proud of her appearance at the dinner party in her honour, at which Group Captain Condermine had proved

69

himself to be a host par excellence.

Not that Fran trusted the man entirely. He was far too self-assured, too smooth to her way of thinking, so that when the meal was over and he invited her to dance with him on a sprung maplewood floor in the centre of the room to 'Begin the Beguine' on the gramophone she had flatly refused to do so.

Asked why not she'd replied primly, 'Because I've never learned how to dance, and I'd rather not make a fool of myself in public, thanks very much.'

'Then perhaps you'd rather do so in private?' Condermine suggested, sotto voce.

Unused to innuendo and unable to reply to it in a light-hearted manner, Fran said coldly, 'And to think that I mistook you for an officer and a gentleman! I daresay Flight Lieutenant Drysdale made the same mistake when he asked you to be his best man.'

'My God, girlie, you're a real goody two shoes, an' no mistake,' Alex laughed. 'A case of sweet sixteen an' never been kissed, eh? Well, not to worry, I wouldn't touch you with a bargepole!'

Rising quickly to her feet Fran riposted sharply, 'You couldn't, even if you tried. I'm leaving now, and I hope you're pleased with yourself, Group Captain!'

So saying, she stalked out of the room, head in the air, close to tears at what she saw as the ruination of Pearl's wedding day, a happy occasion clouded by its conclusion.

★ ★ ★

70

Next day, to her surprise, she'd received a hand-delivered letter of apology from Alex Condermine, inviting her to lunch with him that day or the next to allow him to express his apologies in person, suggesting the wedding hotel as a venue.

Tearing up the letter, Fran consigned it to the nearest waste paper basket, and yet, the following day, against her better judgement, she turned up at the hotel to hear what the group captain had to say for himself. It was the day on which Pearl and her husband would be returning to London from their brief honeymoon.

Entirely sober, and suitably contrite, he extended his hands in greeting as Fran entered the hotel foyer. 'Thank you for coming,' he said gratefully. 'I was half afraid you wouldn't, all things considered. I behaved disgracefully the other night. I know that now, and I'm so very sorry. Please say you'll forgive me.'

'That remains to be seen,' Fran said starchily. 'You said you wouldn't touch me with a bargepole, remember?'

'I know,' Alex smiled ruefully, 'but I was rather tiddly at the time. At any rate, you put me in my place quite convincingly, as I recall.'

'You got what you deserved,' Fran reminded him.

'So I did. Now, shall we have lunch, or would you prefer to leave me with a flea in my ear? Frankly, I'd rather we settled our differences over a dining table than waste time here

71

in the foyer.' He smiled charmingly. 'Come now, let's be friends, shall we?'

No use holding grudges, Fran thought, preceding him into the dining room.

'As a matter of fact,' Alex said, over portions of fish pie, 'I think you are a remarkably attractive young woman. You look great in uniform, you looked stunning in that blue dress you wore the other evening. Do you wonder I made a pass at you?'

'Do you mind if we drop the subject?' Fran sighed wearily. 'Why keep on flogging a dead horse?'

Alex laughed. 'I've never heard that expression before. Where are you from, by the way?'

'Yorkshire, where we call a spade a spade, not a shovel! Don't tell me you hadn't noticed my Yorkshire accent?'

'Not particularly. Why? Are you ashamed of it?'

'No, I'm not. Aware of it yes, but not ashamed. There *is* a difference.'

'You're fairly outspoken, aren't you?' Alex regarded her thoughtfully.

'For a goody two shoes you mean? Well, I used not to be, but I am now. A matter of self-preservation, if you really must know. Would you like me to fill in a questionnaire?'

'Ouch!' He grimaced. 'You certainly know how to hit a fellow when he's down. Tell me, are you inimical to the human race entire, or just men in particular? Myself above all.'

'I haven't really thought about it. Why? Should I have done?'

'No, I guess not. We got off to a bad start, and that's that. You really don't like me very much, do you?'

'Can you give me one good reason why I should?'

Alex smiled ruefully. 'Just one. Because, given half a chance, I had hoped to get to know you much better. Unfortunately,' glancing at his wristwatch, 'time is running out for me. I'm due back on duty the first thing tomorrow morning, north of the border. My train leaves London in an hour from now.'

'Oh, I see,' Fran murmured, beginning to warm to him. 'I'm sorry to have been such a ... stick in the mud. I could go with you to the station, if you like.'

'How very kind of you. Yes, I'd like that very much indeed,' he replied, deeply attracted to this strong-minded young woman who had utterly refused to be seduced by him, who had voiced her disapproval of him in no uncertain terms. A gem among women, he suspected. Steel true, blade straight, in contrast to every other woman he had met, with the exception of Pearl Galsworthy, now happily married to his favourite nephew, Peter Drysdale.

At King's Cross Station Alex asked, 'If I write to you, will you reply?' He was standing near an open carriage window, looking down at her upturned face, wondering if he dared kiss her.

'Write to me? What about?'

'This and that. I'd like to know how my

nephew and his bride are getting along, for instance. What happens when Pearl introduces Peter to her parents. Besides which, I'd like to know how you are getting along.'

'I didn't know Peter was your nephew.' Fran puckered her forehead, edging closer to the window to catch what he was saying above the steam-letting from the locomotive, the clanking of hand-barrow wheels and the general confusion of departure of a crowded London to Edinburgh train: the slamming of carriage doors, the sound of running footsteps along the platform as last-minute arrivals flung themselves and their belongings into whatever space was still available in the jam-packed corridors.

'You haven't answered my question,' Alex reminded her, noticing that the guard's green flag was unfurled, his pocket watch in hand, his whistle about to be blown.

'Oh, very well then,' Fran conceded as the guard waved his flag, blew his whistle and the train began to move forward, at which moment Alex leaned down and kissed her, not on her cheeks or forehead or any other area of her face upraised to his, but her lips. Of necessity a brief kiss, as the train was gathering speed, but nevertheless a deeply satisfying kiss so far as he was concerned, and akin to an electric shock to its recipient.

Five

Pearl returned to Tanglewood in a state of euphoria, reliving every moment of the blissful forty-eight hours she and Peter had spent together in the idyllic surroundings of a country cottage in the grounds of a hotel owned by John and Grace Latimer, friends of Peter, whom he had known since his early boyhood when he and his parents had spent holidays there.

Even then, Peter had been fascinated by the stone-built cottage tucked away in the grounds, which the Latimers used as a bolt hole when the hotel was full to overflowing with summer visitors. Many the times he'd watched Grace busily making bread and pastry in her pin-neat kitchen, baking fruit pies, cakes and currant loaves, which he'd helped her to carry across the garden to the hotel kitchen in trugs covered with pristine linen tea towels.

John, a chef by profession, had seen to the roasts and casseroles, and his wife had baked away from the heat and bustle of the hotel kitchen in which her husband reigned supreme. An ideal arrangement, the young Peter Drysdale had considered, thinking that when he grew up and got married he'd like to own a hotel exactly like this one, with a trout stream at the bottom of the garden and apple trees and fruit bushes galore, to grow herbs and vegetables and to keep hens for the sheer pleasure of collecting fresh eggs, warm from their nesting boxes, every morning.

He had never imagined that one day he would meet, fall in love with and marry a girl with whom he would share a blissful honeymoon in what he had always thought of as Grace's cottage. Not in summer, but springtime, in war not peacetime. Yet he had known instinctively that Pearl would love the cottage as much as he did. Thank God he'd possessed the wisdom to write to the Latimers requesting the cottage as a honeymoon venue when Pearl had whispered an ecstatic, 'Oh yes, please,' to his albeit tentative proposal of marriage, which he had scarcely believed for one moment that she'd accept. He had simply prayed that she would, and his prayer had been answered.

Even so, he'd warned her that he had little to offer her apart from love, no job prospects in view after the war. He said, 'All I know is how to fly an aircraft. I'm not exactly poverty stricken, but I'm far from rich. My father's a civil servant, Mum's a volunteer helper at our local hospital for the time being. She gave up nursing when she married my dad. I come from what could best be described as a middle-class background,' He added wryly, 'I'd think again about marrying me, if I were you.'

'Ah, but you're not me, are you?' She smiled contentedly. 'And if you love me half as much as I love you, that's good enough for me,' Pearl assured him tenderly, overwhelmed by a feeling of absolute joy as his lips met hers. Then, 'Oh Peter,' she whispered urgently, 'let's not waste time worrying about the future, let's get married as soon as possible. All that matters a damn is the here and now!'

And so they had ended up together, on their honeymoon, in a stone-built cottage near a trout stream, blissfully alone at last in an olde worlde atmosphere conducive to love and romance.

Carried across the threshold in her husband's arms, Pearl had fallen in love at first glance with the chintz-covered sofa and armchairs near the wide stone fireplace in which burned a log fire, laid and lit earlier by John Latimer to provide a warm welcome for the newlyweds, whilst Grace, as busy as a bee, had placed fresh towels in the bathroom, switched on the immersion heater to ensure a liberal supply of hot water for the happy couple and dusted and polished every item of furniture, glass and silverware to a pristine lustre following the cottage's long winter break.

She had also, thoughtfully, left a dozen fresh eggs, bacon rashers, a loaf of home-baked bread, a slab of farm butter, a jug of milk and a note explaining that meals would be available in the hotel dining room, if and when required.

If and when? Ravenously hungry, they had walked up to the house that evening to partake of delicious homemade carrot and potato soup, roast saddle of lamb with mint sauce, fresh vegetables and Grace's apple pie served with thick cream from a nearby dairy. Alone in the dining room lit with dancing firelight and softly shaded lamps, they had talked about their wedding, recalling that breathless moment when the registrar had pronounced them husband and wife and when Peter, gathering his bride's hands in his, had gently kissed the shining gold ring on her left hand and whispered, 'I love you, Mrs Drysdale.'

After dinner, walking back to their honeymoon cottage replete and happy, having thanked John and Grace for the gift of a bottle of Sauternes to accompany the roast lamb and bidden them a fond goodnight, Peter said quietly, 'Just a thought, darling, but wouldn't this be a good time to break the news of our wedding to your parents and mine? Not that we've done anything wrong exactly, certainly not in the eyes of the law, but I can't help feeling...'

'Guilty?' Pearl finished the sentence for him. And, of course, he was right. Entering the cottage, she said, 'I'll ring Mummy and Daddy right away, come clean, then hang up. Or would you prefer to ring your parents first? Let's toss for it, shall we? Better still,

78

why not wait till tomorrow? We could waddle down to the village post office, if there is one, and send telegrams, short and to the point: "Married. Blissfully happy. Signed Pearl and Peter, or Peter and Pearl," whichever is the more applicable to each set of parents.' She added, more seriously, 'You see, my darling, guilt doesn't enter into the way I feel about you. So why apologize to anyone at all for having married you? Tonight, above all nights, belongs to us alone, to no one in the world except ourselves.' She added shyly, 'Now, let's go to bed, shall we?'

Up early next morning, whistling happily, Peter went down to the kitchen to prepare breakfast for his bride. Stepping outside the cottage door, he gathered a handful of dew-wet daffodils to adorn the kitchen table, and when the tea, toast, bacon and eggs were ready to consume she came downstairs to sample his cooking.

'Oh, this is simply marvellous,' Pearl said ecstatically, entering the kitchen in her night attire, inhaling the scent of the daffodils, of burned toast, eggs and bacon. 'I didn't know you could cook.' What was more, she meant what she said wholeheartedly. An endearing facet of Pearl's charming personality was that she had no fault to find in those she loved. The love she gave was unstinting, generous and kind, as Peter had discovered on their wedding night when, making love to her, he had realized the extent, the depth and breadth, of the passion of which she was capable in his embrace.

On her return to Tanglewood, Pearl confided to Fran the heartache she'd endured when she and Peter had parted company after their honeymoon, and Fran, enthralled by Pearl's description of that stone-built cottage tucked away in a corner of The Trout Stream Hotel garden, had understood why as she imagined the peace and quietude of the place, the fire and lamplit rooms at nightfall and the gentle burbling of the trout stream beyond the cottage windows.

Then Pearl, never one to indulge in self-pity, said light heartedly, 'Now, tell me what happened after the reception. Pete and I discussed the possibilities. He bet me a hundred pounds to a hayseed that his Uncle Alex would make a pass at my Aunt Rachel. Knowing Alex, he said he was bound to make a pass at someone.'

'He did,' Fran said. 'He made a pass at me, and I told him exactly what I thought of him.'

'You did? Good for you!' Pearl's eyes sparkled mischievously. 'Well, don't leave me in suspense. Then what happened?'

And so the story of Fran's brief encounter with Group Captain Condermine unfolded, little by little and haltingly, Fran wishing she hadn't mentioned the episode in the first place.

When the tale was told, Pearl said sympathetically, 'Poor you! Well, all I can say is that

Pete was right about his uncle. Not that they are blood relatives. Alex simply married Peter's elder sister, Rosemary, some twenty years ago and, because they had no children of their own, Alex took quite a shine to Pete, whom he regarded as his own flesh and blood, which is why Peter invited him to stand as his best man at our wedding.'

'Then why didn't Alex bring Rosemary to the wedding?' Fran asked.

'Because he and his wife parted company some time ago,' Pearl answered. 'So far as I know, Rosemary met someone else, and she is now living abroad in America or Canada. I'm not sure which. A sad story really, which probably explains why Alex is such a – a womanizer!' She smiled reflectively. 'Though I must confess to quite liking him when we met just prior to the wedding, and I know that Peter thinks the world of him. Well, there you have it in a nutshell.'

Would Alex write to her? Fran wondered, or was he an out-of-sight, out-of-mind kind of person? 'All wind and water' as folk would say in the north. Certainly he was prone to making expansive gestures – not to say expensive gestures. That dinner party at his Wimbledon hotel must have cost an arm and a leg, she pondered, reckoning up the number of guests on that occasion – fourteen in all – with no shortage of food or wine.

Not that Fran cared much for wine, or food for that matter, although she had wondered at the time how there came to be smoked salmon, roast beef and fresh fruit salad in wartime. Was the man a fool, a philanthropist or a Black Marketeer? He was most certainly an exhibitionist, a Character with a capital C. And yet, deep down, Fran harboured a sneaking regard for the man whose goodbye kiss had almost, quite literally, swept her off her feet.

If he hadn't let go of her when he did, chances were she'd have ended up in a first class carriage to Scotland, hauled aboard a moving train by Pearl's proxy uncle, Group Captain Condermine, Fran reflected, buffing her shoes in readiness for the weekly pay parade in First Officer Langtree's presence. She was thankful for the normality of everyday life, which left little or no room for anything else save duty, responsibility and the continuance of a war which seemed destined to last from here to eternity, with no let up, no respite from its grim reality, until...

Tearing open the envelope with its Scottish postmark, received later that week, she read:

Dear Fran,
    Fulfilling my promise to write you, I can only apologize, once more, for my abominable behaviour towards you on the evening following my nephew's wedding. I make no such apology for kissing you goodbye the way I did. If anyone deserves kissing, it is you. I know my own shortcomings all

82

too well, believe me. I'm brash, self-centred and conceited, as you are well aware. I am also lonely, as self-centred men like me are bound to be, stripped of their pretensions. Please reply to this letter, if you feel inclined to do so. If not, I shall remain, ever yours regretfully,

Alex Condermine

'You appear to have made quite an impression on Alex,' Pearl said when Fran showed her the letter. 'I have to say the old boy has remarkably good taste in women.'

'Just how old is he?' Fran asked curiously, trying hard not to sound curious.

Pearl puckered her forehead, 'I'm not quite sure. Late-forties at a rough guess. Peter's twenty-six, Rosemary's thirty-five. I gather there was a bit of a rumpus when she announced her engagement to a man quite a bit older than herself, but that was twenty years ago, and I imagine it wasn't just the age difference the Drysdales were concerned about, but Alex's lifestyle.'

'What about his ... lifestyle?'

'Well, one gathers he'd made a lot of money. Don't ask me how. Money he threw about with careless abandon, which he still does, apparently.' Pearl sighed deeply, 'I shouldn't be saying this, it seems – disloyal – somehow. Disloyal to Peter, who thinks the world of him.' She paused momentarily, then continued. 'I can see why. Despite his shortcomings, the man's generous to a fault. It was he who pulled strings to provide the salmon and the champagne for our wedding reception, not to mention the wedding cake. It just worried me a little that he was able to "pull strings" in wartime.'

'The same thought struck me,' Fran confessed, 'when smoked salmon and roast beef appeared on the dinner menu at his Wimbledon hotel. I'd expected Woolton's pie or Spam fritters and chips, not a banquet. I wondered afterwards if he was a Black Market racketeer or somesuch, though I have to admit I wasn't thinking too kindly of him at the time.'

'And are you thinking more kindly of him now?' Pearl asked levelly, hoping against hope that, for Fran's sake, she was not. Her heart sank when Fran said, 'Well, yes. That is, I shall reply to his letter. I did say I would, and I must keep my promise.'

'Yes, of course you must,' Pearl conceded, praying inwardly that Alex's interest in Fran would soon peter out, as it had done with so many other women since Rosemary had left him. Alex Condermine to her certain knowledge, was a womanizer and a fraudster, albeit a charming one, who she wouldn't trust an inch in view of the nefarious business dealings from which his wealth had derived in the first place. A Black Marketeer? Pearl wouldn't be in the least surprised. She had no proof, of course, that Alex was or ever had been dishonest. She simply mistrusted the man, despite his undoubted charisma – or possibly because of it.

The last thing on earth she wanted was for Fran to become emotionally involved with Alex Condermine. On the other hand, what could she possibly do to prevent it? The answer came clear cut as crystal. Nothing. Nothing at all.

Off duty, Alex relaxed in his bolt hole in the centre of Edinburgh. Re-reading Fran's letter, a decanter of malt whisky close at hand, he thought about the surprised, not to say shocked, expression on the girl's face when he had kissed her goodbye.

Pausing to replenish his glass, he recalled with pleasure the titillation of her response to the improper suggestion he had whispered in her ear after the dinner party in Wimbledon. Inured to having women fall into his arms at the drop of a hat; her negative response to his suggestion had both puzzled and intrigued him, whetting his curiosity to find out more about her. Was she as steel true and blade straight as she had led him to believe, or as corruptible and susceptible to flattery as all the other women in his life so far?

Throwing aside her letter, glancing about the room in which he was sitting, deriving satisfaction from his ability to afford the luxury of richly furnished accommodation as an escape route during his off-duty weekends away from RAF headquarters on the outskirts of Edinburgh, he flirted with the idea of inviting Fran to spend her next leave here with him, if only to prove to himself that he could have any woman he wanted, given the time and the opportunity. Money – no problem. He'd always possessed the Midas touch, an instinct for wheeling and dealing in stocks and shares that had paid rich dividends in the long run. If only his wheeling and dealing with women had reaped as rich rewards.

The burr beneath his saddle was that he was still married to a woman who had left him for another man when he had failed to give her the child she had so desperately wanted. The reason why he had come to regard his nephew, Peter Drysdale, as his own son, and had squandered upon him both money and affection. But to what end, what purpose? The boy was now happily married to a lovely, desirable young woman, leaving him exactly where in the scheme of things? Perhaps it was time to form a stable relationship of his own.

Fran's letter appeared to have been hurriedly written. Formally phrased, she had begun by thanking him 'for yours of last week' and had gone on to say that Pearl and her husband had enjoyed their honeymoon very much indeed. Stating the obvious, Alex thought impatiently. Then came the interesting part.

You wrote of your shortcomings. Experience has taught me that what people say about themselves is usually true. I find it

86

hard to believe, however, that you are either lonely or stripped of your pretensions. More than likely you are just feeling bored, in need of a shoulder to cry on. I daresay another girl, deserving to be kissed, will soon come along to dispel your boredom. Must go now. Duty calls. In haste,
   Yours sincerely,
   Frances Abbot

The artful little devil, Alex thought. No quarter asked, none given. What was more, damn her, she was right in her assessment of his character. Neither bored nor lonely nor stripped of his pretensions, he knew at least five young women, far better looking and more physically desirable than the prim and proper Frances Abbot, who were willing and able to strip him of more than his pretensions. So just who the hell did she think she was, the stuck up prig?

All the more reason to break down her barrier of resistance towards him. Looking forward to the challenge, glancing at his watch, Alex rose to his feet to make ready for his dinner date with Waaf Officer Kate Bower at a well-known haunt of his in Princes Street. A dazzling red-head, Second Officer Bower would have no inhibitions whatever about spending the night with him after dinner, here in his luxuriously appointed hideaway, as she had done many times before.

So why, goddammit, couldn't he stop thinking about a stuffy little Wren, as plain as a proverbial pikestaff, whose obvious antipathy towards him was causing him so much trouble? Only time would tell.

Six

Incensed by the news of their daughter's clandestine marriage to Flight Officer Peter Drysdale, a man of whom they knew nothing whatsoever, Sir Henry and Lady Eleanor Galsworthy arrived one afternoon at Tanglewood, to confront First Officer Langtree, Lady Eleanor's sister-in-law; and demand angrily of her what had been going on behind their backs.

'Ye gods, Rachel,' Eleanor burst forth indignantly, 'you of all people should have kept us informed of Pearl's affair with some young upstart who probably married her for her money. Have you no sense of family honour?'

'Now see here, Nell,' Langtree said unflinchingly, 'Pearl wanted a quiet wedding, and Peter Drysdale is no upstart but a perfectly charming young man from a decent family background. Moreover, he is doing a highly responsible, not to say dangerous job. Flying a Wellington bomber in wartime is scarcely the province of some young upstart, as you are pleased to call him. Furthermore, I'm not in the least surprised that Pearl decided not to divulge her wedding plans to you and Henry, realizing as she did what your reaction would be. Family honour, my eye! What about family unity and understanding?'

'Oh! I might have known that you would take her side in this unfortunate affair,' Eleanor blustered. 'In case you've forgotten, *I* am Pearl's mother! How would you feel if a daughter of yours had got married without a word to her nearest and dearest?' Out came a lace-edged hanky from her ladyship's crocodile handbag. 'I'd envisaged a white wedding for my – our – only child, a proper reception at The Grange, not some hole in the corner affair. Is that so difficult to understand?'

'In your case, no not at all,' Langtree conceded, disliking her sister-in-law intensely as she always had done, thanking her lucky stars that Eleanor's brother Ralph had inherited none of his sister's narrow-minded snobbery or bombast. She would never have married him otherwise. She added wearily, 'Oh do sit down! Unless, that is, you have said all that you came to say. If so, you'd best leave now, hadn't you? As you can see, I am on duty. So, as it happens, is Wren Drysdale. There *is* a war on, in case you've forgotten!'

Langtree breathed a sigh of relief when the Galsworthys had gone, Sir Henry following in the wake of his wife. He was what Rachel thought of as the junior partner in the marriage, completely overshadowed by Eleanor's more robust personality. No wonder he engaged in a little 'silken dalliance' once in a while, although as a member of the War Cabinet he had to be careful not to blot his copybook.

Sending for Pearl when she came off duty, Langtree said succinctly, tongue-in-cheek, 'The Indians are on the warpath. A scalping party, no less!'

Knowing exactly what Rachel meant, Pearl said ruefully, 'They've got it in for Peter, I daresay. The reason why I wanted a quiet wedding, not a circus. Had my parents known beforehand, they'd have made our lives a misery.' She sighed deeply, then smiled. 'At least Pete and I are married now, and nothing they can do or say really matters a damn. I guess we'll have to face them sooner or later, but if they dare say a word against my husband they'll have me to contend with, and if the mention of money comes into it, well, Pete and I will manage fine without their interference. After the war we plan to buy a country cottage somewhere or other, to keep hens and grow our own vegetables. I shan't care two pins if I never set eyes on The Grange again.'

Misty eyed, she continued, 'After all, Tante Rachel, it's not money that matters, but love. And my parents have never really loved me. I know that now. It was always money and position they cared about: socializing, dinner parties, cocktail parties, house parties –

entertaining and being entertained – I was just an encumbrance, a bit of a nuisance.

'The thing is, this war will change a lot of things. It already has. Take The Grange for instance. All the servants, apart from the Bateses, have gone now. They're making new lives for themselves and, sooner or later, Mummy and Daddy will need to do the same. The time is coming when ancestral homes will be a thing of the past, sold off as hotels, boarding schools or museums, then my parents will have to cut their coats according to their cloth. When that happens, perhaps they'll realize that love, not money, is the only thing that remains indestructible.'

Langtree could not have agreed more.

Fran had shown Pearl her reply to Alex's letter before sending it on its way. 'Good for you,' had been her response, thankful that Fran had had the nous to call the man's bluff, mistrustful of his motives in writing to the girl in the first place. 'Now, take my advice, forget about him. If he writes to you again, tear up the letter. I'm not denying that Alex has charm, and he can be very persuasive, but he *is* still married to Peter's sister, and I couldn't bear to see you get hurt.'

'Thanks, Pearl, but I wasn't born yesterday.' Fran spoke more sharply than she'd intended, beginning to wonder if she was destined to go through life suspicious of the opposite gender and their motives towards her. First there had been her brothers, then Eddie

Musgrove, now she was being warned against forming a relationship with a married man. As if she needed reminding of anything to do with men, having discovered, the hard way, their general untrustworthiness.

'I'm sorry, Fran,' Pearl said gently, 'I didn't mean to upset you, or to interfere in your personal affairs in any way. Please. forgive me?'

'There's nothing to forgive.' Fran's eyes filled with tears. 'It's just that I've never known what it's like to be loved, not really. Oh, my mother loved me, of course, but not the way she loved my brothers, who did nothing to deserve it. Then, when Mum died and my brothers joined the Green Howards and went away, I was left alone in the house with no one to turn to, so guess what I did. I went to the pictures, to the Odeon, to see Merle Oberon and Laurence Olivier in *Wuthering Heights*. Pathetic, don't you think, that for the price of a one and ninepenny seat in the stalls, I found the romance I craved, not in reality, but make believe. And it has been the same ever since: wanting romance – love – but never finding it, as if there was something wrong with me. Something missing...'

'There's nothing at all wrong with you,' Pearl broke in quietly, 'nothing missing, either, believe me. You've been unlucky, that's all, in not meeting the right man for you. But you will one of these days, and when that happens love will be a reality, not make believe. No more doubts or fears. You'll look at someone across a crowded room, he'll look at you, and that will be that! Next thing you know, you'll be married and – pregnant – just like me!'

'Oh, Pearl, you really mean that you're going to have a baby?' Fran blurted excitedly.

'Yes. And you're the first to know,' Pearl said, sotto voce, 'so keep it under your hat for the time being. *Promise?* I'm meeting Peter this evening. He's driving over from Ringrose to see me. We're having dinner together at the Ox Hotel.' She blushed becomingly. 'I'll break the news to him over the cottage pie and chips!' She added, glowingly, 'Wish me luck, Fran, and believe that, one day, you'll be as happy as I am now.'

Setting off from Ringrose before seven o'clock Peter was awaiting Pearl's arrival in reception at seven thirty. Anticipating the pleasure of a quiet evening together he glanced anxiously at his watch, and as its hands moved towards ten minutes past eight he thought it probable that she'd been kept late on duty. He had booked their table for eight o'clock. Explaining to the head waiter that his wife had been unavoidably detained for some reason, the maître d' told him not to worry, the dining room was not busy that evening and he would hold their table for as long as necessary. Thanking the man, Peter went to the bar for a gin and tonic, keeping an eye on the door through which Pearl might appear at any moment, hands outstretched to greet him, apologizing profusely for having kept him waiting.

At nine o'clock, worried sick that Pearl had still not put in an appearance, Peter rang Tanglewood and asked to speak to First Officer Langtree. 'Sorry, sir,' the duty Wren informed him, 'First Office Langtree is not available at the moment. There's been an ... incident...'

Peter's heartbeat quickened suddenly, his throat muscles tightened. 'What kind of incident?' he uttered hoarsely.

'Sorry, sir, I can't say for sure. Something to do with a transport vehicle, I gather. Apparently it overturned and caught fire. Now you really must excuse me. I'm alone on duty, and everything's in a state of chaos for the time being.'

'Yes, of course.' Peter hung up the receiver. Minutes later, seated in his car and switching on the ignition, he was heading towards Tanglewood with one thought in mind, and one person: Pearl, his beloved wife. Desperate to find out what had become of her, whether she was alive or dead, deep down he already knew the answer.

Seated in Rachel Langtree's office at close to midnight, shoulders hunched, head sunk in his hands, tears trickling between his fingers, Peter asked the inevitable question: *'Why?* Why did this have to happen? We were so happy together.'

'I know, Peter, and I'm so dreadfully sorry.

94

I loved her too,' Rachel responded wearily, worn out from the shattering events of the night when she had been called upon to identify the remains of the three Wrens dragged from that burning transport, following its collision with an army lorry, the first of a convoy headed towards Salisbury Plain; the horror of her discovery that her beloved niece, Pearl, had been a victim of that terrible accident.

Uncovering his face, squaring his shoulders, Peter said huskily, 'I'd like to see her now, if I may, if at all possible.'

'No, Peter, I'm afraid it isn't,' Rachel said quietly. 'Tomorrow, perhaps, but not tonight. I'll tell you when. Now it's high time you were on your way back to Ringrose.'

Rising to his feet, gathering Langtree's hands into his, Peter said mistily, 'Forgive me, Rachel. It's just that I can't help wishing that if one of us, Pearl or I, were destined to die, the chosen one had been me.'

Devastated by the news of Pearl's death, Fran's never very robust self-confidence hit rock bottom. Pearl, her friend and mentor, could not possibly be dead, she told herself over and over again in the dark watches of the night. Not *Pearl*, the procreator of a new life forming within that tender yet tensile young body of hers. Pearl, that warm, wonderful human being who had taken her under her wing that weekend at The Grange and shown her a different aspect of life. A beautiful, unpretentious young woman whose memory would remain with her all the days of her life, as lovely and unfading as the Evening Star. But memories were not enough. It was the living flesh- and-blood human being Fran needed, not memories, to sustain her in her present loneliness and despair.

Requesting an interview with First Office Langtree, next day Fran stood forlornly in her office, the picture of misery, eyes swollen with weeping.

'Sit down. Abbot,' Langtree said sympathetically, understanding the girl's grief, knowing that she and Pearl had been especially close and dear to one another. 'You asked to speak to me. About Wren Drysdale, I imagine.'

'Yes. But I prefer to stand, if you don't mind,' Fran said quietly.

'As you wish. But I must warn you that I am not at liberty to discuss matters pertaining to her death. Beyond my jurisdiction now. In the hands of a higher authority than mine to determine. You understand? There'll be a full-scale enquiry.'

'Yes, ma'am. But that's not why I'm here. You see, Pearl told me, the night she died, that she and her husband had arranged to meet, for dinner, at the Ox Hotel. She also told me that she was pregnant, and that I was the first to know. That's why I asked to speak to you, because, well, being related to her, I thought that you, also, should know.'

Robbed momentarily of her usual savoir faire, Langtree's eyes filled with tears. She said in a low voice, 'Are you quite sure about this, Abbot?'

'Yes, ma'am. Quite sure.'

'Thank you.' Blinking away the tears, speaking her thoughts aloud, Rachel said, 'They say that life must go on. At times like this, one wonders why.' Then, squaring her shoulders, 'Now, if you'll excuse me, I have things to do, a number of phone calls to make.'

'Yes, ma'am. I understand.'

When Fran had gone, closing the door quietly behind her, Rachel stared at the telephone, willing herself to pick up the receiver. She knew that this was the worst moment of her life so far. A highly trained Wren officer she may be, well inured to coping with the many day-to-day crises involved in the administration of a WT station of the size and importance of Tanglewood, but she was also a woman, a caring human being, dreading the thought of imparting the news of their daughter's death to Pearl's parents, and, above all, of telling Peter Drysdale that he had suffered a double loss, that of his wife and child.

Not that she would dream of telling him so over the phone; that would be far too impersonal, far too cruel. Finally, plucking up the courage to pick up the receiver, contacting the duty officer at Ringrose, she left a message for Peter, requesting his attendance in her office 'as soon as possible'.

Sufficient unto the day is the evil thereof, she thought grimly, turning her attention to contacting Sir Henry's flat in Whitehall.

Eleanor answered the call. 'Huh, so it's you, Rachel,' her ladyship said huffily. 'So what is it this time? Another lecture on family unity?'

She drew in a deep breath of despair at her sister-in-law's lack of humanity and understanding, her shoulder-shrugging approach to life, in which she must always take the upper hand. 'No, Nell,' Rachel said quietly, 'I'm ringing to tell you that family unity is no longer an issue. I'm sorry, Nell, Pearl died last night. She was involved in an accident.'

Eventually, Rachel hung up the receiver on her sister-in-law's hysterical outburst once the news had sunk in; her repeated protestations that her beloved daughter could not possibly be dead. Having done her duty, weary beyond belief, Langtree made her way to her cabin, and lay down on her bunk to give way to her tears, her pent-up emotions as a woman, not a high-ranking officer in the Women's Royal Naval Service. When she felt calmer, getting up she bathed her eyes, combed her hair, straightened her uniform and went back to her office.

Her colleague and second-in-command, Second Officer Julia Whitfield, who occupied an adjoining office, was answering the telephone when Rachel came in. 'The War Office,' she explained briefly, hanging up the receiver, 'about the accident. They're sending someone this afternoon to investigate. Heads will roll, I daresay.' She added concernedly, 'You look all in, ma'am. Would a

98

cup of coffee help?'

A strong bond of affection and trust existed between the two women. The last thing Langtree needed right now was tea and sympathy. 'Coffee will be fine,' she said brusquely, glad of her colleague's support in her hour of need. 'But you must be in need of more than coffee. Why don't you nip down to the canteen for a bite to eat?'

Whitfield smiled, albeit grimly. 'I will, if you will,' she suggested quietly.

'But *I'm* not hungry,' Rachel replied huskily.

'Come to think of it, ma'am, neither am I,' Whitfield assured her superior officer, understanding full well the depths of her despair at the death of someone close and dear to her, recalling the horror of that blazing transport vehicle of the night before, from which had been dragged the bodies of the three young women and the charred remains of its driver.

All night long, Whitfield had remained with Langtree, in excess of her own duties. To desert her now was unthinkable, despite the heaviness of her eyelids from lack of sleep, and a hunger pain in the pit of her stomach the size of Wookey Hole, in her native Cheshire. She said levelly, 'Very well then, ma'am, I'll order the coffee right away.'

The War Office investigators arrived at two o'clock, four of them, grim faced and officious. Polite yet impervious, they questioned Langtree and Whitfield closely about the accident: the precise time of its occurrence, where they were and what they were doing at the time; what they had seen and heard – all of which Rachel answered with the dignity becoming an officer and a gentlewoman, even when the questions related to her identification of the victims of the crash. Never once did Langtree betray a sign of her inner turmoil as the questioning continued. Her self-control was complete, remarkable to Whitfield's way of thinking.

Suddenly the phone rang. 'It's for you, ma'am,' Whitfield said, answering the call. 'Flying Officer Drysdale is here to see you, by appointment, I gather. Shall I ask him to wait in reception?'

'No, have him come up at once.' Turning to the men from the Ministry, she said charmingly, 'If you'll excuse me, gentlemen, I do have other matters to attend to. Second Officer Whitfield will show you out.'

When they had gone, Langtree's self-control broke momentarily as she awaited Peter's arrival, dreading, as she did, imparting to him the news that Pearl was pregnant at the time of her death, and adding to the poor boy's distress. Even so, he must be told, and she must be the one to tell him, as calmly and unemotionally as possible, for his sake as well as her own.

When he came into the office, she stepped forward, hands outstretched to greet him. 'Sit down, Peter,' she said quietly. 'I have something to tell you.'

'About Pearl?' he asked bleakly. 'Sorry, Rachel. I'm not thinking quite clearly right now. I still can't register the fact that she's gone. I keep on remembering the Ox Hotel, waiting for her to walk into the room apologizing for being late for dinner, smiling that wonderful smile of hers. Well, you know what I mean.' Searching for a crumb of comfort, he said. 'At least she didn't die alone.'

Knowing exactly what he meant, Rachel said gently, 'You are quite right, my dear. Pearl didn't die alone. She died with the closest companion possible, the child she was carrying. *Your* child. And so, I think it true to say that she died happy, on her way to you, to tell you she was pregnant. Her death was instantaneous, of that I'm certain, which leads me to believe that she died happily, with thoughts of you and her baby uppermost in her mind. And that is what you must cling to now, Peter, for her sake, and your own.'

Peter looked stricken. 'Pearl was pregnant? I had no idea! And clinging to that thought is supposed to make me feel better is it?' he uttered savagely, rising quickly to his feet, pushing aside his chair as he did so. 'In any case, how the hell did *you* know she was pregnant? Was it common knowledge? Was I to be the last one to know?'

'No, Peter! The only person she told was her friend Wren Abbot, who was, to the best of my knowledge, the last person to see her alive. Pearl was on her way to the transport at the time. No one else knew, not even I, until

101

Abbot told me so the morning after the accident. Abbot was Pearl's bridesmaid at your wedding, if you recall. She and Pearl were best friends, one gathers. An unlikely friendship, perhaps, but they thought the world of one another.'

Peter said grimly, 'Where can I find Wren Abbot? I'd like a word with her, the sooner the better!'

'That is up to you entirely, of course,' Rachel said resignedly. 'Before you go, however, I have to say that I deeply regret that you seem to hold her responsible for the worsening of your troubles. The last thing I wanted or anticipated. She loved Pearl, too, remember?'

'I'm sorry, Rachel,' Peter apologized. 'I didn't mean to upset you, but I must speak to Wren Abbot, if, as you say, she was the last person to see Pearl alive. I need to know what Pearl said to her. I *must* know! Surely you can understand that?'

'If you say so,' Rachel replied coolly, sick at heart, tired of being calm, wise, understanding, and misunderstood. 'You must do as you think best.'

How could Rachel have possibly known that sending Peter in search of Wren Abbot would change the whole course of their lives in a far distant, unforseeable future?

Peter had scarcely noticed Fran on the day of his wedding. All the girls had worn uniform, all had been roughly the same height and

102

build, happy and smiling. Today, having discovered from the duty officer that Wren Abbot was due off watch at five o'clock, he decided to wait for her near the canteen where the stewards were setting out cups and saucers for afternoon tea. 'She's bound to pass this way, sir,' the duty officer said helpfully, 'they all do, as a rule. It's like a cavalry charge when the tea bell rings at four thirty.' Then, curiosity getting the better of her, 'Is she a friend of yours?'

'We have met,' he replied, 'but only once, and very briefly. I'm not sure if I'll recognize her.'

'In which case, I'll give her a hail, shall I? Tell her you're waiting, send her over to you?'

'Thank you. Yes. That's a good idea.'

'Shall I give her your name?'

'That won't be necessary, thanks all the same.'

Hmm, an interesting situation, the duty officer mused. A bit of a dark horse, Wren Abbot, neither pretty nor popular. So how come the dishy flying officer's interest in her? Daisy Shaw wondered.

The tea bell rang, the cavalry charge had begun. Uniformed females were jostling to get into the canteen, to nab tables and join the queue for cuppas and currant cake. Not that she blamed them, she could do with a tea break herself, Daisy mused, weighing up the Abbot situation. Perhaps the bloke waiting for her preferred plain girls? Ah, here came Frances now.

Fran's heart sank. She had guessed that FO Drysdale would want to talk to her sooner or later. He must have heard about the baby, and he had a right to know what his wife had said on the subject. Even so, talking about it would be a painful business for both of them, which she would rather postpone in her present state of mental exhaustion.

Peter said, 'I'm sorry to waylay you like this. I think you know why.'

Fran nodded briefly, thinking how ill and strained he looked, a far cry from the happy, buoyant bridegroom of his wedding day. 'We can't talk here,' she said.

'I realize that, of course. Then later, perhaps? There's a quiet pub called the Lamb and Flag in Wimbledon, in a side street off the main road. Will you meet me there at, say, seven o'clock? Or may I call for you?'

Bowing to the inevitable, Fran agreed to a meeting with Peter at the main entrance of Tanglewood at seven o'clock that evening. For Pearl's sake, and in memory of their friendship, how could she deny the man Pearl loved whatever comfort he might derive from an account of her last few minutes on earth, the last words she had spoken in the cabin before setting off to climb aboard the transport?

The Lamb and Flag was a small hostelry bearing the hallmarks of a village pub, with an inglenook fireplace, wooden settles, horse brasses and oak-panelled walls. The bar parlour was empty apart from a quartet of old men playing dominoes in a corner of the room, and the landlord, busily polishing glasses behind the beer pumps on the mahogany counter, who bade them a pleasant 'good evening' when Peter and Fran came in.

Feeling more relaxed in the warm, friendly atmosphere. Fran elected to sit near the inglenook fire. Asked what she would like to drink, lemonade was all she could think of. 'Why not try a shandy?' Peter suggested. 'That's lemonade with a dash of beer. I'll have the same.'

Returning with the drinks, he sat down next to her. Touched by her naivety, she was not a strikingly pretty girl, he decided, but attractive, with a clear complexion, greenish hazel eyes and a generous mouth, dark eyelashes and hair, and delicately curved eyebrows. Also, unusual in this day and age, she was not wearing make-up, not even a trace of lipstick or a dusting of face powder. But what attracted him most was her air of quiet self-containment, her lack of artifice, and he discerned the reasons why Pearl had felt drawn to this girl in particular, because she, too, had lacked artifice and pretence, had possessed the same air of stillness and repose.

He said quietly, 'There's no need to talk to me, if you don't feel up to it. It's just that I loved Pearl so much. Now she's gone, and – oh, I can't explain how I feel, right now.'

Fran said gently, 'I once read a book, a love

story, but the final pages were missing, so I never knew how the story ended. I could only guess at that ending. If only I had known for certain, but there was no one to tell me. I was very young at the time, and I've forgotten the title of the book, all I clearly remember is my frustration over those missing pages.'

It was then, haltingly, that Fran filled in the missing pages of Peter and Pearl's love story, repeating from memory every word that Pearl had said to her about one day looking across a crowded room, when love would be a reality, not make believe, ending with Pearl's joyous: 'Next thing you know, you'll be married and pregnant, just like me.' Adding Pearl's sotto voce warning to keep it quiet as she was meeting Peter that evening to break the news to him over cottage pie and chips. Fran concluded softly, 'At least you know now that Pearl died happy, the thought uppermost in her mind to tell you she was pregnant. So cling to that. Whatever happens, remember that Pearl died loving you with all her heart.'

Then, getting up from the table, she said, gathering up her belongings, 'I'd best be leaving now. Please don't bother to drive me back to the Wrennery. It isn't far, and the exercise and fresh air will do me good.'

And then she was gone, a trim figure in her Wren uniform, hurrying away from him as if, having filled in the missing pages of his love story, she could not bear his company a moment longer.

Seven

The Galsworthys had invited a contingent of Wrens to attend Pearl's funeral, Rachel Langtree, of course, their son-in-law and his parents, his Uncle Alex and, at Rachel's insistence, members of Peter's air crew who had been at the wedding.

'Be reasonable, Nell,' Rachel said when her sister-in-law had jibbed at the intrusion of strangers in what she saw as a family matter. 'Peter was Pearl's husband, for heaven's sake; his uncle, Group Captain Condermine, was Peter's best man at their wedding. As for the girls of Number Four Watch, they were Pearl's friends and colleagues. How do you think she'd feel if they were precluded from attending her funeral?'

'As Henry and I were precluded from attending her wedding, you mean?' Eleanor retorted bitterly.

'Look, Nell,' Rachel said wearily, 'isn't it time to put the past behind you? The funeral's next week. All the people who knew and loved Pearl will be there to pay their respects, villagers, servants, shopkeepers. The church will be packed, prayers said, hymns sung, tears shed. Is it too much to ask that

107

you behave with dignity and restraint when it comes to meeting Peter, his family and Pearl's comrades? All eyes will be on you, Nell, remember. Any sign of hostility or indifference on your part will be duly noted and remarked on afterwards. Is that what you want? To air your grievances in public at your daughter's funeral?'

'No, of course not,' Eleanor riposted sharply. 'Really, Rachel, you presume too far, at times, in telling me how to behave! *I* am Lady Galsworthy, not a ... a Billingsgate fishwife, as your words appear to suggest!'

Drawing in a deep breath of relief, Rachel knew that she had won the battle of wills, and why. Her words, 'All eyes will be on you, Nell, remember', had done the trick, as she had imagined they would. Bathed in the spotlight of approval, Nell would play her role as a grieving mother to perfection, to the extent of welcoming Peter and his family to The Grange if not affectionately, at least graciously, as befitted the lady of the manor.

The day of the funeral dawned fair and clear. The sun was shining, birds singing, and yet there was no feeling of joy, of springtime in the air, rather an overwhelming sense of sadness at the sudden, shocking death of a lovely young woman, whose coffin had rested overnight in the village church.

A silent, shadowy figure had been there, night long, keeping vigil beside the catafalque. Rachel and the verger Robert Simms knew of Peter's presence in the church. At midnight, at three o'clock and again at five o'clock, Rachel had taken flasks of hot coffee to sustain him, not speaking, understanding his deep, silent grief, his need to be alone with his wife on this, her last night on earth.

At seven o'clock, the verger quietly reminded him that the time had come to end his vigil. Nodding briefly, Peter stood up, laid his hand on the coffin, whispered, 'Goodbye, my darling, till we meet again,' and followed Simms to his cottage, down the lane near the church, to bathe, shave, and put on his uniform before driving to meet his parents, whose train was due to arrive at Fairford Station at nine thirty.

The verger's wife, Gladys, a kindly grey-haired woman who knew about the vigil, and knew how to keep a secret, had sponged and pressed Peter's uniform the night before, when he'd exchanged it for dark-grey trousers and a black, thick-knit sweater, and had hung it up to air in her warm, pin-neat kitchen.

'Now, sit you down and get something to eat inside you,' Gladys insisted when he appeared from the bathroom, placing a platter of bacon and eggs on the kitchen table in front of him. 'You've a long day ahead of you, and no one can live on coffee and fresh air. An' don't tell me you're not hungry, cos it stands to reason you must be – a strapping lad of your age!' And she was right.

Miraculously, Pearl seemed to be with him, here in this warm kitchen, smiling at him, just as he remembered her, no longer confined in that flower-bedecked coffin, but still an essential presence in his life. And this he had prayed for, night long: faith in an afterlife, the knowledge that death held no dominion over the power of love.

Rachel had been instrumental in arranging Peter's stay at the verger's cottage, of which the Galsworthys knew nothing. She had also been responsible for booking rooms for Peter's parents and Alex Condermine at the village pub, where they would stay overnight after the funeral.

The Wren contingent and members of Peter's air crew would arrive and depart by means of transport vehicles from Tanglewood and Ringrose. There would be a buffet luncheon at The Grange after the church service, following which the Wrens and air crew would return to base.

The girls of Four Watch talked in hushed voices on the journey. Fran remained silent as she stared out of the window, dreading her return to The Grange without Pearl, remembering that happy weekend they had spent together, and the many events that had occurred since then. Her visit to Middleton following the death of her Aunt Dorothy; the surprise news of Pearl's engagement on her return to Tanglewood; Pearl and Peter's wedding day. She thought about the vase of spring flowers on the registrar's desk. Strange

110

how inconsequential memories remained indelibly printed on the mind to conjure up precise moments in time, so that from now on, whenever she caught the scent of daffodils, in springtimes yet to come, she would remember that wedding day, just as she would remember, whenever she heard Beethoven's Moonlight Sonata, Pearl seated at a grand piano, by candlelight.

Above all, Fran dreaded coming face to face with Peter once more, and with Alex Condermine; the horror of the burial service, the committal of Pearl's coffin into the grave: earth to earth, ashes to ashes, dust to dust, recalling the feelings of loneliness and despair she had suffered at her mother's funeral when the first spade of earth had been scattered on the coffin lid.

Mrs Bates, the housekeeper, was on her way to the dining room with a tray of food when Fran and the other girls came into the hall. The Galsworthys were in the drawing room at the time, entertaining a specially invited coterie of personal friends of theirs from London, some of whom would be staying on at The Grange for the weekend – as though Pearl's funeral was a cause for celebration, Rachel thought angrily, refusing a proffered glass of sherry, having also refused an invitation to the weekend house party.

Nothing would induce her to spend a moment longer than necessary under the same roof as her sister-in-law. She had been here long enough as it was. Her bags were already packed. The minute the buffet luncheon was over, she would return to Tanglewood with the girls of Four Watch.

Her sympathy lay with Mrs Bates, called upon to cater and cook for not only the buffet luncheon, but also the house-party guests, ten of them all told, with the help of her husband and two young girls from the village, hired by her ladyship to help with the washing-up and preparation of the vegetables, to make beds and clean the bathrooms. Meanwhile, Mr Bates would be expected to bring in logs, light and mend the fires, and, acting as a general factotum, serve breakfast, luncheon and dinner.

Utterly ridiculous, to Rachel's way of thinking, and she had said so in no uncertain terms, thus deepening the rift between herself and the Galsworthys. Not that she cared tuppence about that. Pray God, after today, she would never have to set eyes on them ever again.

Anxious for a word with Mrs Bates, following her to the dining room, Fran said, 'Please, let me lend you a hand with the tray,' thinking how ill and weary the woman looked, understanding why, knowing how much she had loved Pearl, how she must be feeling now, on the day of her funeral.

'Oh, Miss Fran,' Mrs Bates murmured hoarsely, 'I said I hoped we'd meet again soon. I meant what I said, but not under these circumstances. It seems like a bad dream somehow.' Setting down the tray, hands trembling, tears trickled down her cheeks. 'The fact is, I scarcely know which way to turn. I have this table to finish setting, and there's more food in the kitchen waiting to be brought through. Bates is in the drawing room, serving sherry to her ladyship's posh London guests, ten of whom are staying over for the weekend. How we shall manage, I just don't know.'

'Don't worry, Mrs Bates, I'll give you a hand. I'll bring in the food from the kitchen, for starters, shall I? I do know my way to the kitchen, remember?'

'But you *can't*, Miss Fran! You're here as a guest.'

'No, Mrs Bates, I'm here as Pearl's friend. What would she think of me, standing here gassing when I could be doing something useful? And I do know something about cooking. I could apply to First Officer Langtree for a twenty-four-hour leave of absence, help you in the kitchen, and go back to London first thing tomorrow morning. That's settled then, is it?'

Deeply touched by the reason behind Fran's request for a twenty-four-hour leave of absence after the funeral, Rachel said coolly, 'Well done, Abbot,' with a dawning awareness of the girl's true worth. 'But why not a forty-eight-hour pass? I'll book you in at the Flag and Compass, and expect you back at Tanglewood by eighteen hundred hours on Sunday. Any questions?'

113

'No, ma'am, just a few problems. You see, ma'am, I haven't a toothbrush or pyjamas with me, not even a face flannel or a cake of soap.'

Rachel smiled, the first time she had felt inclined to do so since heaven knew when. She said, 'Here, take my overnight case. Your need is greater than mine!' And then she was gone, a slim, trim figure boarding the transport to Tanglewood.

Later, in The Grange kitchen, Fran beat Yorkshire pudding batter till her wrist ached, basted the sirloin of beef sizzling in the oven, parboiled the potatoes she had peeled, prior to placing them round the meat, washed pots and pans and scraped carrots and pared parsnips. This left Mrs Bates free to get on with the making of pastry for apple pies and gooseberry tarts, while she helped her as unobtrusively as possible, relieving her of the strain of cooking dinner for the house-party guests her ladyship had so thoughtlessly invited for the weekend, which involved her in not merely cooking but the preparation of the guest rooms beforehand, the making up of beds for the visitors in long disused four posters that had needed airing to dispel any trace of dampness, the filling of stone hot water bottles, the boiling of kettles and repeated trips up and down stairs.

Now Bates, grim faced and exhausted, having cleared the dining table of the lunch-eon buffet, was resetting it for dinner, carrying heavy trays of cutlery, china and glasses to the dining room.

'Poor Bates,' his wife said sympathetically, 'he's been up since the crack of dawn, lighting fires, digging up vegetables, answering the doorbell, serving sherry in the drawing room. It just isn't good enough if you ask me. Truth to tell, Miss Fran, we're thinking of moving on, finding ourselves a job elsewhere. Things were different in the old days, when Miss Pearl was alive. Now she's gone, the sooner we're out of here, the better. Lady Galsworthy should think shame on herself, using us the way she has done. Bates is a gardener, for God's sake, not a butler!'

She continued angrily, 'Marvellous, isn't it, the way some folk live? Rabbit pie for the likes of us, sirloin of beef for our lords and masters! Sir Henry brought the meat from London, an' not just beef but a leg of lamb, a York ham, pork sausages, a dozen or more bottles of champagne, not to mention sherry, red and white wine, all in a great wicker hamper strapped on the back of his limousine. And guess who had to carry that hamper into the house. Bates, that's who!'

She continued downheartedly, 'I'm sorry, Miss Fran, I shouldn't be burdening you with my troubles. I can't help worrying what her ladyship would say if she knew you were here.'

'She does know. First Officer Langtree told her so. And would you mind dropping the Miss? Just call me Fran.'

115

'Well, if you say so. A real good help you are, an' all. I don't know how I'd have managed without you. A couple of village lasses are coming in tomorrow, an' a fat lot of use they'll be in the kitchen. As daft as brushes, the pair of them.'

'I'll be here all day tomorrow,' Fran reassured her, 'and on Sunday morning. I'll come first thing to help with the breakfast, see to the vegetables and wash the pots. Just tell me what to do, and I'll do it.'

Mrs Bates heaved a sigh of relief. Then, 'But where will you stay overnight? Any road, I thought you only had a twenty-four-hour leave.'

'Don't worry, that's all taken care of, thanks to First Officer Langtree. I'm to stay at the Flag and Compass, and she granted me a forty-eight-hour leave. What's more, she left me her overnight case, pyjamas, toothbrush and so on.'

'Now she's what I call a real lady.' Mrs Bates beamed. Her husband came into the kitchen at that moment. 'Well, all's ready in yonder,' he announced, 'and now I'd best be off to the drawing room to start serving the sherry. Huh, I'd sooner be out in the garden doing my proper job. God, how I hate this get-up,' he said, referring to his dark suit of clothes, stiff collar and the white gloves he had on. 'I feel a right danged fool!'

'You look just fine, love,' His wife assured him, 'and the dinner's nearly ready. The beef's resting, an' the Yorkshires have risen a

116

treat.' She laughed. 'No wonder, the beating Fran gave them.'

Dinner was served at seven thirty. At a quarter to ten, having helped with the clearing away and the washing-up, Bates walked Fran to the Flag and Compass, feeling more cheerful than he had done for many a day. He said, 'You've been a real godsend, Miss Fran, helping my wife an' me the way you have done. Now you get a good night's sleep. You must be fair worn out.'

'We all are,' she replied quietly. 'It has been a long, difficult day, and I'm glad it's over.'

She had spoken too soon. Bidding Bates goodnight, the last person she had expected to meet, entering the hotel, was Peter Drysdale. Not that she disliked the man, quite the reverse. She had deeply admired his dignity and bearing at the funeral, she simply felt unequal to reliving that traumatic event, much less talking about it, in her present state of emotional exhaustion. On the other hand, to pass by him without a word was unthinkable.

Peter said, 'Forgive me, Fran. Rachel, that is First Officer Langtree, told me you'd be staying here, and why. It was splendid of you to stay on to help the Bateses. Pearl would be so pleased, so proud of you. Just the kind of thing she would have done given the chance.'

He paused momentarily, then said, 'Please, if you're not too tired, I'd like you to meet my parents. They're in the lounge. I've just ordered tea and biscuits. Tea, Mum's favourite

117

tipple!' He smiled awkwardly. 'They never met Pearl, you see, but they'd like to meet you – her best friend.'

'Very well, then. But don't expect me to talk about her, because I couldn't. Not now. Not tonight.'

'I understand,' Peter said quietly. 'I'm sure they will, too. They're just nice, ordinary folk, but they'd appreciate your saying goodnight to them. They'll be leaving here tomorrow morning, you see, and I think that meeting you will make Pearl seem more real to them, somehow.'

Mrs Drysdale was a thin, anxious-looking woman, clearly out of her depth in a situation she scarcely understood, having been called upon to attend the funeral of a daughter-in-law she had never set eyes on, the daughter of a baronet, no less, and a Cabinet Minister to boot. She was accustomed to wealth and easy living, judging by her background, a magnificent country manor set in acres of park land, so why marry a man incapable of keeping her in the style to which she was accustomed? Why the secret marriage?

'Pearl wasn't like that,' Peter had explained after the funeral 'She cared nothing for wealth or background. We married for love, in secret because she didn't want her parents to find out...'

'That she was marrying beneath her?' his mother had interrupted bitterly.

'No. Because she, that is we, both wanted a quiet wedding. We decided to marry first, to face the music later. I'm sorry, Mother, but aren't you saying now what you'd have said at the time, had you known about it?'

'Yes, son, I suppose so,' Mrs Drysdale had had the grace to admit, glad to see the back of The Grange and Pearl's stand-offish parents. They had been in Peter's car at the time, driving towards the Flag and Compass, looking forward to a wash and brush up, a change of clothing and a quiet meal in the dining room. The last thing they'd expected was that Alex Condermine, who Mr and Mrs Drysdale had studiously avoided at the funeral, would also be staying at the hotel.

Alma Drysdale had gritted her teeth, hoping against hope that he would have the courtesy not to intrude, but courtesy had never been her son-in-law's strong point, besides which Peter was inordinately fond of him, despite Alex's cavalier treatment of their daughter, Rosemary. Now, at Peter's instigation, the wretched man was coming over to their table to dine with them.

Aware of Alma's disapproval, Peter had said, sotto voce, 'Come on, Mother, we can scarcely ignore him. He is, after all, Rosemary's husband.'

'Peter's right,' Cyril Drysdale ventured, in support of his son. 'Might as well make the best of a bad job. There's been enough grief as it is, today. Why add to it?'

'Thanks, Dad,' Peter murmured gratefully, rising to his feet to welcome his Uncle Alex.

Later, albeit reluctantly, accompanying

119

Peter into the lounge to meet his parents, Fran's heart had lurched at the sight of Alex Condermine, seated at the Drysdales' table, drinking *tea*. Actually tea, not whisky or champagne, but common-or-garden tea.

Moreover, apparently perfectly sober, he had risen to his feet to greet her, along with Cyril Drysdale.

Bemusedly, Fran had acknowledged her introduction to Alma and Cyril Drysdale. When it came to Alex, she said, stiffly, 'Group Captain Condermine and I have met before,' remembering, yet preferring to forget, their former brief liaison of whispered words, unanswered letters and that farewell kiss he had planted on her lips at King's Cross Station.

Alma Drysdale said mistily, 'I understand that you were Pearl's best friend? Unfortunately, my husband and I were destined never to meet our daughter-in-law. A pretty girl by all accounts.'

'No, Mrs Drysale,' Fran said quietly, 'Pearl was not pretty, she was beautiful. Steel true, blade straight through and through, incapable of meanness or deceit in any shape or form whatsoever. A rare and lovely human being without whom this dreary world of ours will be a much poorer place to live in. Now, if you'll excuse me...'

Tired beyond belief, Fran hurriedly quit the lounge, closely followed by Peter Drysdale, calling out to her to wait, cursing himself as a fool for pushing her beyond the limits of her endurance. Catching up with her in a passage

120

leading to the stairs, he said, 'Please forgive me, Fran, I didn't mean to upset you. What you said about Pearl was wonderful. I can't thank you enough, but I should have known better than to coerce you into meeting my parents the way I did, knowing how tired you were.'

'You look pretty tired, too,' Fran said, noticing the lines of suffering on his handsome young face. 'Perhaps what we both need is a good night's sleep, if such a thing is possible. Shall you be leaving here tomorrow?'

'No. I'll be here till Sunday. There are people I need to see, certain arrangements to be made. And you?'

'I'll be helping out at The Grange all day tomorrow, and on Sunday morning,' Fran said. 'I'm due back at Tanglewood at eighteen hundred hours on Sunday evening.'

'I see. In which case, may I offer you a lift? I'm due back at Ringrose at twenty hundred hours on Sunday.'

'Well, if you're sure you don't mind,' Fran replied uncertainly. 'I'm not very good company at the moment.'

'That makes two of us,' Peter reminded her ruefully.

'Yes, I suppose so. Well, goodnight, Peter,' she said, going upstairs to her room.

'Goodnight, Fran,' he responded wistfully. 'See you on Sunday.'

Early next morning, after breakfast, Peter drove his parents to Fairford Station to see them safely on their way home, bidding them goodbye with a deep inner feeling of relief that their visit was over and done with – on their side that ghastly meeting with Pearl's parents before and after the funeral, and in his case the gut-churning misery of that funeral: the committal of his wife's body to a hole in the ground, carrying with her the foetus of a child destined never to see the light of day, never to learn how to walk and talk, how to laugh and play in the sunshine. This was the reason why Peter needed to see certain people before his return to Ringrose, to ensure that the wording on his wife's gravestone would read simply: 'In everlasting memory of a mother and child. Pearl Drysdale. A pearl beyond price.' Just that and nothing more, as Pearl would have wished.

Doubtless Sir Henry and Lady Galsworthy would be up in arms when they found out, but Peter could not have cared less about the lord of the manor and his so-called lady. He did care, however, about Frances Abbot – an odd, lonely, self-contained kind of girl, in need of kindness and affection to bring out the best in her, as Pearl had done.

At the station, Alma said reflectively, 'That girl we met last night. Tell her she's welcome to stay with us any time she feels like it. Better still, give me her address and I'll write to her myself.'

It had been a long, fraught weekend. Sitting beside Peter on their way back to London,

Fran wished never to set eyes on The Grange ever again. The village, yes, the church, and the Bateses, but not The Grange and its inhabitants, the overbearing lady of the manor and her weak-willed husband.

Never would she forgive the Galsworthys their insensitivity in turning a wake into a weekend house party, as if Pearl's death had meant less than nothing to them. Little wonder that she had joined the Wrens to get away from her parents, just as she, Fran, had joined up to get away from her overbearing Aunt Dorothy.

Deeply aware of his companion's silence, hazarding a guess at the reason for it, Peter said quietly, 'Glad to be going home?'

'Home? I haven't got a home,' Fran uttered briefly. 'If you mean Tanglewood, well yes, I'll be glad to get back into a routine, being told what to do, and when, knowing exactly where I stand. Queueing up for my weekly pay, for breakfast, lunch, tea and supper. It's what I'm used to. God only knows what I'll do when the war is over, but I daren't think that far ahead.'

'For what it's worth,' Peter said quietly, 'if I survive this war, you'll have a home with me. A bolt hole, if you prefer: someone to turn to, should you need someone to rely on. No ties. No strings. I shall never marry again. I couldn't, not after Pearl. But I mean what I say, and I want you to remember that.'

'I'll remember,' Fran murmured, close to tears.

Part Two

Part Two

Eight

Fran felt like a fish out of water. A hermit crab robbed of its shell, a spider robbed of its web. So far as she was concerned, the end of the war meant an end of the feeling of security she had known at Tanglewood.

Somehow, she could not share her colleagues' rejoicing at the prospect of being demobbed – exchanging their uniforms for civilian clothing, a longed for reunion with their families and friends, a return to so-called normal life, whatever normality entailed. Fran scarcely knew the meaning of the word. In her book, normality entailed not being late on duty, obeying orders, queueing for meals and hammering out messages vital to the war effort on her teleprinter keyboard.

She had no family awaiting her return to civilian life with open arms, no job to go back to. So what the hell was she supposed to do with her life from now on? Join the nearest dole queue? Apply for mundane jobs as a shorthand typist? Find herself a bed-sitting room somewhere or other in the Greater London area? Or should she return to Middleton, from whence she had sprung?

Certainly a business trip there seemed

indicated. The tenants of what she still thought of as her Aunt Dorothy's house had expressed a wish to buy the property, and, all things considered, she might just as well part with it. Thanks to the rent monies she received since her aunt's death, she had a tidy nest egg in her Post Office savings account, but she knew, deep down, that a return to Middleton to live was out of the question; the very thought of it depressed her. No, it was time to move on. Where to she hadn't the faintest idea, however, until, one day, out of the blue, she received a letter from Alex Condermine:

Dear Frances,

    I'll be leaving Scotland soon, returning to my home in Wiltshire, staying overnight in London en route, at the Great Northern Hotel. If, as I suspect, you are uncertain about your future now that the war is over, I have a proposition to put to you which, of course, you may feel unable to accept. That is entirely up to you. No strings attached, I assure you. With your permission, I propose a meeting on the first of September at the Wimbledon Hotel at, say, seven thirty, for dinner. Please say you'll be there.

    Yours sincerely,
    Alex

Well, why not? Fran thought fatalistically. One thing was for certain, he couldn't propose marriage, since he was already married. So why not find out exactly what he had in mind?

'My dear Frances,' Alex said, stepping forward to greet her, looking far less imposing in his civilian clothing than he had done in his group captain's uniform, 'how kind of you to have come. So how's the world treating you?'

'It isn't,' Fran said flatly. 'I'm paying my own way!'

'Look, Fran,' he said placatingly, 'I know we got off to a bad start, but can't we let bygones be bygones? I'm not half as bad as you think I am. At least I hope not.'

'So do I, for your sake,' Fran reminded him. 'So why am I here?'

'Let's discuss that over dinner, shall we?' he responded quietly. 'Do you like chicken casserole, by the way?'

'Not particularly. But if that's what you've ordered, so be it!' Then, realizing that she was being bloody minded, she said, 'I'm sorry, Alex, it's just that I'm not thinking quite clearly at the moment, wondering what the future holds in store for me when I leave Tanglewood.'

'Then how would you feel about coming to Wiltshire as my housekeeper?' Alex asked the question tentatively, not believing for one moment that she would agree to his proposition, yet desperately in need of someone of Fran's calibre to restore his long-neglected house to some kind of order. Someone he knew he could trust when his back was turned.

She said, 'But I've never kept house in my life. All I'm good at is cleaning.'

'Oh come now, Frances, homemaking comes naturally to most women, I imagine, and I *am* offering you a home, a room of your own, freedom to come and go as you choose, a decent salary...'

'In return for what, exactly?'

'The usual things.' Taking her elbow, he steered her towards the dining room. 'Please, sit down and let me explain.' He smiled charmingly. 'I haven't ordered yet, by the way. The chicken casserole was merely a suggestion. Perhaps you'd prefer the fish pie. Ah, here's the waitress.' His prevarication was deliberate. Fran required careful handling, and he needed a woman about the house. A lot would need doing to make it habitable.

Taking out his wallet, he handed her a photograph of the house, a snapshot taken from the garden some time ago. Looking at the photo, Fran noted it was an old house, with latticed windows, a thatched roof and ivy covered walls, not at all what she'd imagined. Not a modern, pre-war villa, slate roofed, bay windowed, lacking in character, but a cottage-style dwelling, picturesque and charming.

He said, replacing the picture in his wallet, 'You seem surprised, but I thought you'd like to know what you'll be letting yourself in for, if you decide to accept my offer. As you can

130

see, "Wisteria" is no ordinary house, the reason why I bought it. Despite your poor opinion of me, at least credit me with good taste.

'I fell in love with the house the moment I saw it. Fortunately, I had the wherewithal to buy it. And, contrary to what you may have heard about me from my in-laws, I came by my money honestly. Granted, I speculated to accumulate, but what's wrong with that? I gambled, took chances, I admit. In the Drysdales' book, the heinous crime I committed lay in falling in love with and marrying their daughter. Thankfully, Peter did not share his parents' poor opinion of me. We were, and still are, thank God, like father and son. I'm not a religious man, but I thank God every day of my life that he survived the war. And, hopefully, when I return home to "Wisteria", he will be a frequent visitor to my Wiltshire hideaway.'

He continued heartily, 'Ah, here's the food. Truth to tell, I'm so hungry I could eat the proverbial horse. All I've eaten since leaving Edinburgh this morning is a cheese and pickle sandwich.'

Looking across the table at him, Fran said thoughtfully, 'I like the look of your house, but I'm not cut out as a housekeeper. I don't like cooking, for one thing, though I don't dislike housework. I just wouldn't want the responsibility of looking after someone else, that's all.'

'Especially me?' he suggested, tongue in
131

cheek.

'Especially you,' Fran conceded. 'Frankly, Alex, I wouldn't trust you as far as I could throw you.'

'Can't say I blame you,' he admitted ruefully. 'The fact remains that I really need a helping hand to clean up my cottage, and you, I daresay, are in need of somewhere to live when you leave Tanglewood. In which case, why not kill two birds with one stone?'

'Meaning what, exactly?' Fran asked suspiciously.

'Meaning, why not combine work and pleasure?'

'*Pleasure?* What kind of pleasure?'

'My God, Fran, you're a hard nut to crack! I'm simply offering you a month's holiday in the country, pub meals, plenty of exercise and fresh air, in exchange for a modicum of housework – washing and ironing curtains, for instance, clearing out cupboards, emptying drawers, vacuuming carpets, washing floors, polishing furniture, cleaning silver, and so on. Is that too much to ask?'

'On the face of it, no, I suppose not,' Fran demurred. 'On one condition, though. That this will be a business deal, pure and simple! No funny business, proper payment for my cleaning duties, otherwise it's no go! A month, you said? Very well, then, I accept your offer of a month in the country. A holiday? Scarcely that, I'd say, since I'll be up to my eyes in housework, most of the time!'

And so the die was cast. Leaving Tanglewood the following week, Fran travelled to Wiltshire to spend a month in the country with Alex Condermine, having written to her Middleton estate agents beforehand expressing her willingness to part with her property to the present tenants, at a realistic purchase price, and to let them know that she would travel north to conclude the deal a month hence, giving her forwarding address as 'Wisteria Cottage, Lockersleigh, Devizes, Wiltshire'.

Turning her back on Tanglewood was one of the hardest things she had done in her life. Awaiting the arrival of a taxi to take herself and her belongings to Paddington, she deeply regretted leaving behind her the now obsolete WT station overlooking Wimbledon Common, and all its memories, both happy and sad, which had been part and parcel of her life for the past three and a half unforgettable years.

But the past was over and done with. All that mattered now was the future. What that future held in store for her, she had no more idea than the Man in the Moon. Ideally, a love affair leading to marriage, children, a home of her own, a man to call her own; a heart-stopping moment of recognition across a crowded room, perhaps. The way Pearl's love affair with Peter Drysdale had begun. Who knew? Who could say for certain how love began, or how it might end?

When her taxi arrived, she climbed into the back seat, her luggage stowed in the boot of the car. As it drove away from Tanglewood, resisting the strong temptation to look back, Fran stared ahead of her stonily, not at the past, but into the future.

Evening shadows were fast falling, a log fire had been lit in the drawing room, table lamps cast a warm glow of welcome as Fran crossed the threshold of Wisteria Cottage. 'Well, what do you think of it?' Alex asked, helping her indoors with her luggage.

'It's lovely,' Fran murmured appreciatively, glancing about her at the beamed ceiling, comfortable settee and armchairs surrounding the wide stone fireplace.

'Good. Glad you like it. Now, if you'll follow me, I'll show you your room. Come down when you're ready. I've made a shepherd's pie for supper. Or you can have poached eggs on toast, if you'd prefer. The bathroom's along the landing. Take your time. No need to hurry.'

He added, off-handedly, 'Your bed should be well aired, by the way. And not to worry, the key to your door's on the inside.' So saying, he hurried away downstairs, leaving her to unpack, to wash her hands and face, and to exchange her travelling clothes, a tweed skirt and jacket, for the blue wool dress she had worn at the Wimbledon Hotel on the occasion of Peter and Pearl's wedding celebration party.

Later, she came down to find him in the drawing room, staring into the fire. He had set a gate-legged table with the supper things, and there was the aroma of food from the kitchen. She said, 'Anything I can do to help?'

'No, everything's under control. So which is it to be, the shepherd's pie or poached egg on toast?'

'The pie, please,' she answered, not wishing to put him to the trouble of cooking something different for her.

Hurrying off to the kitchen, he returned, in due course, with the shepherd's pie, piping hot and nicely browned on top, which he placed on the table in front of her, adjuring her to help herself whilst he brought in the vegetables and gravy.

After they had finished eating. Fran said, 'If you'll show me the way to the kitchen, I'll do the washing-up, shall I? Then, if you don't mind, I'll go to bed. I *am* rather tired. It's been a long day.'

Alex frowned. 'You mean you're staying on?'

Smiling mysteriously, Fran said quietly, 'Well, as the saying goes, discretion is the better part of valour. With your permission, I'd like to stay on, as your friend, not your enemy.'

'Forget the washing up, I'll see to it. You get off to bed. Have a good night's sleep.' He added, tongue-in-cheek, 'Don't forget to lock your door. You look pretty fetching in that dress you're wearing.'

Fran smiled; despite their agreement, Alex still couldn't help himself. Knowing he was teasing her deliberately, she said, 'I look less fetching in my wincyette pyjamas, believe me!'

Alex's favourite watering hole, the Bargee, stood on the banks of the Kennet and Avon Canal, hence its name, although barges were no longer a feature of the landscape. And *what* a landscape, Fran thought, revelling in a sense of freedom at the sight of vast acres of grass-covered hills rolling away to seemingly limitless horizons.

The pub was plain and functional, with wooden tables and benches, bare wooden floorboards, and a smoky coal fire at the far end of the tap room. The customers, playing darts and dominoes and supping beer, were mainly elderly farm labourers wearing corduroy trousers, flannel shirts, and hefty, earth-caked boots, with whom, to Fran's surprise, Alex seemed entirely at home, they with him.

Apart from the landlord's wife, a plump red-cheeked woman, wearing a hand-knitted jumper, and with a flowered pinny tied about her ample midriff, Fran was the only female present, therefore an object of speculation.

'Now, Captain, what'll it be?' the landlord, a beefy individual with tobacco-stained teeth, asked pleasantly. 'The usual? A pint of bitter? A bite to eat? Ada, love, tell the Captain an' his lady what's on the menu.'

'Home-made tomato soup, cottage pie or

cheese and pickle sandwiches,' Ada reeled off obligingly, casting an eye in Fran's direction, envious of her slim figure and her air of quiet self-containment, wondering who on earth she could be. The Captain's latest fancy woman, more than likely.

Alex said easily, 'Well, sister of mine, what shall it be?'

'The cottage pie, please,' Fran said desperately, thinking, the damn cheek of the man. 'Sister of mine' indeed! On the other hand, why feed the fires of rumour and speculation regarding their *unorthodox* relationship?

They ate out of doors, at a rough wooden table overlooking the canal, on a perfect September afternoon. 'Sorry, Fran,' Alex apologized, when they were alone together. 'I said what I did to safeguard your reputation. Forgive me?'

'I suppose so. But one of these days you're bound to come unstuck. You do realize that, don't you?'

Screwing up his eyes against the sunlight glinting on the weedy waters of the canal, Alex smiled reflectively. 'The trouble with you, Fran,' he said lazily, 'is that you know nothing of life, of reality. You are a nice, attractive young woman without the faintest idea how to make use of your looks, your sexuality. So ask yourself what will happen if, one day, you meet a man you really want. What will you do? Give him the cold shoulder? Cling to your virginity at all costs? If so, more fool you!'

'Thanks, Alex, but my future is scarcely your concern, is it?'

'Nor mine yours, apparently,' he said regretfully. 'A pity, really. I am quite fond of you, you know.'

'Really? I can't think why! This is a business proposition, remember? So let's stick to business, shall we? I intend washing curtains this afternoon. Tomorrow I'll be cleaning paintwork, knocking down cobwebs, ironing and re-hanging the curtains. In short, earning my pay, so I strongly advise you to keep from under my feet and leave me to get on with my work. Understood?'

Coldly angry, Fran walked back to Wisteria Cottage alone. Prepared to meet Alex halfway, to forgive and forget his past behaviour, now she could scarcely wait to see the back of him, the arrogant upstart, with his one-track mind.

Not looking where she was going, she failed to notice the tall figure of a man coming towards her, until, hearing his voice calling her name, looking up at him, she gasped disbelievingly, 'Peter, what on earth are you doing here?'

Smiling down at her, he said, 'Looking for Alex. My fault if I've missed seeing him. I should have told him I was coming.'

'He's at the Bargee. We've just had lunch together. I'm on my way to the cottage as it happens.' Then, by way of explanation, 'I'm here on a kind of working holiday, helping him to get settled.'

Peter said, 'I came with that very thought in mind. I haven't seen the old boy since heaven knows when. He wrote me he was coming back to Wiltshire to live, and I figured he'd be glad of a helping hand. I had no idea you'd be here. A pleasant surprise, I must say. It's great to see you again, Fran, and looking so well. I take it you've been demobbed? So have I, more's the pity.' He grinned ruefully. 'Truth to tell, I hate being at a loose end, wondering what the future holds in store for me.'

Fran said quietly, 'I'm in the same boat myself. I have no qualifications, you see, apart from shorthand and typing, and the thought of finding myself a nine to five job in a stuffy office just doesn't appeal to me.'

'Then what, ideally, would you like to do?' Peter asked, as if her answer really mattered.

'Ideally? Well, to own a place of my own, I suppose, in a quiet corner of the world. A two up, two down cottage would do, with a garden and a hen-run. To start up a business cleaning other folks' houses. I've always been quite fond of housework: housework, not cooking. I loathe and detest cooking! A throwback to my childhood, I suppose, when nothing my mother cooked for my brothers was ever good enough for them.'

At that moment, Alex appeared on the towpath beside the canal. Catching sight of Peter he hurried forward to throw his arms about his nephew in an excess of affection, murmuring, 'My dear boy, how wonderful it is to see you again!'

139

'You too, Uncle Alex.'

Leaving the two men to their own devices, feeling like a spare part, Fran entered Wisteria Cottage to commence her house-cleaning duties.

She was perched on a step-ladder, taking down the drawing room curtains, when Peter entered the room, unnoticed. 'Here, let me do that,' he said.

'It's all right, I can manage.'

'I'm sure you can, but I'm here to help, remember?'

'Where's Alex?' she asked, remaining on her perch.

'In bed. He took some persuading, but knowing him as well as I do, I reckon bed's the best place for him. He'll be fine when he's recovered from his hangover.'

'Are you telling me he's drunk again? But he only had a couple of pints at lunch-time!' Turning to look down at Peter, her arms full of curtains, Fran slipped and would have fallen had he not been there to steady her. 'Hand me the curtains,' he said, 'then come down one step at a time. Don't argue, just do as you're told. You shouldn't have gone up the damn thing in the first place, it's not safe. First thing in the morning, I'll buy a new one. Ye gods, girl, you might have broken your neck if I hadn't come in when I did. Now, give me your hand, and take it slowly.'

His hand felt strong and warm in hers as he guided her down the ladder. 'Thanks, Peter,' she said shakily, strangely disturbed by his touch, his concern for her welfare. 'It's just that I have a job of work to do, and Alex told me to start with the drawing room curtains.'

'But not to risk life and limb in the process, I daresay.' Peter said grimly. 'He might have known that this old step-ladder would be unsafe. Well, all's well that ends well. Now, come through to the kitchen and I'll make us a pot of tea. What shall I do with these damn curtains, by the way?'

'Put them in the bath to soak overnight,' Fran suggested. 'I'll wash them and hang them out to dry tomorrow morning, if there are any pegs.'

Peter laughed. 'Why not make out a shopping list? Come with me to Devizes in the morning? It's a grand little town – lots of shops and an open market. Would you like that?'

'Yes, Peter. Very much indeed.' Not daring to admit to herself just *how* much. Apart from all else, he had arrived in the nick of time to prevent a full-scale row between herself and Alex, resulting from his unwarranted remarks regarding her life, or lack of it, and his going so far as to mention her virginity, as if virginity in an unmarried woman was some kind of disease in need of a cure.

She had Peter to thank for restoring her self-confidence, for his kindness and courtesy towards her at a time when she had desperately needed some consideration; the touch of a strong, warm hand in hers; a cup of tea made by someone other than herself a comforting presence in her life when, her spirits at a low ebb, she had been about to pack her belongings and leave Wisteria Cottage the next morning. Instead of which, now she had something to look forward to, a trip to Devizes, with Peter, to buy nothing more romantic than a step-ladder and a few clothes' pegs.

Nine

Never would Fran forget that Indian summer when she had fallen head over heels in love with Wiltshire and Peter Drysdale. Not that she had dared to admit, even to herself, the dawning awareness of her feelings towards him. She had simply revelled in his company, his kindness, his concern for her welfare, knowing in her heart that he regarded her as nothing more than Pearl's best friend, and therefore a person to be trusted and admired, in much the same way as he trusted and admired his Uncle Alex.

This, Fran accepted, knowing that she could never hope to supplant Pearl in Peter's affection. Nor would she attempt to do so. Settling for second best, she had at least, during that month at Wisteria Cottage, succeeded in sharing his innermost thoughts regarding the death of his wife, as well as his love of Wiltshire on their frequent visits to

Devizes and occasionally to Salisbury, when he had confessed to her his longing to settle thereabouts one day, and to purchase a small hotel in the country.

'With a trout stream running through the garden?' Fran had suggested, recalling Pearl's description of the cottage in which she and Peter had spent their honeymoon.

'Well, yes.' Peter smiled reflectively. 'Pearl told you about it, I guess? Not that I know the first thing about hotel keeping.'

'You could always learn, unless you have a job lined up. With your experience, you could become a flying instructor.'

'No. I'm through with flying. I've had enough of that to last a lifetime.' Fran's idea had taken root. He said, 'I could apply for a training course in hotel management, but that's not what I'm after. I need a job of work to do, hands on experience, learning the hard way, working as a kitchen hand or a porter, or whatever.'

'Then what's stopping you?' They were in the market place in Devizes, near the prestigious Bear Hotel. 'Go on, now's your chance. Ask to speak to the manager. Tell him you're after a job, however menial. Try to look hungry.'

'No need to try, I *am* hungry!' Peter laughed. But what if he turns me down?'

'Then we'll have lunch in the dining room. That way, at least one problem will be solved.' She urged him forward. 'I'll wait outside. If it's no go beckon me in and we'll have sausages and mash or egg and chips. *Anything* except fish, shepherd's or cottage pie!'

Awaiting Peter's reappearance, Fran thought about her brothers, her mother and that roast chicken dinner she'd provided the last Christmas they'd spent together, wondering where her brothers were now, if they were alive or dead. Remembering that, in a week from now, she'd be returning to Middleton to conclude the sale of her Aunt Dorothy's house, leaving Wisteria Cottage, Alex Condermine – and Peter – behind her, more than likely never to meet up with them again. After all, there was no real reason why she should.

Experience had taught her that nothing in life was certain or secure. People died or went away, leaving no trace of their existence apart from memories. Why, then, shouldn't she assume that when she left Wiltshire Peter would not also disappear from her life? The thought seemed unbearable, but he must never know how deeply she had come to care for him, how much the halcyon days of this Indian summer had meant to her. How much *he* meant to her.

Suddenly, there he was, emerging from the Bear Hotel, giving her the V for victory sign and grinning like a schoolboy. 'I've done it,' he said breathlessly. 'I've landed myself a job! Thanks to you, Fran! Oh, so many thanks to you!'

Caught up in his excitement, pushing unhappy thoughts to the back of her mind, living for the moment, she asked eagerly,

144

'Doing what, exactly?'

'Washing pots,' he announced joyously. 'Swabbing floors, cleaning ovens, what's known as kitchen-portering: scrubbing pantry shelves and being sworn at, I daresay. Apparently the chef is a bad-tempered so-and-so who threatened the last porter with a knife for leaving egg on the plates, which is the reason why I got the job, starting seven o'clock sharp tomorrow morning! Now, come on, let's celebrate, shall we? There's a caff round the corner. I'll treat you to a cheese sandwich and a cuppa!'

Alex was furious that Peter had landed himself with so demeaning a job.

'As a means to an end, Alex,' Peter reminded him, refusing to be browbeaten.

'Huh, that pie-in-the-sky hotel notion of yours, I suppose? You know damn well I want you here with me. Why rush into something you'll regret? Washing-up, indeed? Have you no self-respect? No ambition? A man of your intellect kitchen-portering for a living beggars belief. Look, Peter, I'm offering you a secure home here. Money no object. Why not take your time? Stay here until a worthwhile job comes your way? I have friends in high places, remember? String-pulling no problem. If you're determined to pursue hotel-keeping as a career, I could pull strings to find you a job as a trainee manager in one of the big London hotels, the Ritz, the Grosvenor or the Savoy.'

'Thanks, Alex, but my mind's made up. I'll visit you quite often, of course, but working at the Bear Hotel entitles me to room and board, plus my wages. Thirty shillings a week, no less. More importantly, I'll be learning about hotel management the hard way, and that's what I want, to start at the bottom of the ladder and work my way up.'

'Well, if that's your attitude, so be it!' Alex said angrily. 'In other words, you'll make use of me when it suits you to do so. Huh! After all I've done for you in the past! Supposing I tell you that, if you prefer living in at the Bear Hotel, you'll no longer be welcome at Wisteria Cottage?'

Peter stood his ground. 'You must do as you see fit,' he said levelly. 'And so must I,' calling Alex's bluff.

On the point of Fran's departure to Yorkshire, Peter asked for a forwarding address, and she had given him that of her solicitors. 'You mean you don't know where you'll be staying?'

'I haven't the faintest idea. I'll see about that when I get there. It shouldn't be too difficult. Middleton isn't exactly a bustling metropolis. In any case, I have a business appointment with my estate agents. I daresay they'll know of a small flat or a bed-sitting room to rent.'

'So you intend staying on there indefinitely?'

'Not if I can help it. I just need time to think

things over, to decide where to go from there.'

Peter said quietly, 'Why not come back to Wiltshire? You like it here, don't you?'

'Yes, I do. But I'd need somewhere to live, employment of some kind.'

He said eagerly, 'Remember that idea of yours? Starting your own business? Buying a home of your own. That sounded fine to me, or have you had second thoughts?'

'No, not really. I'd just need to test the ground a little first, find out if there's any call for domestic help in the area. Part- time help, that is. I'd hate to be lumbered with a full-time job. Well, they do say that variety is the spice of life, and it's freedom I'm after. Freedom to pick and choose.' She smiled ruefully. 'It's hard to explain.'

'There's no need, Fran. Pearl felt the same way. We both did, hence the quiet wedding. Pearl knew that telling her parents would be tantamount to telling the world and his wife. Sorry, perhaps I shouldn't have said that. It's just that what we felt for each other was so special, so personal, we wanted to keep it that way.'

'I know, Peter.' Fran's eyes filled with tears.

He said, 'I don't want to lose touch with you, Fran. You remind me of Pearl in so many ways. It would please me to think that you will return to Wiltshire in the not too distant future. Promise that you'll think about it?'

'I promise,' she said, experiencing an upsurge of happiness at being wanted. His words dispelling the spectre of a lonely future without him.

At that moment, the cab she had hired to take her to the station drew up at the garden gate, and Alex appeared on the doorstep to bid her farewell and a safe journey. 'Goodbye, m'dear,' he said gruffly. Come back soon, if you've a mind to. Your room will be ready and waiting.'

'Thanks, Alex. Take care of yourself.'

'Huh, who else will, if I don't? Not this young whippersnapper here. He couldn't care less about me. It's *you* he came to see. Can't say I blame him.' He chuckled hoarsely. 'Well, go on, Peter, kiss the girl goodbye. If you don't, *I* will! And I've forgotten more about kissing than you'll ever learn, believe me. Isn't that so, Fran?'

'I'm not qualified to judge,' Fran riposted, refusing to be drawn, 'and this is neither the time nor the place for a kissing contest. I'll miss my train otherwise, so you'll have to settle for this!' Turning at the gate, waving aside Peter's offer of help with her luggage she cupped her hands together and blew each of them a kiss, her eyes on Peter, not Alex, knowing that the kiss she blew Peter contained a portion of her heart that would always belong to him. Not that he wanted her heart, merely her friendship.

Middleton depressed Fran more now than ever before. She missed the rolling Downs, the soft wind-rippled grass, golden corn-sheaves stooked in stubble fields at harvest

148

time, the hazy warmth of Indian summer days, the drowsy humming of bees in flower-filled cottage gardens, the sound of church bells on Sundays, bells that had hung silent in their towers during the war.

Above all, she missed those Indian summer evenings at Wisteria, looking up at the moon and stars in a blue velvet sky, Peter beside her, savouring the peace and quietude of the countryside, sharing with him deep, companionable silences, saying little or nothing to break the spell of silence or dispel the enfolding magic of darkness, shadows, moon and starlight.

Now, Middleton, with its harsh lights, hard pavements and streets of red-brick houses, mundane shops, bus stops, billboards, cinema queues and couples, arms linked, chattering nineteen to the dozen, seemed as a wilderness to Fran as she hurried towards her rented cubbyhole of a flat. carrying a bag of groceries on her way home from her estate agent's office, in which she had signed away the deeds of her Aunt Dorothy's house for the princely sum of fifteen hundred pounds. A small fortune so far as she was concerned. Far more than she'd expected.

Even so, she could scarcely rejoice in crossing the threshold of her present accommodation, a basement flat in a prim Victorian villa, comprising a narrow hallway leading to a bay-windowed bed-sitting room, a tiny kitchen and an ice-cube of a bathroom – not with memories of Devizes strong in her mind, an endless yearning to be back there. At least it was clean, and the bed-sitting room was adequately furnished with a single divan bed in one corner of the room, a gas fire, a couple of chintz-covered armchairs, a table, two upright chairs, a sideboard and a what-not displaying a plethora of Goss china ornaments.

This flat might not be ideal, but it was far less expensive than hotel accommodation and she needed time to think about the future. Lighting the gas fire, removing her outdoor garments and sinking into an armchair, she decided that tomorrow she must pay a visit to her solicitors to pick up the parcels containing her aunt's belongings, which she had left there at her last visit. Also, she must deposit her fifteen hundred pounds in her Post Office savings account, and buy flowers to lay on her parents' and Aunt Dorothy's graves in Middleton Cemetery. It was the least she could do for those people once close and dear to her during their lifetime.

'My dear young lady.' Charles Bessacre greeted Fran warmly. 'How nice it is to see you again. Do come through to my office. I'll ask my secretary to bring in some tea. Sit down, m'dear, and tell me how you've fared since our last meeting. Am I to take it that you've decided to return to your roots now the war is over?'

'No, Mr Bessacre.' Fran regarded the solicitor fondly, remembering how kind he'd been to her following the death of her aunt. 'I had business matters to attend to. I've sold Miss Hunter's house, you see, and there were certain documents to sign. Also, you were good enough to safeguard a few of her personal possessions on my behalf. Just a few ornaments and photographs she was fond of, which I'd like to find room for when I've found a place to call home.'

'Of course, Miss Abbot, I'll have them brought up to you directly. Meanwhile, here's Mrs Wagstaff with the tea.' His elderly secretary had appeared silently, bearing a tray of cups and saucers which she placed on the desk in front of him, then, just as silently, disappeared to the outer office, reappearing seconds later holding a letter, which she handed to Fran, explaining that it had been delivered earlier that morning, addressed to her c/o Franks and Bessacre, Solicitors, and marked 'Please forward'.

Slipping the letter into her handbag to read later, Fran's heart soared – Peter had kept his promise to write to her. 'Thank you, Mrs Wagstaff,' she said, resisting a strong desire to kiss her.

'Good news, I assume,' Charles Bessacre enquired, smiling discreetly. A romantic at heart, he added, 'That place to call home you mentioned earlier wouldn't be a home for two, by any chance?'

'No, at least I don't think so. That is, I'm not entirely sure.' And yet, in her present state of euphoria, Fran imagined that anything, *everything*, was possible.

151

Later, opening Peter's letter, she read:

My dear Fran,

Where to begin? I'm missing you, that goes without saying. Also, I'm hoping that given time to consider the future you'll decide to return to Wiltshire to discover that dream cottage of yours and to make a success of your future. As for me, I'm settling in well at the Bear Hotel, enjoying every minute of my dish-washing duties, taking good care not to leave egg on the plates! Fortunately the chef, known as 'Butch', has taken a shine to me, to the extent of letting me keep an eye on his ovens when he nips outside for a smoke. In short, I'm enjoying hotel life enormously. I've even done a bit of bar work and hall-portering in my off-duty hours. All grist to the mill.

Living in, I'm readily available to help out, if needed, and I grab every opportunity to learn as much as possible. The manager's a decent sort, with whom I have a great deal in common!

He ended the letter,

I'm writing this in the hope that when you have taken the time you need to determine your future, you will bear in mind, your friend,
Peter Drysdale

Refolding the letter and replacing it carefully in her handbag she listened to the sound of rain beating against the window panes of her basement flat. Huddling closer to the plopping gas fire, she thought how strange it was that a matter of a few hours ago she had been prepared to pack her belongings, shake the dust of Middleton from her feet and catch the next available train to Wiltshire. Now she was not so sure.

Suddenly this room in which she was sitting seemed to her a haven of warmth and comfort against the world outside, the rain a reminder that her Indian summer idyll was a thing of the past, over and done with, along with her foolish supposition that, one day, Peter would come to regard her as more than a friend. His letter had made it clear to her that he would not. Nor, realistically, had he ever treated her as more than a friend. He had written, in his letter, of love and loss, loneliness and longing, as a result of the war, referring obliquely to Pearl, not herself. Pearl, the love of his life, and justly so – a near perfect human being worthy of his love and remembrance. So where did she, Fran, fit into the picture? The answer to this question came clear and simple. Nowhere at all, except as an onlooker in the game of life, dependent on Peter for happiness.

As deeply as she desired to stay close to him, loving him so much, would she ever truly feel able to accept a secondary role in his life?

Lying in bed staring up at the ceiling, hearing the beating of the rain against the window panes, unable to sleep, her mind in turmoil, Fran imagined the frustration of a one-sided love affair, the mental and physical strain involved in living a lie, forever reaching out for the unattainable, never daring to tell Peter how much she loved him, how much she needed him to hold her in his arms, to kiss her, to make love to her. She imagined reading contempt, far worse, pity in his eyes if she attempted to cross the boundary between love and friendship. Rejection would be a bitter pill to swallow, so why even attempt to cross that boundary?

Far better, she realized, to make a clean break away from temptation, before she made a complete fool of herself. Her mind made up, eventually she fell asleep to the lullaby of the rain on the window panes.

Up early next morning, picking up pen and paper, she wrote: 'Dear Peter, Many thanks for your letter. Great news that you are enjoying the Bear Hotel so much,' at which point she stopped writing abruptly, uncertain how to continue. Writing a lie, she thought despairingly, was tantamount to living one. Above all, she must impart the impression that she was happy in her new surroundings, and so she continued, writing in glowing terms about her flat, making it sound like a cross between a pre-war Ideal Homes Exhibition and a film set of the Victorian thriller *Gaslight*. starring Anton Walbrook and Diana Wynyard, which she had seen at a cinema in Wimbledon, during her Tanglewood days.

She wrote effusively:

It's not a large flat, but extremely comfortable and well furnished, in a Victorian villa close to the shopping centre of Middleton. As you know, I had certain reservations regarding my return to Middleton, fearing that I might feel lonely here. You know little of my past life. How could you? I never felt inclined to speak of it during the comparatively short time we have known one another.

But why dwell on the past? All that matters now is the future, making the right decisions regarding what lies ahead of us. I must admit that I'm strongly tempted to stay on here, in Middleton. As for you, I'm certain that you will, one day, achieve your ambition to own a hotel of your own.

Later, stamping and posting the letter, she thought, well, that's that. Better to have loved and lost than never to have loved at all.

But where would she go from here? Rain was falling steadily from a slate-grey sky as Fran slowly wended her way back to her basement flat, neither knowing nor caring what the future held in store for her. She was just so exhausted that all she could think of was sleep. Sleep, deep dreamless sleep – to forget the past, the present and the future.

Simply the comfort of a warm bed, a soft pillow and a hot water bottle.

Suddenly, halfway down the basement steps, the gaunt figure of a man stepped forward to meet her. Startled, she demanded hoarsely, 'Who are you? What do you want?'

'I'm Alan. Your brother Alan,' the man said wearily. 'Oh, for Christ's sake, sis, give me summat to eat, I'm bloody starving!'

'*Alan?*' Fran's heart went out to him, he looked so ill, such a far cry from the cocksure, swaggering bully of old, that she had scarcely recognized him.

'What are you doing here? Where's Ernest?' She asked.

'I'll tell you later. For God's sake, let me indoors. I'm ill, soaked to the skin, cold and hungry. I need help.'

'Come on, then!' Her tiredness forgotten, taking charge of the situation, she said briskly, 'The bathroom's down yonder. Run yourself a bath. The water should be hot and there's towels in the airing cupboard and a bathrobe behind the door. You'd best strip off. Hand me those wet clothes. I'll put them near the fire to dry and go and rustle up some food. Come through to the sitting room when you're ready.'

'Thanks, sis!'

Stripping off his wet clothes and handing them to her round the edge of the bathroom door, then turning on the hot water bath tap, he called after her. 'Hurry up with the grub!'

Some things never changed, Fran thought

resignedly, arranging his wet clothes to dry near the fire. Food had always come top of his list of priorities. Well, he'd have to settle for tinned tomato soup and cheese sandwiches for the time being. Later, when he was warm, clean and decent, she would treat him to something more substantial in that caff round the corner. Meanwhile, she wanted to find out the reason for his visit, and what had become of Ernest.

'He's married,' Alan said shortly, wolfing down the meal Fran had prepared for him. 'Living in a pre-fab near Scarborough, the lucky sod, working for the council, no less. And that's where I'm heading when I leave here. Trouble is, I'm flat broke at the moment.' He grinned knowingly, 'You, I gather, are not. Huh, fell on your feet, didn't you, toadying up to Aunt Dot the way you did.'

'I see. So that's why you're here.' Fran's weariness returned. She said scathingly, 'I might have known. You're not ill at all, are you? Recovering from a hangover, more like!'

'Aw, come on, sis.' He laughed. 'A man must have his little pleasures in life. So what if I had a drop too much to drink last night? Why make a song and dance about it?'

'And to think I felt sorry for you!' Fran regarded him disdainfully. 'I thought that you had changed for the better. I was wrong.'

'*You* haven't,' he said succinctly. 'Still the same holier-than-thou little madam that you were the last time we met! I haven't forgotten, if you have, the way you treated

157

Ernest an' me.'

'And I haven't forgotten the way you treated Mother!' Fran's patience snapped. 'Forever making fun of her cooking, expecting her to wait on you hand and foot, not caring tuppence how deeply you hurt her! She thought the sun shone out of you and Ernest. Well, *I* didn't, and I still don't!'

She faced him defiantly. 'I've often wondered what became of you. Now I *know*! *Nothing!* Why doesn't that surprise me? You are still as feckless and self-centred as you always have been and always will be! You'll go through life bullying and scrounging! Does Ernest know that you are about to appear on his doorstep to upset his matrimonial apple cart? I guess not! I just hope that his wife will send you packing, as *I* am about to do! I mean what I say. I know now why you came here, to extort money from me – I'm right, aren't I? Well, hard luck, Now, please go. If you're flat broke, serve you right for squandering your money.'

On his way to the front door, he flung back at her, 'You'll live to regret this!'

'If I live to regret anything at all,' Fran replied wearily, 'it will be the way you treated Mother.'

When he had gone, her spirits were at zero. What exactly had she achieved, Fran wondered, by her determination to stand on her own two feet? Two things sprang to mind: the letter she had posted to Peter, putting paid to her return to Wiltshire, and her stubborn

158

rejection of her brother.

Why hadn't she been more tolerant and forebearing? She had asked herself that question before over the Eddie Musgrove episode. Her clash with Alan had upset her more than she had realized, coming out of the blue as it had done. Her hands were shaking, her mouth felt dry.

Resting her head against a cushion, she fell asleep, waking an hour later with the feeling of something left undone. Something important. Suddenly she remembered what it was. Of course! She had forgotten to deposit the cash she'd received from the sale of the house in her Post Office account. Expecting a cheque, she'd felt bemused by the thick wad of notes handed to her by the estate agent, accepting his explanation that the buyers had insisted on payment in cash. A careful, frugal couple, they had saved up week by week since their tenancy began until they could afford to make an offer for the property.

Getting up from the chair near the fire, badly in need of a cup of tea, Fran went through to the kitchen. The window was open, rain was beating on the windowsill. She had left her handbag on the dresser. The bag, too, was open. The wad of notes she had tucked away in a zipped-up compartment was missing.

Her brother must have unlatched the window while she was in the sitting room. She now knew what he had meant when he'd said, 'You'll live to regret this.'

What Fran regretted, more even than the loss of the money, was the certain knowledge that Alan was not merely a liar, but also a thief.

Ten

Even if she had decided to return to Wiltshire, Fran thought, to buy a cottage and start a business, the theft of her money had put paid to that idea. The whole course of her life had been changed in a matter of minutes when she had discovered that empty compartment in her handbag.

Now she faced the realization that she must, of necessity, find herself a job. If not, she'd be living on capital, and how long would her savings last in that event? Not long. The few hundred pounds in her Post Office account would soon be gone, with rent to pay, food and clothing to buy and a hungry gas meter to feed. A shilling's worth of gas was soon gobbled up, and this was a cold flat even now, so what would it be like in winter when the weather turned colder?

Not that she really wanted to stay here, in Middleton. Why stay on in a dismal town she had always disliked? And supposing she found employment here, what would she do exactly? Office work? A nine to five job in the town centre? The thought was unbearable. What, then? Needing someone to talk to, a wise counsellor, someone she knew and trusted, she thought of Charles Bessacre, her solicitor and friend.

'My dear young lady,' he murmured sympathetically when she had finished pouring out her heart to him, 'you are quite right, of course. Living on capital is unthinkable, you must find yourself employment. Preferably a live-in job with room and board provided. An hotel job, perhaps.'

He wrinkled his forehead. 'Let me think. Ah yes! For what it's worth, a hotel-keeper friend of mine in Scarborough recently mentioned his need of a competent receptionist with shorthand and typing experience and a good head on her shoulders, willing to work all hours: "All found," as the saying goes!'

He smiled disarmingly. 'I could put in a word for you, if you like. Scarborough's a charming resort. My wife and I spent our honeymoon there, and the Greystones Hotel occupies a prime position on the south promenade, overlooking the Italian Gardens.' He paused. 'John Hammond is a likeable fellow, an ex-naval lieutenant, working hard to get the hotel up and running again after the wartime requisitioning of the property by the RAF. He needs reliable staff to help him achieve his goal.'

Charles continued reflectively, 'Of course, when my wife and I stayed at Greystones, many moons ago, John's parents, Rex and Muriel Hammond, were the proprietors; John was a schoolboy at the time. Now that his parents have retired, he is desperately anxious to restore the hotel to its former glory. So what do you say, Miss Abbot, shall I effect an introduction?'

'Yes, Mr Bessacre, and thank you,' Fran replied gratefully. 'It sounds ideal.'

'Then I'll write to him at once. Doubtless he will get in touch with you, and you can take it from there.' Bessacre nodded astutely, admiring the girl's stoicism over the loss of her money, simply accepting that it was gone and turning her thoughts to ways and means of earning a living.

'You will let me know how things work out, won't you?' he asked, as she got up to leave.

'Yes, of course,' she said. 'I'll let you know, whatever the outcome.'

'Just one more thing, m'dear. If I were you, I'd inform the police of the robbery. They'll make enquiries and, who knows, they may even discover the whereabouts of your money, and the name of the thief.'

'Thanks, Mr Bessacre,' Fran said ruefully, 'but I know who stole the money, and why. It was someone well known to me, the reason why I prefer to let the matter rest.'

'As you wish.' The shrewd old lawyer forebore to add, 'A case of family loyalty, I take it?' But he knew he was right. He also knew that Frances Abbot was far too decent a person to betray her own flesh and blood.

The letter he later penned to John Hammond reflected his high opinion of her. 'Miss Abbot,' he wrote, 'is a person of rare integrity and discretion, loyal and trustworthy, a former member of the Women's Royal Naval Service, presently in search of a new direction in life, and a worthwhile job of work to do...'

Reading the letter, John Hammond thought he had better interview this paragon of virtue, most probably a forty-year old ex-petty officer with a face like a horse and a backside to match. But what matter what she looked like as long as she knew her onions behind a reception desk?

Meeting Fran at Scarborough Station, in due course, he was pleasantly surprised to greet a slender young woman, dark haired, attractive and shy.

'Miss Abbot?' he enquired disbelievingly. 'I am John Hammond. Please, do come this way. My car's outside. I trust you had a good journey?'

'Oh yes, thank you. Very pleasant indeed,' she murmured, feeling tongue-tied in the presence of the tall, handsome man confronting her.

'Good, now what I have in mind is a spot of lunch at the hotel – I daresay you're feeling peckish, I know I am – after which I'll give you a guided tour, though I should warn you that all is not shipshape, as yet. Some of the rooms are being redecorated, and there's reconstruction work going on in the kitchen. Hopefully, all will be completed in time for the Christmas season.'

As they got into the car he asked, 'Tell me, Miss Abbot, are you au fait with reception duties?'

'No, I'm afraid not,' she confessed awkwardly. 'I've just recently been demobbed, you see. All I'm really – au fait – with is a teleprinter keyboard, but I'm good at cleaning.'

'I see.' Hammond regarded her doubtfully. 'Well, not to worry, reception work isn't all that difficult. Let's discuss it over lunch, shall we?'

Gazing at the sea as he swept the car on to the promenade, she said ecstatically, 'Oh, isn't it lovely. I've never seen much of the sea before, except in Scotland during my training, but it looked nothing like this. The dockyards spoiled the view, and in any case I was too busy to notice.'

Glancing sideways at her rapt expression and flushed cheeks, warming to this oddly attractive girl beside him, Hammond said quietly, 'Yes, the sea is lovely.' He added reflectively, 'Not always calm as it is today, more often than not, quite the opposite, totally ruthless and demanding, but fascinating, nonetheless.' About to add, 'like a beautiful woman, purring one moment, unpredictable the next,' he decided not to. Instead, he said, 'Well, here we are,' drawing the car to a halt in the driveway of Greystones Hotel, an imposing stone-built, bay-windowed mansion, which once, in a long gone era, had been the home of a Victorian gentleman, his wife, children and servants. 'What do you think of it?'

'It's magnificent,' Fran said simply, overwhelmed by the thought of living and working here if John Hammond offered her a job.

After lunch – chicken sandwiches and hot coffee – Hammond showed Fran round Greystones from basement to attics, opening doors, commenting briefly on this room and that as she followed him up and down stairs, along wide corridors, and narrower passageways branching off from the attic rooms, once the servants' quarters, Fran imagined.

The tour of inspection over, back to ground floor level, standing near the reception desk, Hammond explained the duties involved in reception work: flexibility, common sense, charm of manner, and accurate typing and book-keeping being the prime requisites, in return for which she would receive an adequate salary, furnished accommodation, comprising a bed-sitting room and bathroom on the top floor, plus full residential emoluments, namely breakfast, lunch and dinner, and one full day off, midweek, by prior arrangement with himself.

'You mean you are offering me the job?'

Hammond smiled. 'Yes, and I hope you'll accept my offer. You are obviously an intelligent woman, with impeccable references supplied by our mutual friend, Charles Bessacre. So what is your answer?'

'My answer is yes,' Fran said breathlessly,

envisaging a whole new future ahead of her.

'Good. That's settled then. Now I'd best drive you back to the station. I daresay you'll need time to make the necessary arrangements before returning here, on, shall we say, the last Friday in October?'

Fran returned to Middleton in a state of euphoria, scarcely able to believe her good fortune in being offered a job she felt she'd enjoy when she'd got the hang of it – and she'd make certain she did get the hang of it, the way she had done when she had learned shorthand and typing as a means of becoming a teleprinter operator instead of a cook.

Moreover, she had fallen in love with Scarborough at first sight; a charming resort, Charles Bessacre had assured her, and he was right. It was a far cry from Middleton with its grimy pavements and endless rows of slate-roofed houses. The sea, in particular, had enchanted her, that vast expanse of water rocking gently beneath a blue, early October sky to a far-flung horizon, imparting a sense of freedom reminiscent of the Wiltshire Downs she had loved so much.

Three weeks hence, she would be returning to Scarborough. Meanwhile, she must give her landlords notice of her intention to quit her flat at the end of the month, leaving everything in apple-pie order in readiness for the next tenants. Meanwhile, she must visit the public library to borrow books on book-keeping and business management, and visit Charles Bessacre to thank him for his kindness in recommending her so wholeheartedly to John Hammond.

Bessacre fairly beamed when Fran told him of her successful interview.

'Many congratulations, m'dear,' he enthused. 'Now, take my advice, treat yourself to a new wardrobe. A smart, well-tailored costume, to begin with, bearing in mind that you will be on display behind your reception desk. Oh dear,' he continued, 'am I being too presumptuous? I hope not.'

'Not at all,' Fran assured him, more than ready to take instruction from the wise old man. 'Apart from the costume, what else shall I need?'

'At least three blouses,' Bessacre mused. 'One white blouse, high-necked, with pearl buttons, one with a frilly jabot, the third quite frivolous, a pink lace blouse, suitable for evening wear.' He twinkled mischievously. 'After all, you may well appear in the dining-room occasionally, and be in need of a pink lace blouse!'

'Right, then,' Fran smiled indulgently, 'so what else shall I need to fulfil my role as a receptionist-cum-femme fatale?'

'Comfortable shoes, a winter overcoat, a mackintosh, bedsocks, a good tweed skirt and a couple of woolly jumpers?' Charles suggested, tongue in cheek. 'Plus a hot water bottle and a bottle of Fenning's Fever Cure! You see, m'dear, experience has taught me the wisdom of being prepared. You are about to take a job in a prestigious hotel, and you must dress accordingly. One well-cut costume and a variety of blouses will be worth their weight in gold, even if it means dipping into your savings.'

He was right, of course. Clothes had never come high on her list of priorities, and the few she did own – apart from the blue wool dress – were old-fashioned and dowdy. She would look forward to choosing a smart new wardrobe.

Later, unable to decide between a charcoal grey and a lighter grey costume, both of which fitted her to perfection, she decided to take both, safe in the knowledge that she could afford to splash out for once in her life, with a job to look forward to, and with the money she had withdrawn from her savings account tucked safely in her handbag. She had then treated herself to a warm camel-hair coat with a stand-up collar, a smart, plaid-lined mackintosh, three blouses, a Harris tweed skirt and two woollen jumpers.

Her new apparel would give her the confidence she needed to tackle her new job in the elegant atmosphere of Greystones Hotel, along with the rudiments of book-keeping gleaned from the pages of the library books she had borrowed on the subject, thinking how strange it was that she and Peter were embarking on similar careers.

Peter. She thought of him often and with deep affection, wondering how he was getting on at the Bear Hotel. He had not replied to her letter announcing her intention to remain in Middleton. Had her letter been too abrupt, too dismissive?

Feeling that she owed him some kind of explanation, she decided to write to him, from Scarborough, when she'd had time to settle into her new surroundings. Their friendship was far too precious a thing to be tossed aside and forgotten. She might even indicate that her decision not to return to Wiltshire was based on her fear that she was becoming too fond of him, too reliant on his presence in her life. Would that be a wise or a foolish step to take? How could she be sure? She couldn't, so better to think things over before rushing in where angels might fear to tread, as she had done so often in the past.

The last Friday in October fast approaching, the flat as clean and as neat as a pin, her rent paid up to date, her personal belongings duly packed, Fran handed in her keys to her estate agent landlords, paid a final visit to Charles Bessacre's office to bid him farewell and booked herself into a hotel in close proximity to Middleton Station, in readiness to catch the ten o'clock train to York. The eleven thirty connection from there to Scarborough was due to arrive at its destination an hour later, where, hopefully, John Hammond would be there to meet her, as arranged three weeks ago.

Awaiting the arrival of the train, John wondered how, without offending the girl, he might suggest providing her with a uniform of sorts, to wear during office hours. Smartness of appearance was essential to a receptionist, and he had noticed that her clothing, though neat and serviceable, was decidedly dowdy. Well, he'd cross that bridge when he came to it.

When the train drew in and the passengers began walking towards the ticket barrier, he failed to recognize the smart young woman wearing a fashionable camel-hair coat, high-heeled shoes, silk stockings, a jaunty black beret and carrying a brand new suitcase, until Fran said brightly, 'I hope I haven't kept you waiting. The train was delayed at Seamer.'

'No, not at all! Here, let me take your luggage. My car's in the forecourt.'

Could this smartly dressed, confident young women possibly be the shy, self-effacing girl he had interviewed three weeks ago? Apparently so.

Mightily relieved, Hammond drove towards Greystones, safe in the knowledge that the suggestion of her wearing a uniform on duty need never arise. During a sandwich and coffee luncheon served in his private office adjacent to the reception area, he noticed that she was wearing a charcoal-grey flannel suit and a pearl-buttoned white silk blouse, both sensible and vastly becoming.

He said, 'You have changed your image somewhat, Miss Abbot. I congratulate you on the result.'

'Oh, my clothes, you mean?' Fran frowned

slightly, then smiled. 'Thanks, but that was Mr Bessacre's idea, not mine. He made me realize the importance of looking smart, so I went on a shopping spree. Well, in for a penny in for a pound as the saying goes. That's when I decided to learn all I could about book-keeping. I thought if a job's worth doing, it's worth doing well.'

'I see.' Deeply touched by the girl's candour and lack of pretence, Hammond said brusquely, yet kindly, 'Now, if you've finished your lunch, I'll show you to your quarters. If you'll follow me, the lift's working now, I'm pleased to say.' He added, as the lift sped upwards, 'If there's anything you don't like about your rooms, you will be sure to tell me, won't you, Miss Abbot?'

A stickler for the truth, Fran said honestly, 'I shouldn't think so, sir. I wouldn't dare,' uncertain whether or not she was being teased by this unorthodox employer of hers, and not really wanting to find out. Well, not just yet, at any rate.

Hammond smothered a smile. Preceding her along the passageway to her accommodation, opening the door and standing back to gauge her reaction to the beautifully appointed apartment with neutral-coloured walls and paintwork, rose-patterned curtains and chair covers, rose-shaded lamps and the warm beige carpeting, he asked 'Well, what do you think of it?' Not that he needed to ask, Fran's face said it all as she moved forward to gaze out of the window at the sea coming in on the shore.

Then, turning to face him, she murmured, 'All this, and Heaven too. Thank you, sir. Thank you so much.'

At a loss for words, Hammond said abruptly, 'I'll leave you alone now to do your unpacking. Supper's at six thirty, in the dining room. Come down when you're ready. Meanwhile, you might as well take the afternoon off.'

Joyously, Fran sped across the promenade and down sloping paths to the seashore, having exchanged her high-heeled shoes for an old pair of flatties, more suitable for walking near the sea's edge, something she had never done before, as she had never gazed into rock-pools or heard the noisy clamour of the seagulls overhead, never breathed in the invigorating tang of ozone or felt the implosion of wet sand beneath her feet.

That evening after supper, beguiled by the latent warmth of the October evening. Fran walked across the promenade and stood near the railings to look at the shore lights reflected in the tranquil waters of the bay. The wash of the tide coming in on the rocks seemed to her as a lullaby.

'A penny for your thoughts, Miss Abbot.'

Turning, she saw John Hammond standing beside her. 'Sorry if I startled you,' he said. 'I often stand here myself for a breath of evening air.'

'I was thinking about the wartime black-out,' she said, 'the awfulness of air raids, the wailing of the sirens,' She shivered slightly despite the warmth and stillness of a perfect October evening. 'One felt imprisoned some-how, living in fear. Not consciously perhaps, but the fear was always there, especially during the London Blitz. I was stationed near Wimbledon Common, so we knew what was happening. Now, standing here, I can't help thinking how lovely it is to see lighted windows and street lamps once more.'

'You must be tired, Miss Abbot,' Hammond said quietly. 'You've had a long day. Tomor-row, I'm expecting an influx of guests, which means you'll be on duty most of the time. Not to worry, I'll be in my office or elsewhere in the reception area, should you need my help or advice. Now, my advice is to have an early night. So goodnight, Miss Abbot, and sleep well.'

'Goodnight, Mr Hammond, and thank you.'

Watching as she crossed the road and enter-ed the hotel, John Hammond suspected that he had discovered something of a treasure in Miss Abbot, an unpretentious young woman with a mind of her own, and a smile like a sunburst. Not that she smiled all that often. He wondered why not.

Up and doing early next morning, Fran went into her bathroom to bathe. Then, putting on a modicum of make-up – a tinted foundation

173

cream, pressed powder and pale-pink lipstick – her lighter coloured flannel costume and a crisp white cotton blouse, she went down to the staff dining room for breakfast: a bowl of cornflakes, toast and marmalade and a pot of tea.

'There's sausages, bacon an' eggs, miss, if you wants it,' a kitchen hand reminded her. 'Seems a pity to do wivout. You'll be starving hungry, come lunchtime, I shouldn't wonder. My name's Gladys, by the way. What's yours?'

'Frances.' She smiled at the girl. 'Thanks just the same, but I couldn't look a sausage in the eye, right now.'

Gladys giggled. 'You're the new receptionist, ain't you? Rather you than me, I must say. But think on, if you feel peckish mid-morning. Cookie'll rustle you up a bacon butty in two seconds flat!' She added a warning. 'Don't let them fakey women in big 'ats get you down. They're nobbut wind and watter.'

Apart from herself, there were two waitresses, a waiter, a porter, a chef, various cleaners, the breakfast cook, Gladys, the kitchen maid, a gardener and an errand boy-cum-boots-cum-washer-upper, a barman and his wife, who occupied a flat at the rear of the building, and a night porter.

Fran knew that all eyes were on her as she took up her position behind the reception desk. Not that the other members of staff were unfriendly, merely curious about the newcomer in their midst. One cleaning lady was vacuuming the reception area, another

174

the dining room. Others were upstairs changing beds, cleaning baths and washbasins; the waitresses were changing tablecloths, the waiter arranging cutlery, napkins and glasses. John Hammond was here, there and everywhere, in his shirtsleeves, lending a hand where necessary: in the dining room one minute, heading towards the kitchen the next, looking preoccupied and glancing at his watch. Meanwhile, Fran was familiarizing herself with the register, the booking forms, the bookings diary and the list of phone numbers on a green baize notice board.

When the telephone rang suddenly, she picked up the receiver. 'Greystones Hotel,' she said levelly. 'How may I help you? Next Saturday? One double room? Hold on, sir, I'll just check.' Opening the bookings diary, she found the right page. 'That will be the fifth of November. Yes, sir, we have a double room vacant on that date. May I have your name and address? Thank you, sir. Written confirmation of the booking would be appreciated. You will? Oh yes, thank you, sir. Goodbye.'

Writing down the booking, she looked up to see John Hammond smiling at her. 'Well done, Miss Abbot,' he said. 'Now, would you please type up these menus, if you can read Chef's writing, that is? A4 paper, double spacing, two copies. I'll explain about the ordering later, and the typing of the menus proper. These are merely reminders. One copy's for Chef, one for Cook, the original for myself.' He paused! 'Use the office typewriter, leave my copy on the desk. All clear?'

'Perfectly clear, sir.'

So far, so good, Fran thought, knowing that she was going to enjoy this job enormously. There was so much going on, people coming and going, a florist's van had just arrived bringing bouquets for the guests, or at least some of them – the 'all wind and watter' brigade, she surmised, smiling at Gladys as the girl brought her a cup of coffee and a plate of biscuits.

''Ow yer gettin' on?' Gladys asked, sotto voce. 'They're sendin' a couple more waiters an' a shoo chef from the labour exchange, I've heard tell. Hope they know their onions, that's all!' She sighed deeply.

'Well, I'd best be gettin' back. Cook's up to her elbows in flour, mekkin' pies an' puddn's. That's wot she does when she's finished cooking the brekfusts. When I've finished clearin' up after her, I'll be off ter't big kitchen to lend an 'and wiv the lunch-time washing up, then back ter't staff dinin' room to 'elp serve them 'ungry-nosed waitresses, an' such! Wot a bloody life, eh?' Another hefty sigh. 'There's times when I don't know if I'm comin' or goin'. I reely don't.'

She added shyly, 'But I shan't mind servin' you, miss. An' if you're late, I'll mek sure ter pop yer portion of cottage pie an' chips in the oven, to keep 'ot!'

Fran blew out her lips; cottage pie, she thought, when Gladys had gone back to the

176

staff kitchen. If there was anything she hated, it was cottage pie. Then, having finished typing the menus, despatched the bouquets to their various destinations, via young Alfie, the errand boy, answered the phone several times and drunk her coffee, she wondered what was next on the agenda.

She hadn't long to wait. John Hammond, now wearing an immaculate grey pinstriped jacket over his shirtsleeves, was at the front entrance, smiling urbanely, welcoming in the first of his guests.

Oh no! Surely not! Fran's newfound air of self-confidence deserted her suddenly. Her heart sank to her shoes as Lady Galsworthy preceded her husband, Sir Henry, into Greystones.

Glancing curiously in her direction, Hammond wondered why the sudden change in her demeanour. The girl looked stricken. He noticed that her hands were shaking as the Galoworthys approached the reception desk.

What ailed the girl? he wondered. Her eyes were focused on Lady Galsworthy with a look of loathing and contempt so evident that any other than a woman so wrapped up in herself and her own importance would surely have noticed. Certainly Sir Henry appeared to have sensed an atmosphere as he bent forward to sign the register.

Eleanor Galsworthy uttered abruptly, 'Tell me, have my flowers arrived yet? If so, have they been taken up to our suite?'

'I believe so, Lady Galsworthy,' Fran replied

177

stiffly, clenching her hands, the knuckles showing white with tension as she confronted the woman who had made a circus of Pearl's funeral.

'What do you mean, you believe so? Do you know, or don't you?' Eleanor demanded, glaring at Fran with not the slightest sign of recognition.

'Yes, they have,' Fran replied coldly.

'Along with suitable containers, I trust?'

'Yes, of course, madam,' she replied, neither knowing nor caring as the hall porter collected their luggage and whisked it and the Galsworthys upstairs in the lift.

'A word with you in my office,' Hammond said, leading the way. 'Close the door, Miss Abbot. Now, what was all that about? The main thrust of your job is to make guests feel welcome, not to treat them with contempt. Your attitude towards Lady Galsworthy was disgraceful. You glared at the woman as if you hated her. *Why?*'

'I *do* hate her,' Fran said. 'Had I known she was coming, I'd have excused myself from meeting her face to face.'

Startled, Hammond said, 'It was a last-minute booking. I took the phone call myself when you were off duty. So are you saying that I should seek your permission before allocating accommodation on the off-chance that you might deem the occupants unworthy of common courtesy and respect?'

'No, sir, of course not. I'm sorry. It won't happen again.'

'I sincerely hope not, Miss Abbot, for your sake.' She hadn't offered an explanation for her enmity, and he didn't feel that it was his business to demand one, but at that moment, Hammond felt he had built a barrier between himself and Fran, and wished to heaven that he had not.

Eleven

Taking over Greystones from his parents was a legacy John Hammond would rather have done without. Hotel-keeping was not in his blood, but he had always known that his father had wanted him to take charge of the business in the fullness of time, not realizing the problems involved in the postwar task of refurbishment, food shortages and finding loyal, hardworking members of staff. The 'old brigade' employed by his parents before the war were no longer available, as he'd discovered when he'd tried to contact them.

In the old days, Hammond recalled, his mother, Muriel, had ruled the hotel with a rod of iron in her capacity as housekeeper-cum-hostess, keeping an eagle eye on the menus, coping with wedding receptions, dinner and cocktail parties, and dealing with recalcitrant members of staff as well as his father, Rex, who 'bent his elbow' far too often, and stood too many rounds of drinks in the bar, to her way of thinking.

John had often heard her say in the past, 'Rex, dear, we are in business to *make* money, not to give it away, remember?'

'Yes, darling,' he'd responded bemusedly. 'Sorry. I tend to get carried away, at times.'

Now, lying awake, John felt that he, also, tended to get carried away at times, as he had done in erecting a barrier between himself and Frances Abbot.

Fran, also, had spent a sleepless night. The appearance of the Galsworthys had deeply disturbed her, resurrecting, as it had done, a host of unwelcome memories of Pearl's funeral.

Early in the morning she dressed and went downstairs to the reception desk, meaning to type a letter of resignation, to find John Hammond sitting there, in his office, awaiting her arrival.

He said, 'Sit down Frances. We need to talk.'

'What about?'

First and foremost, I owe you an apology.'

'*Why?*'

'I believe I was too harsh over what I saw as a lack of courtesy towards Lady Galsworthy. You answered the woman quite correctly when she asked if flower containers had been sent up to her room. I simply gained the impression that she had sensed hostility in the tone of your voice and your general demeanour towards her, and so I expressed

180

disappointment in you, forgetting your lack of experience as a receptionist. Had I been less demanding, more understanding of your circumstances, I should not have expressed myself so forcefully. I was wrong, and I'm sorry. What more can I say?'

Fran said quietly, 'But you weren't wrong, Mr Hammond. That's the reason why I came down early to type a letter of resignation. As your receptionist, I should have known better than to let my personal feelings towards a guest become so apparent. I'm sorry, sir, but I'd sooner leave here now than stay a moment longer beneath the same roof as that woman!'

Hammond said succinctly, 'And I would far rather ask "that woman" to leave here at once than lose you, Miss Abbot.'

'That won't be necessary,' she replied, smiling her forgiveness, 'and I much prefer Frances to Miss Abbot. Fran for short, if you don't mind.'

'Very well, Fran, and thank you.'

Quitting the office, John knew that the barrier between himself and his receptionist no longer existed, and thanked God that she would remain with him, for the foreseeable future, as an important member of Greystones Hotel. Moreover, her smile of forgiveness had warmed his heart.

He still did not understand Fran's hostility towards Lady Galsworthy, and he had not pursued the matter. Truth to tell, he did not care for the woman himself. She had seemed to him arrogant and overbearing, glancing at him dismissively when he had welcomed her and Sir Henry to the hotel, as if to say that this was not the kind of hotel she was used to.

Thankfully, they would not be here for long. Sir Henry had mentioned some function or other at which he would appear as a guest speaker. No doubt accommodation had been arranged by the organizers, hence the bouquets.

Going through to the kitchen to make certain the butcher, fishmonger and grocer had been to deliver the food supplies he had ordered the previous day and to check that the stockpot was on the simmer, he wondered if Fran had worked for the Galsworthys before the war. If so, her ladyship had given no sign of recognition. Hardly likely she would, he surmised; the woman was an out and out snob. But the incident was over and done with, and he had more important things to do than worry about a storm in a teacup. Frances was staying on, and the new contingent of staff had appeared at the rear entrance to supplement the present workforce. The hotel was filled to capacity this coming week, and advance bookings augured well for the Christmas season. Moreover, the hotel entire had benefited enormously from its floor to ceiling redecoration and re-plumbing, and the amount of money he had expended on advertising his new-look hotel, with the help of his mother, Muriel, who had insisted on his including gourmet dishes in the menu in anticipation of the forthcoming

Christmas bonanza.

'Take my advice, son,' she'd said forcefully, 'offer them a package deal they can't refuse. Apart from turkey and all the trimmings, centrally heated rooms, sherry and hot mince pies, on their arrival there should be a party atmosphere, fun and games. You'll find it will pay in the long run.'

'Well, if you say so, Mother, but I'd feel happier offering my guests a quieter, more traditional Christmas.'

'You must do as you see fit, Jack. After all, you are in charge now,' his mother had replied coolly. 'I was merely giving you the benefit of my advice. If you choose to ignore it, well that's up to you. Traditional Christmases are a thing of the past, in my view. People want excitement nowadays, music, dancing, laughter, not just hymns, holly wreaths and mistletoe, but organized entertainment, car rallies, treasure hunts, fancy dress competitions, cocktail parties, that kind of thing, not to sit snoozing in armchairs. Otherwise, you might as well turn Greystones into a home for geriatrics and have done with it!'

'Very well, Ma, you win!' Hammond gave in to his mother's blandishments as he always had done in the past. He said resignedly, 'You could be persuaded, I suppose, to organize the fun and games?'

'Of course, darling. There's nothing I'd like better. I'll see to the decorations, too, and have a word with Chef about the menus.'

'I'd rather you didn't, Mother.' Muriel had a way of putting people's backs up at times. 'You see to the fun and games, I'll see to the food.'

'But do be sure to write to Scotland to order fresh and smoked salmon well in advance, won't you? And don't forget to contact Daddy's supplier of poultry as soon as possible. She added brightly, encouragingly, 'You see, darling, your father and I have a wealth of experience to put at your disposal, and we do so want you to make a resounding success of your first Christmas at Greystones.'

'Thanks, Ma,' John said brusquely, knowing she meant well but wishing she would leave him alone to gain his own experience. A little of his mother went a long way. Besides which, deep down he abhorred the thought of Christmas fun and games. He would settle for holly and mistletoe, candlelight and plain, simple, well-cooked food; peace and quietude at any time of the year. Especially at Christmas, with its still painful memories of the past.

As a former member of Winston Churchill's Wartime Cabinet, Sir Henry had felt it expedient to accept an invitation to speak to a powerful coterie of Conservative supporters at a dinner party hosted by a close personal friend of his, in aid of Conservative Party funds. Scarborough remained a bastion of Conservatism, despite the election of the

Labour leader Clement Attlee as Prime Minister after the war, which was why Sir Henry had felt it his bounden duty to honour his own deep-seated allegiance to the Conservative Party, to nail his colours to the mast. Besides which, a short break in a pleasant part of the country would not go amiss for either himself or his wife, following the shock Labour landslide victory in July and the less recent but equally unexpected death of their daughter.

Not that Eleanor had seemed keen on a visit to Scarborough in October, and she had certainly not taken kindly to Greystones Hotel, which she regarded as second-rate accommodation. But then Eleanor had never been an easy person to please, as he knew to his cost, having been married to her for the past twenty-seven years. Now she seemed to have a bee in her bonnet about the receptionist, who, she claimed, had been rude to her on their arrival. Well, she'd see about *that*, she told him. Jumped-up little nobodies from nowhere needed bringing down a peg or two, to be taught a lesson in manners when dealing with members of the aristocracy.

'I'm so sorry, Fran,' John Hammond said bleakly, 'but I have received a letter of complaint from Lady Galsworthy regarding your behaviour towards her. A complaint which I cannot possibly ignore, though I feel inclined to tell her to go to hell and pump thunder.' He ran his fingers through his hair distractedly. 'She has requested a meeting with me in my office at ten o'clock, in a quarter of an hour's time. What the hell shall I say to the woman?'

'Let me talk to her,' Fran suggested quietly. 'This showdown had to come sooner or later! I'd keep well out of the firing range, if I were you. Show her into your office and leave the rest to me!'

'Fran, are you quite sure about this?'

'Perfectly sure!'

Alone in the office, pressing her hands to her lips, Fran awaited the arrival of Lady Galsworthy.

Fran's opening gambit came as soon as her ladyship appeared on the threshold. 'You don't remember me, do you, Lady Galsworthy? But I remember you! How could I possibly forget the circus you made of your daughter's funeral?'

'Well, really,' Eleanor blustered, 'how dare you speak to me in such a fashion? You do realize who I am?'

'Oh yes, Lady Galsworthy. You are the mother that your daughter couldn't wait to get away from. The reason why she joined the Women's Royal Naval Service. She saw you for what you really are. In Pearl's own words, "My parents are far from doting, they are both too busy to give a damn about me. The reason why I joined up was to get away from the pair of them."'

'But this is monstrous! I came to speak to the management, not the hired help!'

186

'I'm aware of that, your ladyship, but as your complaint concerns me not Mr Hammond I received his permission to speak to you first, to tell you what I thought of your insensitivity in using Pearl's funeral as an excuse for a house party. Not that he knows why I wished to meet you face to face. I haven't told him.'

She continued harshly, 'Pearl was my friend. I attended her funeral. Later, I stayed on at The Grange to help the Bateses, courtesy of First Officer Langtree, my Wren station commander, who realized that they would need help with the catering.'

'Huh, I might have known that *she* would have had a finger in the pie,' Eleanor Galsworthy spat forth disgustedly. 'By what right did *she* give you permission to stay on in *my* home without *my* permission?'

'Because she also loved Pearl,' Fran said levelly, 'and had the common sense to know that an elderly couple, grief stricken at the death of your daughter, could not possibly have shouldered the burden of a weekend house party without help and support. I gave them the help and support they needed. Tell me, Lady Galsworthy, as Pearl's mother, if you had really loved her, how could you have borne to entertain a houseful of guests knowing that she was lying dead in a graveyard scarcely a stone's throw away from The Grange?'

Struggling to master her emotions, Fran continued hoarsely, 'Because Pearl was right,

187

wasn't she, in saying that you didn't give a damn about her? Well, your ladyship, I've said what I wanted to say to you, except *this*! The mills of God grind slowly, but they grind exceeding small. One day, pray God, you'll take a long hard look at yourself and wonder why, despite your title, your wealth, your furs, your jewels, your expensive lifestyle, you are nothing more than a poor excuse for a human being!'

Having unburdened herself, Fran marched out of the office, head in air. On the threshold, Eleanor threw after her, chin sagging, plump flesh a-quiver, 'Sir Henry and I will be leaving here directly. Never, in all my life, have I been so insulted!

Turning back Fran said, 'Then all I can say, Lady Galsworthy, is that you should try harder, next time!'

Later that night, alone in her room, Fran started a letter to Peter Drysdale. 'Dear Peter,' she wrote, 'Believe it or not, I am presently working as a hotel receptionist...' Somehow the letter would not flow. Her mind was too full of her confrontation with Lady Galsworthy to concentrate on writing. Giving up the attempt, she put on her coat and crossed the promenade to look at the town lights clustered about the bay, deriving comfort from the sound of the sea washing in on the shore, feeling the wind in her hair, watching the slow movement of a lighted timber boat far out at sea, near an indiscernible horizon, remembering the Galsworthys' dramatic departure from Greystones earlier on that day, her ladyship's barbed remark as they had quit the premises to enter a taxi: 'Come, Henry, let's get back to civilization.'

Poor Sir Henry, Fran had thought, feeling sorry for any man too weak willed to resist manipulation by an overbearing wife. No wonder the poor devil had developed a penchant for other, younger, prettier women than the one he'd been saddled with for the better part of a lifetime. Would the day ever come, she wondered, when he would find enough courage to cut the strings attached to his vast female puppeteer?

In reflective mood, scarcely aware of the first drops of rain on her face, she thought about her brothers. Had Alan come to Scarborough to foist himself on Ernest and his wife? Had the money Alan had stolen from her been frittered away on drink, women and gambling? Ernest had, at least, married, found himself a home and a job. Even so, Fran felt no compulsion to visit him, to talk about ... what? Old times? The misery they had inflicted upon their mother? No! So far as she was concerned, she never wanted to set eyes on her siblings ever again. Having made abundantly clear her feelings towards them after Mary's funeral, she had no desire to build bridges between them, so why bother to even try?

Rain was falling faster now; the lights of the

timber boat were out of sight. Turning away from the promenade railings, Fran hurried back to the hotel, to her room and the warmth and comfort of her bed.

In the weeks preceding Christmas, by dint of perseverence and sheer determination to fulfil her role as a receptionist and learn all she could about Greystones, its staff members, the tradesmen, the menus, the number of en-suite rooms available to upper-crust clients and all the other essential details of hotel life Fran, with her store of common sense, quickly picked up the ins and outs of her job, to John Hammond's infinite relief that he could now depend on her to shoulder the full responsibility of the reception desk without his help or advice.

Truth to tell, he had not been aware of his growing dependence on her until, a few days before Christmas, his mother felt it expedient to remind John of the pitfalls of what she termed 'favourtism'.

'Favouritism? I'm sorry, Mother, I don't understand what you are driving at.' John frowned, mystified by the accusation. 'Favouritism towards whom precisely?'

'Oh, come now, Jack, don't play the innocent with me! Granted, she's a personable young woman, quite attractive in an offbeat kind of way, and she is obviously ambitious and setting her cap at you. Don't pretend you hadn't noticed. I am speaking of your receptionist, a go-getter if ever there was one!'

Startled, he replied angrily, 'Miss Abbot? But that's ridiculous! Fran is no more interested in me than I am in her. I simply admire the way she has worked to master a job of which she had no prior experience until, on the recommendation of Charles Bessacre, an old friend of yours and Father, if I'm not mistaken, I took her on. And his advice regarding her trustworthiness, discretion and loyalty has been correct in every detail. Now, if you'll excuse me, I have better things to do with my time than to stand here listening to mindless gossip about "favouritism".'

Later, having dismissed his mother's accusation so forcibly, John asked himself if there was not a grain of truth in her utterance. He liked and admired Frances Abbot enormously, and he had made no secret of the fact. Why should he? Never at any time had she overstepped the bounds of their employer–employee relationship, much less 'set her cap' at him as his mother had suggested, a remark which he had found both insulting and demeaning to himself and Frances. The question remained, however. Had he inadvertently given her the impression that his warmth of feeling towards her implied something more than mere friendship? No, of course not. A man of the world, he would have known at once the meaning of a come-hither glance cast in his direction. There had been no such glance, not the slightest indication that Frances regarded him as other than a friend.

Knowing, from bitter experience, the lengths that women often went to in pursuit of the opposite sex, the arch smiles, their pretence of helplessness in certain situations, the breathless 'whatever should I do without you to take care of silly little me?' routine, accompanied by an upward glance of simulated adoration and a pouting of the lips in anticipation of a kiss. That was the way it had happened with Irene, a long time ago...

It was all in the past now, yet the memory of Irene continued to haunt him as it always would at this season of the year.

The hotel larder was filled to overflowing with the Christmas fare John had ordered at his father's behest, although, in fairness to his own tradesmen, he had placed sizeable orders with them for beef, bacon and hams, eggs, fresh fruit and vegetables. On good terms with the local shopkeepers, he wished to remain so. Frankly, he enjoyed his visits to the market, and the fish pier in particular, to find out what was on offer by way of home-produced vegetables and freshly landed fish, enjoying the repartee between himself, the farmers and the fishermen, with whom he had established friendly relations since his installation as the new owner of Greystones. A case of mutual respect. He respected the farmers and fishermen. They, in turn, respected him.

A hitch occurred on Christmas Eve when

the breakfast cook, responsible for the making and baking of the home-made pies, cakes and puddings that featured strongly in the hotel menus, sent word that she was 'down with flu', confined to her bed and unable to work, being 'under the doctor'. A fact confirmed by the 'sick note' enclosed in the scrawled missive delivered by her grandson first thing that morning.

Stricken, showing Fran the note, John uttered despairingly, 'So no mince pies, no steamed chocolate puddings, no ginger snaps, no staff breakfasts or lunches. God, this is all I needed. So now what? How am I supposed to find an experienced cook at such short notice?'

'I could take over in the kitchen,' Fran said, albeit reluctantly, understanding his dilemma, 'if you could see to the reception desk. I joined the Wrens as a trainee cook, you see, before I became a teleprinter operator.' She added, 'I could at least rustle up a few mince pies and chocolate puddings, cook staff breakfasts and provide lunches, if that would help.'

'*Would* it? Oh, my dear girl!' Hammond said gratefully. 'Thank you so much! Whatever should I do without you?'

Entering the hotel at that moment, catching the tail end of the conversation and the expression of joy on her son's face, Muriel Hammond surmised that she had been right all along in believing that a romantic liaison existed between John and that scheming

193

receptionist of his. Well, she'd soon put paid to *that*. The sooner Frances Abbot quit Greystones Hotel, the better.

Twelve

For the first time, Fran had derived pleasure and satisfaction from cooking, knowing that her efforts had ensured a plenitude of mince pies, cakes and individual chocolate puddings to uphold the culinary reputation of Greystones.

Moreover, she had coped well with the staff meals, aided by the ubiquitous Gladys, who washed up, set and cleared tables, and sieved icing sugar on to the mince pies with gay abandon, running hither and thither like a scalded cat, praising Fran's cooking to the skies, saying how much the staff members, herself included, had enjoyed the chicken pie, mashed potatoes and fresh veggies she'd given them for lunch instead of the usual boring cottage pie and baked beans.

Just one thing had stuck in Gladys's craw. 'I just wish,' she'd said darkly, 'that Mr Hammond's ma had kept away from Greystones this Christmas – pokin' her nose in where it ain't wanted, upsettin' folk the way she does! I've 'eard tell that she an' the chef are at logger'eads. Well stands to reason, don't it? A

194

wumman like 'er interferin' in 'is kitchen. Apparently 'e told 'er to get lost unless she fancied cookin' the Christmas grub 'erself. An' who can blame 'im?'

Who indeed? Fran thought, having taken an instant dislike to the woman at their recent introduction to one another in the reception area earlier on that day, before she had come through to the staff kitchen. Why Fran had no idea. She had simply sensed Mrs Hammond's hostility towards her, and the feeling had been mutual.

Taking his mother aside, he said firmly, 'I understand that you have been in confrontation with Chef, and it is simply not good enough. I asked you to keep out of the kitchen. Now I'm not *asking* you, I'm *telling* you! Chefs are notoriously touchy individuals. Has it occurred to you the kind of mess we'd be in if Raoul took umbrage and left us in the lurch with a hotel full of visitors to see to? Would you be prepared to run the kitchen, the fun and games, in fact the whole bloody shooting match, single-handed? If not, I suggest that you give the kitchen a wide berth and concentrate on the fun and games.'

Deeply affronted, she snapped, 'Well, really, Jack, to speak to me in such a fashion. I *am* your mother, remember? A fact which you appear to have forgotten. Huh! I daresay you would not speak to the hired help as rudely as you have just spoken to me. That precious receptionist of yours, for instance! Well, I'm sick and tired of all this! Trying my best to help you, receiving nothing but unkindness in return! *You* run the whole bloody shooting match from now on! I'm going home!'

'Oh come now, Mother, you don't mean that.' But John knew that she *did* mean it. He had never seen her so angry and upset before as, turning abruptly, she marched out of Greystones without a backward glance.

'Mother,' he called after her, to no avail. Oh God, what now? he thought wearily, watching the tail lights of her car disappearing into the early dusk of a December afternoon. Possibly the kind of Christmas he'd envisaged all along, he pondered deeply, returning indoors to assume the full responsibility of his inheritance. Not fun and games, rather carols by candlelight in warm, firelit rooms; simple, well-cooked food served at tables adorned with arrangements of holly and Christmas roses, preceded by afternoon tea in the sea-view lounge: egg and cucumber sandwiches, mince pies, home-made cakes and scones, courtesy of Frances Abbot, who had worked so hard to ensure that the culinary standards of Greystones remained intact despite the sudden illness of Mrs Megginson, whose role she had filled so admirably.

Dear, dependable Fran, Hammond thought gratefully. Modest, unassuming, utterly dependable and trustworthy – albeit a lonely, withdrawn woman, with her own secrets to keep, her own sorrows to hide. A woman worthy of love and respect, a devoted hus-

196

band, children, a home of her own. A woman worth waiting for. If only he had possessed the wisdom to wait a while longer for a woman like Fran. Regretfully, he had not, and this was the burden he was called upon to bear from now on. Marrying in haste, eternally haunted by the memory of Irene.

At a quarter to midnight, when the hotel was quiet and most of the guests had gone to their rooms – apart from a few late drinkers in the bar – John invited Fran to go with him to Midnight Mass in St Mary's Parish Church on the hill overlooking the harbour, an invitation that she quietly accepted, in need of spiritual refreshment after what had proved to be a long, tiring day, fraught with memories of her mother, Pearl and Peter Drysdale, fleeting memories as insubstantial as spindrift on storm-tossed waves, as rainbows and half-remembered poems, learned as a child yet never fully assimilated or understood in classrooms of long ago. A child with hunger pains in her belly and a poorly mother to look after on her return home from school.

What Fran longed for, above all else, entering St Mary's Church, was a feeling of cohesion, a drawing together of the shattered fragments of her life so far, to form a composite whole, a deeper understanding of the meaning of life, a drawing together of its complexities to ease the burdens of a troubled mind, her continual yearning for her mother, for Pearl and for Pearl's husband, Peter. And the chance to pray for the strength and courage to learn how to live without them.

Driving her back to Greystones after the service, John said quietly, stopping the car en-route on the promenade, 'What is it, Fran? What's wrong? Something is troubling you; won't you tell me what it is? I may be able to help.'

'Thank you, but it's nothing tangible that I can put into words.' She turned her face away to hide her tears.

'Here, take my handkerchief,' he said, handing it to her. 'I guess we're both in need of a good night's rest. Things have been pretty fraught on the whole. Strange really, at a time of peace and goodwill to all men. At least we were spared all the jollification my mother had planned for this weekend.' He laughed briefly, mirthlessly. 'Balloons, paper hats, quizzes, parlour games. Frankly, I've never regarded Christmas as anything save a celebration of the birth of a babe in a stable, to do with peace and quietude, not parlour games and fancy hats.'

Facing him, Fran said, 'I've never been much of a churchgoer, but my mother was a good woman who taught me the meaning of the Christmas message, about the star and the stable, the wise men and the shepherds abiding in the fields. We, my mother, my two brothers and I, knew all about poverty, believe me. There was never enough money, you see, after my father died. Little or nothing for food or presents. Not that I cared about that. All I cared about was my mother trying her best to make ends meet. Only they didn't ever quite meet. I watched her wasting away day by day, month by month, year by year. Then suddenly she was gone, of heart failure, the doctor said. Of a broken heart, more likely.'

'Oh, Fran, my dear,' he murmured compassionately, 'I am so sorry.'

Then, on an impulse born of his own loneliness of spirit, taking Fran in his arms, he kissed first her tear-stained cheeks, then her forehead, finally her lips, in desperate need of the close human warmth and companionship so long denied him when Irene had left him on the night of their wedding on Christmas Eve seven years ago. Irene, the love of his life, who he had never seen or heard of since, apart from the note she had left on his pillow, which had read, quite simply: 'Sorry, John, but far better a moment's pain than a lifetime of regret being married to the wrong person. I, not you, am that wrong person.'

'I am so sorry, Fran,' Hammond apologized, releasing her from his embrace. 'Forgive me? I had no right to take advantage of you so blatantly. Blame it on the time of year, on holly and mistletoe, carols by candlelight, on moonglow and star-shine, your guess is as good as mine.'

'Then my guess is that the sooner we get

back to reality, the better,' Fran said wearily. 'After all, we have a long day ahead of us tomorrow, or rather today.' Smiling, she added, 'In any case, what's a kiss between friends? Especially on Christmas Day?'

Regretting her outburst of righteous indignation the day before, Muriel Hammond marched into Greystones ready to fulfil her duties as hostess, to discover that her presence there was superfluous. The residents were in the lounge, gathered round the Christmas tree, sipping sherry and listening to carols played by the Salvation Army band. 'Away in a Manger', 'Silent Night' and 'While Shepherds Watched', of all things. All being too damned calm and bright for her liking; there wasn't a sign of balloons or fancy hats, she registered furiously, going in search of her son to embark on another outburst. The reception desk was unmanned, so where was that bloody useless girl who should have been on duty?

Fran was in the staff kitchen baking scones, sausage rolls, mince pies and fairy cakes in readiness for afternoon tea. Today, the staff would be lunching in the dining room after the guests had been served and had gone out for a stroll along the promenade, to their rooms or to relax in the seaview lounge. John had planned a buffet supper for his guests, to include poached salmon, cold roast beef, Melton Mowbray pies, green and fresh-fruit salads, cheeses and so forth, to which guests

200

could help themselves as they felt inclined. They had dined royally, at lunchtime, on roast turkey and all the trimmings and Christmas pudding and rum sauce, and he had felt it appropriate to provide a cold buffet instead of another hot meal, taking his staff into consideration, especially his chef, Raoul, and the waiters and waitresses, who had been run off their feet all day.

Now, Mrs Hammond burst into the staff kitchen in search of her son, and found Fran up to her wrists in flour. 'What the hell are you doing here?' she demanded angrily. 'Why aren't you where you belong – at the reception desk?'

'Because the staff kitchen cook is off sick, and I'm standing in for her,' Fran replied, wondering why the woman was so hostile towards her. 'I trained as a cook, you see, during my Wren days.'

'Then let's hope that you are a damn sight better as a cook than a receptionist,' Mrs Hammond flung back at her.

'That's enough, Mother!' John had entered the kitchen un-noticed. 'Miss Abbot is doing a sterling job of work here, with my full co-operation, I might add!'

'Oh yes, that goes without saying, doesn't it? Her way of worming her way into your affections I daresay. The indispensable Miss Abbot. More indispensable than your own mother!'

Fran stared at the woman uncomprehendingly. Had she taken leave of her senses? Then suddenly she knew! Here was a jealous mother imagining a liaison of some kind between herself and her son. What had put that idea into her head, Fran couldn't begin to understand. And yet, in a moment of intuition, she realized that this was the beginning of the end so far as she was concerned. The end of yet another chapter in her life, the end of a job she had liked in a place she had come to love, to think of as home.

Not immediately perhaps, but soon, very soon, she would be moving on. Through no fault of her own, she would, of necessity, be seeking future employment in a strange place, among unknown people.

Words spoken at her mother's funeral sprang to mind: 'For I am a stranger with thee, and a sojourner, as all my fathers were. O spare me a little, that I may recover my strength before I go hence'.

'I'm so sorry, Fran, I never meant this to happen,' John said later, when they were alone together in his office following the departure of his mother to her own home. More of an eviction than a departure, he thought ruefully, regretting the necessity of getting rid of her before she caused more trouble with her ranting and raving.

'What exactly *has* happened?' Fran asked intently. 'I wish I knew. I know your mother dislikes me, that much is obvious, but what have I done to deserve her opprobrium?'

'Nothing at all,' he replied gruffly. 'I'm to

202

blame entirely.' Burying his head in his hands, he confessed, 'The truth is, she's always been jealous of any woman I've admired. You see, I married some years ago. Mother didn't approve of my fiancée. The wedding took place as planned, but it was never consummated. My wife left me on our wedding night. Mother was delighted.'

He laughed bitterly. 'Non-consummation of the marriage meant that I could have instituted annulment proceedings against Irene. I chose not to do so, living in hope that she would come back to me one day. Then the war started, I received my commission and haven't the faintest idea where my wife is now, whether she's alive or dead, and I have no way of finding out what became of her.'

'I see,' Frances said. 'Thank you for telling me. It can't be easy for you, working so hard to create a successful business with other things on your mind. Did your wife leave no clue to her whereabouts?'

'None at all. I contacted her parents, who couldn't come to the wedding, Irene's mother was ill at the time. I assumed she'd gone home to stay with them, but they hadn't heard from her, neither had anyone else I spoke to. A woman friend of hers suggested that she might have gone abroad with a man called Anton, an actor who had a farmhouse in Provence, which I didn't believe for one moment. Irene would have told me had there been another man in her life, of that I'm certain. She had men friends, of course, lots of them – actors, artists, writers, musicians – none of whom she had taken seriously. They were mainly young intellectuals struggling to gain recognition, part of what Irene referred to as her mother's "Bloomsbury set". Irene's parents were quite well off, you see, philanthropic by nature.'

John went on, reflectively, 'It was love at first sight so far as I was concerned. I'd never met anyone – any girl – like Irene before, so beautiful or charming, so uninhibited. I was on holiday in London at the time, attempting to come to terms with my future role in life. To teach or not to teach, that was the question. I came down from Oxford well qualified to teach English literature, maths and geography, but it was freedom I wanted, adventure.' He smiled ruefully. 'Horatio Hornblower had been a boyhood hero of mine. The day I met Irene, I'd been on the verge of joining the Navy.'

'What stopped you?' Fran asked.

'The thought of my mother's reaction, I guess, the tears, the emotional outbursts, her horror at my duplicity, my stupidity at throwing away my Oxford education for a common-or-garden career as a sailor. All of which I endured until the end, when I finally chose the Navy as a blessed alternative to teaching. I have Irene to thank for that. It was she who told me to go ahead. I'll never forget what she said to me. "We have only one life to live. Best live it to the full or not at all, is my advice, the way I live mine. Why spend a lifetime regretting all the missed opportunities along the way?"'

He added huskily, 'Irene was like that, such a positive person. If I only knew what became of her.'

'Perhaps you'll find out, one day?' Fran suggested quietly.

'I doubt it. Her parents' house in Bloomsbury was destroyed during the war. Her mother, Maxine, and her father, Victor Dupêche, died instantaneously, I gather.' He sighed wearily. 'But no use raking over dead embers. If Irene did go to France before the war, chances are she was trapped there when it started.

'Now, I think I'd better go to the kitchen to lend Raoul a hand with the staff lunches. You will join us, won't you?'

'I'm not really hungry.' The thought of sitting down to face rich food was more than Fran could bear at that moment. 'If you'll excuse me, I'd like a breath of sea air.'

'By all means. Take the afternoon off if you like. Come down later for supper, or I'll have something sent up to you.'

'Thanks, but I'll be fine when I've had some air.' Above all, Fran needed to be alone, to think. She had a great deal to think about right now.

Standing near the promenade railings, looking out to sea, remembering the feel of John's arms about her, the touch of his lips on hers in the early hours of the morning, she had believed, for one breathless moment, that

205

he loved her. Of course she was wrong. Irene had emerged, as a ghost from the past, dispelling Fran's illusions of a blossoming love affair with a man she had grown to trust and admire as a friend. But who knew when friendship might blossom into something far deeper?

No chance of that now, she thought regretfully. And yet she knew, deep down, how much she needed to be loved. John's kiss had convinced her of that. For one glorious moment she had experienced an upsurge of joy in his embrace, a sudden uplifting of her heart. Now her heart felt frozen, as cold as ice, a burden as heavy as lead, as it had done so often before. And perhaps, she thought bleakly, she was destined to go through life never knowing what it would be like to be loved by a man wholly, completely, passionately, the way Peter Drysdale had loved Pearl, the way John Hammond had loved, and still loved, Irene.

When Christmas was over and done with, she decided, she would set her sights on fresh fields and pastures new. A snatch of poetry by Walt Whitman invaded her mind: 'The untold want, by life and land ne'er granted. Now, Voyager, sail thou forth to seek and find'.

Part Three

Thirteen

Rosalind Torrance had been a leggy thirteen-year-old schoolgirl when Frances came to work at Kingfisher Cottage nine years earlier. Now 'Gipsy', as she was affectionately referred to by her family and friends, was a leggy, attractive young woman with a flat in London, a string of boyfriends and a job as a sub-editor in the offices of a well-known Fleet Street newspaper.

Being the daughter of a famous father had helped in that direction, of course. Bruce Torrance, a well-known novelist famous for his series of psychological thrillers set against a Cornish background, had used his influence to ensure that his beloved Gipsy gained a foothold, however tentative, on the ladder of literary success. He had, moreover, stumped up the wherewithal for her to purchase an apartment overlooking Blackfriars Bridge, close to her place of employment. It was a spacious, top-floor flat, which she had furnished, bizarrely, with functional modern tables and chairs and bean bags instead of sofas – to her father's distress at the lack of floor covering and curtains and the posters, not paintings, on the colour-washed walls of her sitting room.

Frances had borne the brunt of her employer's displeasure. 'Ye gods,' he'd sounded off following his first visit to his daughter's flat, 'bean bags and bloody posters, of all things! Has the girl no taste?'

'Her own, apparently,' Fran had reminded him coolly, inured to such outbursts from a temperamental man whose own home was scarcely the acme of comfort. Despite the carpets, curtains, sofas and armchairs, book-lined shelves and gilt-framed original oil paintings there was no feeling at Kingfisher Cottage of homeliness, as there had been at Alex Condermine's cottage in Wiltshire.

Frankly, Kingfisher Cottage was scarcely a cottage at all, to Fran's way of thinking. More specifically it was an elongated villa over-looking the River Fowey – a hotchpotch of a building, which she had viewed suspiciously nine years ago when she had been shortlisted as a possible cook-housekeeper by the celebrated author Bruce Torrance.

Desperately sad and lonely at the time, knowing she must leave Scarborough and find herself a new job, she had applied for cook-housekeeper jobs in Cornwall, as far away from Scarborough as possible, answering adverts that offered self-contained accommodation in return for cooking and cleaning. Above all, Fran had needed a place to call home, no matter how much she disliked the prospect of cooking, to earn herself a decent living.

And so the die had been cast. She had accepted the job as cook-housekeeper to Bruce Torrance, charmed not by his forceful personality and unorthodox appearance – his moleskin trousers, baggy cashmere sweater, open-toed sandals, thinning grey hair and general air of dishevelment – but by the self-contained apartment she'd been offered, the front windows of which overlooked a marina on the River Fowey containing a flotilla of yachts lapped by the incoming tide. With the wheeling of seagulls overhead and the invigorating scent of salt air in her nostrils, Fran had suddenly wanted that job more than she had wanted anything before – well, almost.

Asked if she could cook, she'd replied primly, 'Yes. I received my training at a Naval base near Dunfermline, in the early days of the war. I was in the Women's Royal Naval Service at the time.'

'The Wrens, eh? Hmmm, fine body of women.' Torrance had considered her coolly. 'Any housekeeping experience?'

'Yes, sir. Not a vast amount, but I know how to clean as well as cook, how to iron shirts, clean windows, scrub floors, shop, to keep accounts, and so on. I can also touch type and take shorthand, if necessary, having ended my Wren career as a teleprinter operator.'

'Any hobbies?'

'I enjoy reading and walking.'

'How old are you?'

'Twenty-five.'

'Men friends?'

'A few.'

'Relatives?'

'Two brothers. My parents died some time ago.'

'Any good with children?'

'I don't know. I've never had anything to do with children.'

'Then you'd best get used to them if you come here to live. I have two of them, a son and a daughter.'

'You mean that you are offering me the job?' Fran wrinkled her forehead disbelievingly. 'If so, thank you, but I'm a cook-housekeeper, not a nanny. I don't know the first thing about nannying, so I'm afraid that I can't accept your offer.'

Torrance chuckled deeply. 'Set your mind at rest, Miss Abbot. My son Tarquin is sixteen, his sister Rosalind thirteen. My wife died five years ago, since when I have coped with them quite well on my own. So are you prepared to come here to scrub my floors, wash my windows and iron my shirts or not? It's up to you entirely.'

Fran smiled. 'Yes, Mr Torrance. When would you like me to start?'

During the decade since this interview, Frances had become an integral part of the Torrance household: a somewhat disorganized one, well nigh impossible to clean thoroughly at first, with two untidy teenagers and their equally untidy father under her feet most of the time, not to mention two gal-lumping great labradors, several cats, and friends and relatives dropping in unannoun-ced for luncheon, tea or supper, until finally, her nerves at breaking point, bearding Bruce in his study, she said firmly, 'This cannot go on, Mr Torrance.'

'Huh? What? Can't you see I'm busy? You can't come barging in here whenever you feel like it, breaking my concentration, my train of thought, interfering in my work! How do you expect me to write anything worthwhile with you standing there like an outraged valkyrie?'

'And how do you expect me to work with you barging into my kitchen morning, noon and night wanting cups of tea and coffee, snacks, lunches or whatever at the drop of a hat? I'm a cook-housekeeper, Mr Torrance, not a magician! Food doesn't simply appear as if by magic, it has to be bought, prepared, cooked and the washing-up done afterwards, and it isn't good enough. The house is like a paddenken and I haven't time to clean it properly. No! Either establish a routine or find yourself another wage slave!'

He cupped his chin in his hand. 'What did you say the house was like?' he enquired, frowning, ignoring her tirade.

'A paddenken.'

'What's a paddenken?'

'This house is a paddenken! Up to the eyes in papers, school books, dog and cat hairs, unwashed windows, cobwebs, dirty pots and unmade beds! It needs bottoming, Mr

213

Torrance, and I'd give it a good bottoming if I had the time, but I haven't, and if you are prepared to live in a paddenken, I'm not!'

'I see. So what do you suggest, Miss Abbot?'

'I've already said. A routine! A proper going on! This is a big house, think on, though it doesn't look it from the outside, but it's the inside that bothers me. It would help if you stopped people dropping in, for a start. Invite them round by all means, but at least give me time to make ready for them. This isn't a wayside cafe, you know, it's supposed to be a clean, properly maintained household, not a snack bar!'

'My dear girl, you are perfectly right, of course. But my friends are accustomed to dropping in, and I wouldn't care to offend them.'

'Right, fair enough, so in future why not invite them in here and give them sherry and biscuits? Just keep them out of my way, that's all!'

'Anything else?'

'Yes. You can keep the animals in here, too!'

'Ye gods! They'll be everywhere! On the sofa, in the chairs! Where will my friends sit?' He was laughing at her, and she knew it.

How strange, she thought, she hadn't cottoned on to him at their first meeting, had believed him to be a humourless kind of man, somewhat fierce and intimidating. Now she thought differently. There was a warm side to his nature. Besides which, he was a good

214

father. His children, especially Gipsy, adored him. As for Tarquin, a sixteen-year-old, he was scarcely a child but a young adult, at an awkward age and not given to outward displays of affection. Captain of his school cricket team, he was also adept at handling his father's sailing dinghy moored in the marina.

Torrance said contritely, 'Leave it to me, Miss Abbot. Promise me just one thing, that you will continue to grace our household with your invaluable presence. We'd be lost without you.'

How could she have possibly refused?

Gipsy had rung up one day recently to say she'd be coming at the weekend, bringing with her her current boyfriend, and could she, Fran, who had taken the call, rustle up something really special for dinner on Saturday night?

'Any idea what?' Fran asked cagily.

'Goulash would be nice,' Gipsy said artlessly. 'He's Hungarian, you see.'

'Then why not give him something foreign for a change?' Fran suggested.

'Such as?'

'Roast beef and Yorkshire pudding!'

Gipsy laughed. 'All right, Abby, you win! See you tomorrow. By the way, Iggy and I will be sleeping together. Break the news to Daddy, will you?'

'That I will not!' Fran said firmly. 'Now see here, young lady, you'll sleep in your own bed

215

and this Iggy character will sleep in the spare room, and that's that! What you get up to in London is your own business, and I shudder to think what you do get up to, but under this roof you'll behave yourself and like it!'

'God, Abby, you're so old-fashioned,' Gipsy burst forth. How old are you? Thirty-four? You might as well be ninety-four the way you go on! We're living in the 1950s, not the Victorian era, for Pete's sake. Don't tell me you're still a virgin?' She paused abruptly. 'Sorry, I didn't mean to say that. Forgive me? What I meant to say is, you're a very attractive woman. You should be happily married, in my opinion, not wasting your life taking care of Kingfisher Cottage.'

'That's as may be, but the way I choose to live my life is my own business, not yours!'

Deeply angry and upset, Fran hung up the receiver. Catching sight of her reflection in the hall mirror, she thought bitterly, a very attractive woman? An ageing frump, more like. But was that really true?

Studying her mirror image more intently, she noticed that her skin had assumed a healthy glow due to her closer contact with the elements throughout her stay at Kingfisher Cottage, during which she had taken daily walks along the cliff tops, cycled into the nearby market town to do the shopping, and had often accompanied Bruce and Tarquin on sailing excursions aboard the *Moth*, Torrance's dinghy. Also that her hair, grown to shoulder length and worn either loose or in

216

the semblance of a French pleat, became her far better than the old neatly cropped hairstyle of her Wren days. Nothing whatever to do with vanity, she simply hadn't had time to pay regular visits to a hairdresser. Her clothing also reflected her new, less inhibited lifestyle in Cornwall, since she had taken to wearing dirndl skirts, low-neck cotton blouses and flat-heeled sandals in summertime, slacks and chunky woollen sweaters, ankle boots and anoraks in winter. It was a matter of expedience, of fitting into the relaxed atmosphere of the adoptive home that had come to mean so much to her, a casting-off her old neat and tidy image in favour of the new.

There were times when she could scarcely recall the Frances Abbot of long ago, and perhaps that orthodox, unhappy person she used to be was best laid to rest and forgotten. Yet the old shibboleths remained when it came to turning a blind eye to promiscuity. And perhaps something of the old Frances would always remain buried deep within her, despite her new beginning. A good thing or a bad? She couldn't be sure. Gipsy's reference to her virginity had deeply disturbed her. Was her spinsterhood so apparent to a lovely young girl on the cusp of life? Was she old-fashioned? Had even her new image failed to disguise her innate longing for love, feelings often experienced yet never fulfilled?

But why waste time studying her reflection when she had work to do – making up the spare-room bed, for instance; shopping, cooking and cleaning? Turning away from the mirror, Fran went through to the kitchen to write a shopping list.

Gipsy and Iggy had duly appeared, next day, in the red Lagonda Bruce had given his daughter on her twenty-first birthday. Iggy, so called because he had an unpronounceable Christian name, resembled a lamp post with an Adam's apple, to Fran's way of thinking, looking as if a good meal would kill him.

Gipsy, on the other hand, looked as contented as a Siamese cat with a saucer of cream. The feline resemblance was remarkable, Fran thought, to do with those hazel-green eyes of hers beneath uptilted eyebrows, her high cheekbones, tawny hair and that pussy cat smile, as well as her grace of movement, her air of self-containment laced with mischief.

Fran cared a great deal about Gipsy, her brother Tarquin, nicknamed Quin by his sister, and about their father, Bruce Torrance, despite their frequent differences of opinion when Torrance, in one of his temperamental outburts, would use her as a kind of whipping boy, blaming her for his lack of concentration, clean shirts, or whatever. Not that Fran took a blind bit of notice, having become inured to her employer's difficult personality during the past decade, knowing that his bark was far worse than his bite, and making allowances for his genius as a writer of bestselling novels. Sooner or later, he would always apologize profusely for upsetting her, beg her forgiveness and exhort her, yet again, not to leave him.

As if she would, or could, Fran had thought leniently, knowing he'd be lost without her, she without him, without Gipsy and Quin, who was now a handsome, charming twenty-five-year-old teacher of music at a prestigious, privately owned academy in Truro. He frequently returned to Kingfisher Cottage at weekends and during the school vacations to pursue his favourite hobbies: sailing, composing and playing the the local church organ, music being his overwhelming passion in life as well as his livelihood and sailing a means of relaxation, of inspiration.

'One of these fine days, Abby,' he'd confessed, 'I aim to compose a sea symphony based on John Masefield's poem "Sea Fever". You know the one I mean?'

'Yes, Quin, I know! The one that ends, "And all I ask is a merry yarn from a laughing fellow-rover, And quiet sleep and a sweet dream when the long trick's over".' Smiling, she'd added, 'No need to look so gobsmacked! I learned the poem at school, long before you were born or thought of. It was a favourite of mine, though I never understood why until I came here to live.'

'Are you fond of music?' Quin asked, realizing how little he knew about her, wanting to know more.

'Well yes, in a way, not that I know much

219

about it. I knew nothing at all until ... but that's all in the past! Now, if you'll excuse me, I'd best be getting back to the kitchen, otherwise the steak pie will be ruined beyond redemption, and your father won't be best pleased about *that*, I can tell you!'

'Look, Abby,' Quin said persuasively, 'tomorrow is Harvest Festival. Won't you come to church, join in the service?'

'What? With Sunday lunch to cook? Talk sense, love! I can't be in two places at the same time, now can I?'

'Couldn't we have cold Sunday lunch for a change?' Quin pursued eagerly. 'Cold roast beef, pickles, salad and jacket potatoes, for instance?'

'Why? What are you up to, Quin?' she asked, regarding him suspiciously. 'I wasn't born yesterday, think on!'

'I've composed a harvest anthem,' he confessed, 'which I wanted you to hear. It was meant to be a surprise.'

Sensing his disappointment, she assured him 'Then I'll certainly come to morning service.' Then, thinking quickly, 'I'll make a chicken casserole for Sunday lunch, bung it in a slow oven along with a few jacket potatoes. How's that?'

'You're a gem, Abby,' he said, with a smile like a sunburst. 'Thanks a million.' Impulsively, bending down, he brushed her cheek with his lips. The church was packed, this being a time of harvest and rejoicing, of thanksgiving for the bounty of land and

220

sea. The window ledges had been decorated with brightly coloured autumn flowers, the steps leading to the altar with corn sheaves, striped vegetable marrows, trugs of carrots, swedes, runner beans, cabbages and beetroot, mounds of glowing, rosy-skinned apples, all of which would be taken to various old people's homes in the district and to cottagers living alone by the children of the community, along with gifts of home-made preserves, jam and honey, sweets and biscuits, bunches of garden flowers, dahlias and Michaelmas daisies, when the service of thanksgiving was over.

Seated in a front pew near the lectern, Fran's heart swelled with pride when Quin took his place at the organ to begin playing softly the opening notes of 'For All the Saints Who From Their Labours Rest', which seemed appropriate, somehow, as a tribute to long-gone generations of men and women who had once laboured long and hard to bring home the bounty of the earth and sea: farmers, fishermen and their womenfolk, whose seed had been handed down to the present generation of worshippers, soon to raise their voices in the hymn 'Come, Ye Thankful People, Come'.

Rising to her feet, Fran sang as sweetly and as clearly as she had done once, long ago, in a village church in Gloucestershire, at the behest of her well-remembered friend, Pearl Galsworthy.

The vicar preached a rousing, uplifting

sermon touching upon the theme of self-sacrifice and hard work as a means of fulfilment on earth and even richer rewards in the world to come. Suddenly a tot piped up, 'Me wants an apple.' Everyone laughed. The child scrambled down from its mother's lap and toddled up the aisle to help herself to a Cox's orange pippin, other children followed suit. Soon apples were rolling in every direction. When the flurry of activity was over, the vicar announced the final hymn, 'We Plough the Fields and Scatter', forgetting about Quin's harvest anthem in the heat of the moment.

Walking home with him, Fran said 'I'm sorry about your anthem. I was looking forward to hearing it.'

Quin shrugged his shoulders dismissively. 'It doesn't matter. I'll turn it into a Christmas Carol!' But Fran knew that he was disappointed. Changing the subject, he said, 'I heard you singing. You have a lovely voice. You should join the choir, sing solo. "Lark in the clear air" springs to mind.'

'No fear!' Fran pulled a face. 'I'd faint dead away as I did once at school.'

'You're not very self-confident, are you?' He asked the question gently, not wanting to pry.

Fran smiled. 'I'm not the only one, am I?'

'I guess not. Comes of having a famous father and an extrovert sister, I imagine. Dad had me earmarked as a professional cricketer at one time. I liked the game, but I never saw myself as an opening bat for England. When

222

Dad asked me what I intended to do with my life and I told him I wanted to study music, he nearly threw a fit! Well, you know my father. "My son, a *musician?*" he bellowed. "Over my dead body!" '

'And what did you say?'

'Just that Mozart's father probably felt the same way when his son started composing at the age of four.'

'Then what happened?'

'Dad came down off his high horse, bought me a piano, fixed up a studio for me and bundled me off to the Truro Music Academy to be taught by the finest teachers available in this neck of the woods. Later, he sent me to Paris for a year to have what he termed my "rough edges" smoothed out. A great man, my dad. A bit of a bastard, at times, but that's just his way.'

'I know,' Fran said, 'which reminds me, I'd better get a move on before my chicken casserole boils dry and the jacket potatoes are kizzened to cinders.'

'Just a thought, Abby,' Quin said awkwardly, 'if you've nothing better to do, after lunch, would you care to come to my studio to hear my harvest anthem?'

'Why yes, Quin, I'd like that very much,' Fran replied, touched by the invitation, knowing that Quin regarded his studio as sacrosanct, It was an apartment overlooking a paved area detached from the main building, which he looked after himself; his own very special and private hideaway, which he kept locked. So far Fran had never crossed the threshold of Quin's bungalow, as Gipsy had called it, somewhat scathingly, adding, 'Honestly, that brother of mine might as well have gone into a monastery and had done with it, for all the fun he gets out of life. I've often wondered if he's, well, not as other men. What I mean is, he's not the least bit interested in women – except me, of course. He's mad about me. In the nicest possible way, I assure you.'

This Sunday, when lunch was over and the washing-up done, Fran went out by the back door and walked down the garden path to Quin's sanctum. Pleasantly surprised, she found herself in a spacious, comfortably furnished, book-lined room containing a vast chintz-covered sofa, several similarly clad armchairs and a Bluthner grand piano.

'Oh, this is nice,' she said, pausing to admire a group of seascapes above the mantelpiece. 'Did you paint these?'

'Yes, a long time ago,' he admitted shyly. 'They're not very good, but then they don't have to be, do they? I enjoyed painting them at the time, and that's all that really matters. At least it is to me.'

He continued, 'I have a small bedroom over yonder, a bathroom and a bit of a kitchen. The furniture came from a saleroom, except the piano. I didn't want new stuff. Most of the books are second-hand. I couldn't afford new. Some of them came from the bookstalls on the Left Bank, when I lived in Paris.'

'You liked Paris?'

'I loved it! The sense of freedom was unimaginable! The bistros, the museums and art galleries, the music! The war was over, there were lilacs in the Tuileries Gardens in springtime, chestnut trees in blossom, love and laughter in the air.'

'Sounds wonderful.'

'It was.'

'Play for me, Quin,' Fran said gently. 'Play your harvest anthem.'

'It isn't very good.'

'Nevertheless.'

'Very well, then.' Sliding on to the piano stool, opening the lid of the instrument, he began to play. He played divinely, but even Fran, no judge of music, realized that this was a composition unworthy of his talent, tailored to the requirements of a village church organ, an unsophisticated congregation.

'I told you it wasn't very good,' Quin said resignedly when the performance was over. 'You didn't think so either, did you? Be honest.'

Fran said, 'It's fine, as far as it goes. It just doesn't go far enough. Why not have a stab at your sea symphony? Let rip!'

'Like this, you mean?' His fingers rippled across the keyboard, unleashing a torrent of sound as he played the dramatic opening chords of his symphony, in which Fran imagined the crashing of waves, the epicentre of a storm at sea, the cracking of canvas sails, the crying of seabirds in a wind-racked sky.

He stopped playing suddenly. 'That's as far as I've gone with it up to now,' he said apologetically. 'I'm not sure that it's worth going on with. What do you think?'

Standing near the piano, her face aglow, Fran said quietly, 'It's magnificent. You *must* go on with it! Promise?'

Looking up at her, he said, 'What I admire most about you, Abby, is your honesty. It can't have been easy for you coming to Kingfisher Cottage as a stranger to cope with my father, Gipsy and me the way you have done all these years. All I can say is, you've won our respect. More importantly, our ... love.'

She was unnerved by the directness of his gaze. 'Affection, you mean?' she said dismissively. 'There's a world of difference between love and affection.' So why the sudden thumping of her heart, a dawning awareness of how much Quin's presence in her life really meant to her?

'No. I said love, and I meant it!' Rising to his feet, he took her hands in his. 'No need to feel afraid. I'm stating a simple fact. I *do* love you, Abby. I feel safe and warm in your company, I always have done. No, don't turn away! I'm not asking you to love me in return. I daresay you still regard me as a child, an unruly teenager. But I'm not. I'm a grown man now, and I *do* love you, Abby, more than you'll ever know.'

'Please, Quin! Let go of me! You don't know what you're saying! I'm your father's housekeeper, for God's sake – I'm much older than you are! I would never have come here had I known...' Words failed her. Turning abruptly, she headed towards the door of his apartment, shaken by the realization that, heaven help her, staying a moment longer, she might well end up in his arms.

Then staying that moment longer, suddenly, sweetly, Fran felt Quin's arms about her, his lips on hers, heard herself whispering, 'I love you, too, Quin.'

Fourteen

She hadn't meant it to happen. Common sense told her that she should not have allowed it to happen, that unguarded moment of capitulation, of surrender to a force stronger than herself, borne of her need to be loved, a fruition so long denied her, which, when the moment came, she was powerless to resist.

Succumbing to Quin's urgent yet tender lovemaking, she had felt an upsurge of joy in the closeness of his strong young body next to hers, had touched his warm, naked flesh as gently and lovingly as she might have done that of a newly born child in need of protection and comfort in its mother's arms.

Never had she experienced, or ever imagined, the unutterable feeling of happiness, of peace and fulfilment she had known when, after their lovemaking, she and Quin had lain together, not speaking – no need of words – at peace with the world, and each other, until she said huskily 'I'm sorry, love, I must go now. It's almost supper time. Your father will expect to find me in the kitchen; he mustn't find me here with you.'

'Supper?' Quin frowned bemusedly. 'What about us?'

'What about us?' Fran was out of bed, dressing quickly, tidying her hair. 'Quin, think about it. If your father knew, he'd send me packing. Is that what you want?'

'More to the point, Abby, what do *you* want?'

'To get on with my work. God, is that the time? Supper should have been ready half an hour ago. The table isn't even set yet! Please, Quin, I *have* to go now!'

Hurrying back to the kitchen, she wondered what else she could possibly have done. Risked the wrath of Tarquin's father had he found her in bed with his son? She loved Quin, but why sacrifice her entire future for a fleeting moment of passion, which, had she been more circumspect, more level headed and clear-thinking, would never have happened in the first place.

Setting the dining-room table and making hasty preparations for supper, Fran realized, in her heart of hearts, that, as dearly and deeply as she loved and desired Quin, their brief love affair was over and done with as swiftly as it had begun.

Quin left Kingfisher Cottage early next morning. 'Bye, Father. Goodbye, Abby,' he said levelly, settling into the driving seat of his Ford coupé. 'See you around Christmas, though I may well decide to spend Christmas abroad, this year. I'll let you know.'

'Huh!' Bruce exclaimed when the car was out of sight. 'What the devil's got into him all of a sudden? Quin adores Christmas. Why the sudden change of heart?'

Fran knew why. He must have realized that they couldn't be together. A sensitive human being, he'd have known instinctively that she deeply regretted what had happened between them. If only she had gone back to his studio last night to talk to him, to explain that it was not their lovemaking she regretted but the impossibility of it continuing because of the age difference between them.

Too late now. He had gone away angry and upset, and who could blame him? Why, for heaven's sake, hadn't she gone to him last night? Because, she had been afraid. Afraid that being alone with him might lead to a second betrayal in the arms of the man she loved, a weakening of her moral fibre when it came to explaining her fears concerning a hole-in-the-corner love affair, which, by its very nature, would ultimately destroy their finer feelings for one another. How could it be otherwise?

Fran loved Quin with all her heart, of that she was certain, and she knew beyond a shadow of doubt that he loved her. Even so, how could she possibly allow his devotion to a woman much older than himself? She could not, and that was that. End of story.

Hopefully, in the fullness of time, he would come to an acceptance of the truth: that a brief love affair between himself and an older woman, stood little or no chance of success. Meanwhile, she must continue to write shopping lists, cook food, clean windows, iron shirts and cater to the whims of her employer as if nothing was wrong.

But something *was* wrong. She was pregnant.

Overwhelmed by the certain knowledge that she was carrying Quin's child, with no one to turn to for help and advice, Fran realized that her days at Kingfisher Cottage were numbered. Then what? Where would she go, what would she do? How could she bring up a child on her own, with little or no money to fall back on, no home, no job, without prospect of employment, at least until after the child was born.

Gipsy had arrived on Christmas Eve with her current boyfriend, this one a braw Scot called Ian Gordon, who, unsurprisingly, worked as a correspondent for the *Scotsman*. 'A foreign correspondent,' Gipsy said teasingly. 'There are times when I can't understand a word he says.'

Her first words to Fran were, 'You're looking peaky. Not coming down with something, are you?'

'No, of course not,' Fran replied curtly. 'I'm a bit tired, that's all.'

'I'm not surprised, with all the extra cooking to do. Christmas cakes, plum puddings and all that jazz. But the house looks marvellous, Abby dear. Oh, it's wonderful to be home! A pity Quin's not coming. Christmas won't seem the same without him. Why the hell swan off to Paris? Do you know, Abby?'

'No. Why should I?'

'All right, no need to bite my head off. Are you sure you're not coming down with something?' Gipsy looked at Fran curiously, thinking how pale and tired she looked, how unhappy, with purple shadows beneath her eyes and something indefinable about her, a kind of apathy at odds with her usual brisk personality, as if she was nursing an inner sorrow. Quin, Gipsy thought perceptively, she's missing Quin.

Later, after supper, helping Fran with the washing-up, Gipsy said warily, 'I wish Quin had come home for Christmas, don't you? Why, Abby dear, what ever's the matter? You're crying!'

'Oh for God's sake, Gipsy, stop fussing and leave me alone!' Turning away from the sink, Fran sank down on a chair and covered her face with her hands to hide her tears.

'So tell me what's going on here! Or shall I hazard a guess? This has to do with Quin, hasn't it? I'm not blind, you know. I've always sensed a special kind of relationship between the pair of you. Nothing I could pinpoint, but I knew it existed. I've always adored Quin, but I've never really understood him – too much of an extrovert, I guess – and Quin has always been a loner, like you, Abby. You're a loner too, aren't you? Adept at keeping your own secrets, never giving too much of yourself away. I'm right, aren't I?'

'If you say so. I'm really too tired to argue,' Fran murmured, drying her eyes and returning to the sink to finish the washing-up.

'That's what's bothering me. Why are you so tired?' Gipsy insisted.

Sick and tired of pretence and prevarication, Fran said huskily, 'Because I'm pregnant. Because, very soon, I'll be leaving here. Do I have to spell it out to you? Because it's Quin's child I'm carrying. Now are you satisfied? Now will you leave me alone?'

A moment's silence ensued, then Gipsy said firmly, compassionately, 'Not likely! At a time when you most need help and understanding? As for leaving here, you can forget that! Don't you realize, Abby, that you are part and parcel of all our lives? Part of our family? Especially now! We love you, Abby. You belong here, and here you'll stay, come hell or high water. Oh, come here, darling, let me give you a hug.'

Gipsy's arms felt warm and comforting. Entering her embrace, Fran experienced an upsurge of relief that she need not leave Kingfisher Cottage after all, unless Bruce

232

Torrance wanted rid of her.

As if reading her thoughts, Gipsy said light-heartedly, 'You leave Daddy to me. Now, come upstairs with me. What you need is a good night's sleep. Things will look a lot better in the morning, believe me.'

Fran *did* believe her; her dear little Gipsy, a wayward child who had suddenly assumed the mantle of a caring, compassionate woman.

It had been a difficult Christmas to live through as they followed the established pattern of the festive season at Kingfisher: log fires, presents beneath the drawing room tree, a one o'clock luncheon party to which close friends of the family had been invited to partake of the traditional turkey and Christmas pudding.

Gregarious by nature, on festive occasions such as this Bruce Torrance carved the turkey at table with the aplomb of a maître d' in a posh London hotel.

'Showing off, as usual,' Gipsy remarked to Fran, sotto voce, helping her to carry into the dining room the tureens of vegetables and the silver gravy boats. 'He can't help it, poor darling.' She'd added conspiratorially, 'I haven't told him yet, by the way.'

Gipsy was proving herself to be a tower of strength, a kind of shield and defender against the slings and arrows of outrageous fortune. All that morning, she had been with Fran in the kitchen, peeling potatoes, preparing the other vegetables, basting the turkey, making certain the Christmas puddings didn't boil dry, and making full use of her Scottish boyfriend when it came to bringing in logs from the garden shed, mending the fires, polishing wine glasses and helping with the washing-up.

When luncheon was over, the dining table stripped of debris, the surplus food put away and the final washing-up almost completed, and she and Gipsy were alone together, Fran said quietly, '*I* must be the one to tell your father about myself and my predicament. It's the only honourable thing to do. I couldn't live with my conscience otherwise. You understand, don't you?'

Gipsy said softly, admiringly, 'That's typical of you, Abby. Standing on your own two feet, facing the music in your own way. I expected nothing less of you, to be honest.' She paused momentarily, then, 'Oh God,' she uttered despairingly, 'if only Quin were here to stand by you!'

'Quin knows nothing of this, and he mustn't!' Fran spoke vehemently.

'Don't you think he has the right to know?' Gipsy asked, taking Fran's hands in hers.

'No! What Quin has the right to is peace of mind, his own life. He's very young. Too young to have his future put in jeopardy for the sake of a moment's folly on my part. I blame myself entirely for what happened between us. I should have known better!'

'Quin may seem young to you, Abby, but he

isn't really. He's a grown man. Oh, I get it! Well, if it's the age difference that's bothering you, forget it! What's nine years more or less? You're a darned attractive woman, Abby. I've told you so before and I say it again! I daresay that Quin thought so, too. Why else would he have made love to you? Frankly, I'm glad that he did! You see, I'd got it into my head that Tarquin was, well, you know what I mean. Now I know differently, and I'm glad, not sorry, that he proved his manhood in the most positive way possible. So what are you going to do, Abby? When you meet Daddy face to face and tell him you're pregnant, are you going to tell him the whole truth, or a watered-down version? Think about it, Abby! After all, it is his grandchild you are carrying, not some bastard from a one-night stand with a local fisherman!'

'I don't know, Gipsy! I really don't know!' Shaking off the girl's restraining hands, her mind in turmoil, Fran hurried upstairs to her room, where, staring out of the window at the shore lights glimmering along the banks of the River Fowey, she reached the only possible solution to her dilemma.

Slowly and painfully regaining consciousness, with no idea of the time or the place she was in, the only thing Fran remembered was the chilling coldness of the water, the slippery moss-covered steps leading down to the marina where the *Moth* was moored, her sudden plunge into oblivion.

235

Opening her eyes, meeting those of Gipsy, Fran murmured, 'I'm sorry. I...'

'Hush! Don't try to talk. Thank God Jack Treherne saw you in time, otherwise you might not be here now. Daddy and Ian are in the waiting room. Doctor Whyte will be here soon. I daresay he'll keep you here overnight to make sure you're OK. Then, hopefully, you'll be home again tomorrow morning. I'll bring you a change of clothing. Now, try not to worry.'

'But what about the *Moth*?'

'What about the *Moth*?' Gipsy frowned.

'She's adrift. She's slipped her mooring. That's why I went down the steps. I tried to reach the hawser but I couldn't. You must warn your father. Please, Gipsy, he thinks the world of her.'

'Ye gods, so that's why...?' Gipsy stopped speaking abruptly. Relief flooded through her. 'I'll tell him at once!'

She had been so certain that Abby's plunge into the Fowey had been deliberate, a suicide attempt. She might have known better. Abby was made of sterner stuff than that. Kissing Fran warmly, Gipsy hurried from the ward to warn Bruce that the *Moth* was adrift in the marina.

Much later, when the *Moth* had been boat-hooked to safety and when Dr Whyte had confirmed that his patient would be discharged from the cottage hospital at eleven o'clock next morning, Gipsy went up to

236

Fran's room to pack an overnight case for her. Crossing the threshold, she saw with a sinking heart, that the bed was strewn with Abby's personal belongings, some of which had already been packed into a heavy leather suitcase. The wardrobe doors stood open, clothing removed from its hangers. The chest of drawers had been similarly denuded of underclothing, destined for a smaller case, alongside piles of crisply ironed, neatly folded blouses and colourful dirndl skirts.

The room told its own story. Abby had decided to leave Kingfisher rather than drag Quin's name into a confrontation with his father. Her way of safeguarding Quin from the harm that a confession might cause him if Bruce knew the truth about his son's liaison with a trusted member of his household.

Returning to the hospital with an overnight bag containing fresh clothing and toiletries, entering Fran's room, Gipsy said, 'It's no use, Abby; leaving Kingfisher isn't the solution to your problems. But let's not discuss that now. You've had a hell of a shock to your system. I'll be back at half past ten in the morning to take you home. I'll have your bed ready for you, and you'll stay in it till you're feeling better!

'Not to worry about grub and so on. Ian and I will see to all that. We'll have cold turkey for lunch, and warmed-up Christmas pudding. Daddy won't mind. He's worried sick about you, by the way, and full of praise for your bravery in attempting to rescue the

237

Moth. I daresay he wouldn't grumble if we gave him bread and milk for lunch and boiled eggs and soldiers for supper.'

She smiled encouragingly. 'Now let's get you out of that hospital gown and into a clean nightie. There, that's better, isn't it? And how about a bit of a face wash? I've brought a cake of soap and a flannel. Why, what's wrong, darling?' as Fran's face contorted suddenly, 'Are you in pain?'

Fran nodded, unable to speak, the pain was so intense, a gripping pain in the region of her groins, as sharp as a knife, something akin to a period pain only much, much worse. Gritting her teeth, she murmured despairingly, 'My baby! Oh God, Gipsy, help me! I'm losing my baby!'

Horrified, Gipsy saw that the pristine white sheets of Fran's bed were stained red with blood. Then, pulling herself together, she pressed the emergency bell above the bed to summon help.

Destined to remain in hospital for several days, during which time she was not permitted to set foot out of bed, fretting inwardly about her miscarriage, Fran's lethargic state of mind had proved beyond even Gipsy's power of persuasion to dispel, until, one day, she said forcefully, 'Look here, Abby, Ian and I are due back in London tomorrow. We have work to do! So have you! In case you've forgotten, my father needs looking after. So what are you going to do? Let him die of starvation?'

Fran said hazily, 'No, of course not.' Then, more purposefully, stung by Gipsy's much needed telling off, 'I'll be back at work tomorrow, with Dr Whyte's permission.' Managing a smile, she added, 'I daresay he'll be pleased to see the back of me. And thank you, Gipsy, I really needed a good mental shake-up.'

Gipsy pulled a wry face. 'Don't we all at times? Ian wants me to marry him, and I can't make my mind up. I like him, but I'm not in love with him. At least I don't think so. Tell me, Abby, should I marry him or not?'

'Certainly not! Why marry a man you're not in love with? A recipe for disaster, if you ask me.'

Gipsy said, 'Would you marry Quin, if he asked you?'

'No!'

'Why not? You're in love with him, aren't you?'

'That's grossly unfair!' Fran's eyes flashed, her voice shook. 'Do you really expect me to answer that question? What prompted you to ask it in the first place I can't imagine. I have no intention of discussing my feelings for Quin with anyone, not even you!'

'I'm sorry, Abby, I didn't mean to pry, it's just that ... well, they do say that forewarned is forearmed. I was trying to tell you, albeit clumsily, that Daddy received a letter from Paris this morning. Abby darling, Quin is coming home. He'll be here on New Year's Eve.'

Fifteen

Bruce welcomed Fran with open arms. 'My dear girl,' he said effusively, 'the house has seemed empty without you.' He ushered her into the drawing room. 'Sit down, my dear. Now, tell me, are you fully recovered from that fearful accident?'

'Yes, Mr Torrance,' Fran assured him, 'but I'm here to work, not to relax.' She smiled. 'It's very kind of you, even so. Now, I should like to make myself useful, to check the contents of the larder, if you don't mind.'

'Oh, stuff and nonsense! All that's been taken care of. There's food enough to feed an army. Gipsy's done the shopping, the washing and the ironing to save you the trouble, haven't you, my darling? And that nice young man of hers has brought in enough logs to take us into next year. By the way, glad tidings, Quin will be here to see in the new year! God, I've missed that boy! Why the hell he footled off to Paris for Christmas beats me. Never mind, eh? All's well that ends well!'

Fran and Gipsy exchanged glances. Abby was putting on a brave face, Gipsy realized. She still looked tired and strained, but she would go about her duties as calmly as usual, betraying no sign of her recent ordeal.

Talking things over before Fran had left hospital, Gipsy had respected her decision to say nothing about her pregnancy or the miscarriage she had suffered. 'After all, why rake over old embers?' she'd said wearily. 'This way, no one need ever know, and that's the way I want it.'

Gipsy had ventured a final question. 'Tell me, Abby, did you want your baby?'

'Oh yes, I wanted it. It was the one and only being that truly belonged to me.'

Torrance had invited a coterie of his closest friends to join the New Year celebrations. Quin arrived home around four in the afternoon to a rapturous welcome from his father, who, clapping an arm about his shoulders, led him to the drawing-room fire, calling out, 'Abby, bring in the tea, Tarquin's here!'

Squaring her shoulders, Fran carried the tray with the tea things from the kitchen, dreading seeing Quin again, remembering the day they had parted, at harvest time, with nothing settled between them, nothing understood. Quin had been hurt and angry by her rejection of him, not knowing how deeply she cared for him.

Now, striding towards her, he said, 'Here, let me take that,' relieving her of the tray. 'How are you, Abby? It's good to see you again.'

'She's damn lucky to be alive,' Bruce broke in. 'Noticed the *Moth* was adrift, tried to grasp the hawser and took a nosedive into the marina. A miracle she wasn't drowned. A damn brave thing to have done. Fetched up in hospital suffering from hypothermia and shock.'

Quin looked stricken. Fran said levelly, 'That's all in the past. I'm fine now.'

'Comes of self-discipline, the Nelson touch,' Bruce announced proudly, 'Knew she was made of good stuff when she told me she'd been in the Wrens. They don't take duds in the Navy. isn't that true, Abby?'

'They made an exception in my case,' Fran said awkwardly, wishing Torrance would leave the subject alone. 'Well, enjoy your tea. Now I'd best be getting on with the buffet.'

Later, Quin came through to the kitchen with the tea tray, as Fran had imagined he would. He said quietly, 'I owe you an apology for leaving so abruptly after my last visit, for making a damn fool of myself. I realized, of course, that what happened between us was a mistake, a moment of madness on my part, not yours. I am truly sorry. Can you ever forgive me?'

Fran said huskily, 'There's nothing to forgive. I think the world of you. I always have and I always will. What happened between us was more my fault than yours. You see, Quin, I wanted you to make love to me. It seemed linked somehow with your music, the magic of your sea symphony, the way I felt hearing you play. Perhaps it was a kind of madness. If

242

so, it was a divine madness, impossible to resist.

'Think about it, Quin! The last thing on earth I wanted was to become a burden to you, a kind of millstone round your neck. You deserve better than that. Freedom to live your own life in your own way. What more can I say? My one and only regret lies in not having told you how I felt about the future, the impossibility of continuing the affair. I couldn't bear the thought of spoiling something so perfect, and it would have happened: the secret meetings, the pretence, the subterfuge. You *do* understand, Quin, don't you?'

He said, 'There's something you should know. I haven't told Father yet and I don't intend to do so until the New Year celebrations are over and done with. The fact is, I'm going back to Paris in a week from now. I've rented a small flat there, in the students' quarter near the Sorbonne, and found myself a job as a music teacher at a privately owned academy in the Rue de Rivoli.

'The flat is shabby but the view across the rooftops of Paris is superb. I shall have my piano and my books crated and sent there as soon as possible.' He smiled contentedly. 'It's what I want, Abby, what I've always longed for, to live in Paris, to be a part of it, to wake up in the mornings filled with a sense of purpose as I used to during that idyllic year I spent there after the war.'

He paused reflectively. 'Father will be angry and upset, but you'll be here to take care of him, and I shall come to see you both as often as I possibly can, that I promise, and I shall always love you, Abby. Make no mistake about that.' He added wistfully, 'You will take care of Father, won't you?'

'Yes, Quin, I'll take care of him.' Fran's eyes filled with tears. 'But Kingfisher won't seem the same without you popping in at weekends to eat us out of house and home! We'll miss you so much, so very much.'

'As I shall miss you,' Quin said tenderly, brushing away her tears. 'Don't cry, darling. Just think, this way our love will suffer no eclipse, no debasement. It was perfect, and it will remain so in the storehouse we call memory. I'll never forget you, Abby. Now, kiss me.'

Suddenly his arms were about her and for one exquisite moment she savoured the feel of his lips on hers, unleashing a torrent of supressed emotion as, briefly, they clung together in a last embrace, a kind of curtain call to mark the end of an abortive love affair.

Quitting his embrace, considering the future ahead of her, smoothing her hair and remembering that she had not yet begun setting the dining-room table for the new year buffet, Fran said shakily, 'I really must be getting on with my work.'

'I'll help you,' Quin said. 'Just tell me what you want done, and I'll do it.'

Together they carried food from the pantry to the dining room, deeply aware of one another, yet in a kind of limbo strung between love and friendship, a no-man's land in which the only reality appeared to be food. Food, glorious bloody food, Fran thought despairingly.

She came in from shopping, three days later, to the sound of voices from the study, Torrance's was raised in anger, Quin's quietly placating. 'I'm sorry, Dad,' he was saying, 'I know you're upset, but it's something I want to do very much. Please try to understand.'

'Understand?' Bruce shouted. 'You expect me to understand your chucking up a decent job close to home to live in some rat-infested garret in Paris? Well I don't understand, and I never shall! What ails you, Tarquin? Have you taken leave of your senses? Oh, I get it. So this was all planned. The reason why you left me in the lurch at Christmas. You might have had the decency to warn me beforehand what you had in mind instead of springing it on me the way you have done! It's unforgiveable! You've treated me with contempt. Your own father. How could you have done such a thing?'

In the kitchen, Fran's hands shook as she unloaded the shopping. Torrance was given to outbursts of temper, but she had never heard him so angry before. Her heart went out to Quin, wrongly accused of deceit and contempt.

When he came into the kitchen some time later, she said, 'I'm sorry. I couldn't help overhearing. But your father's bark is worse than his bite. He'll calm down, given time.'

'The trouble is, there isn't much time. I'm leaving here the day after tomorrow. I wish I knew what to say to him to make him realize how much I need his understanding and for-giveness.'

'Then talk to him again, after supper,' Fran advised. 'He'll be more amenable with a good meal inside him: roast lamb, washed down with a bottle of Chablis.'

'What a wise woman you are,' Quin said quietly. 'I'll do as you suggest. Any other advice?'

'A glass or two of brandy might help,' Fran proffered, from long experience of Bruce's fondness for coffee, brandy and cigars in the wake of a good meal. She would make certain that the roast lamb was cooked to perfection, moist and tender, served with his favourite crisply roasted potatoes and al dente vegetables, followed by an irresistible freshly baked apple pie and a jug of thick Jersey cream. She laughed suddenly.

'What's so funny?' Quin asked, frowning slightly, yet smiling.

'The fact that I've always hated cooking,' Fran told him. 'The last thing I ever envisag-ed was becoming a cook-housekeeper. A cleaning lady, yes, but never a cook or a housekeeper. So you see, Quin, I've been sail-ing under false colours for the past decade.'

'I know so little about you, Abby,' Quin confessed. 'Next to nothing about your back-ground. I never knew, for instance, that you had been in the Wrens during the war, or that you disliked cooking. Gipsy and I simply accepted that you were coming to look after us and that was it. There were other house-keepers, none of whom stayed long, mainly because Dad put the fear of God in them. But you stood up to him.'

He chuckled. 'I remember the day you marched into his study and told him the house needed bottoming, that it looked like a paddenken – and you were right. Soon you'd become a part of our lives.'

He added, 'I know it won't be easy for you coping with Dad when I'm gone. He's not as resilient as he used to be, or as successful. He'll need you, Abby, to bolster his ego, and you'll need something to occupy your time – apart from cleaning and cooking.'

'Good works, you mean? No thanks. I've always been a loner. It's he who will need more company, which I'll encourage from now on. That way I'll have more to do, so it will cut both ways. Don't worry about me, Quin, I can take care of myself.'

Thankfully, Fran's tactics had worked wonders. Mellowed by food, wine, brandy and cigars, Torrance had forgiven his son's trespasses against him. Seated near the drawing-room fire, after dinner, Bruce said regretfully, 'I'm a selfish, tetchy old fool. It's just that the thought of losing you came as a shock, but your life is your own, and you must live it as you see fit, the way I've lived mine, with no

247

regrets. Youth must have its fling!'

'Thanks, Dad. But you're not losing me exactly. I'll come home as often as possible, I promise. Meanwhile, Abby will be here to look after you.'

'Abby,' Bruce mused, staring into the fire. 'But what if she decides not to stay with me? After all, why should she? She also has a life to live. The wonder is that she has been here so long, an attractive woman in the prime of life. Why waste her time at Kingfisher when she might have a home of her own, a husband and children? You know, Quin, there's something about Abby that I've never quite fathomed or come to terms with. As if she harbours some sorrow in her past that has erected a barrier of reserve between herself and the rest of the world. What do you think, Tarquin?'

'That you're meeting trouble halfway!' Quin said quietly. 'We all have secrets to keep. Now, let's call it a day, shall we? You're tired, so am I.' He added huskily, 'I love you, Dad, and I always will.'

But Quin's departure came as a blow to his father and to Fran when it happened. It was a cold, bitingly windy day, with snow flurries and a leaden sky threatening heavy snowfalls to come. His cases were strapped and waiting in the hall, his books and his piano had been crated the day before, and would be in transit now to Paris. 'If the bloody boat doesn't sink, in this wind,' Bruce muttered despairingly Oh, for God's sake, Quin, use your common sense, postpone your trip for the time being. Batten down the hatches, stay put till the weather improves!'

'I'm sorry, Dad, I can't. My plans are made, the taxi will be here any minute. I'll ring you tonight to tell you I've arrived safely. Ah, here's the taxi now. Come on, Dad, it's not the end of the world.' He threw his arms round his father. 'Goodbye, Dad.' Then he held Fran close to him for a brief moment in time. 'Goodbye, Abby, and God bless you.' Then he was gone, and the loneliness had begun.

Gipsy rang later to say that she had seen Tarquin safely aboard his flight at London Airport. 'How's Father taking it?' she asked.

'Not too well on the whole. It's all been a bit sudden, you see.'

'Oh, Lord,' Gipsy said guiltily. 'Then I'd best leave my own news till later. Poor Daddy will have a fit when he knows.'

'Knows *what*? Oh come on, Gipsy, stop being mysterious. You can tell me.'

'Promise you won't let on?'

'How can I "let on" when I don't know what the hell you're on about?'

'All right, Abby, keep your hair on! It's just that Ian is going back to Scotland next week. He wants me to go with him, and I've said yes. Guess I'm fonder of him than I thought.' She sighed deeply. 'It will mean giving up my flat and my own job, and Daddy won't like that one little bit, but I can't help it. I just want to be in Edinburgh with Ian.' She paused momentarily. 'Shall *I* tell him, or will you?'

'You'll tell him yourself, my girl! What's more, you'll do it properly, face to face, and as soon as possible, if you're sure you're doing the right thing. Oh, my dear, don't rush into something you might regret. Come home anyway, talk to him about it, seek his advice. That's the least you can do.'

'You're right of course, Abby,' Gipsy conceded thoughtfully. 'Very well then, I'll be home next weekend.' She added wistfully, 'You will be on my side, won't you? Promise?'

Fran promised. How could she have done otherwise? She loved Gipsy, who was, in essence, the child she had always longed for and never had. Much more than that, she was a compassionate young woman without whose help and support Fran might well have not recovered from the trauma of her recent illness to face up to life once more.

Torrance fairly glowed when he knew that Gipsy was coming home for the weekend. 'Is she coming alone or bringing that Scottish bloke with her?' he asked. 'If so, how about tatties and neeps for supper?'

'I've never cooked tatties and neeps in my life,' Fran protested. 'I don't even know what they are! No, if he comes, he'll have steak and kidney pudding, and lump it!' The battle of wills between Fran and her employer remained as keen as ever, sharpening the dull

250

edges of life – a game which they both secretly relished. The near decade of their assocation beneath the same roof had spawned their serio-comic relationship, their deep regard and respect for one another, despite their occasional outspoken differences of opinion. Never at any time had Fran referred to Bruce as other than Mr Torrance, or sir. There were boundaries which could not and should not be overstepped, in Fran's opinion, and this was one of them.

'Do *you* know what tatties and neeps are?' she demanded, tongue in cheek.

'No, but *I'm* not paid to do the cooking, *you* are!'

'Tell me, sir, did you like the Scotsman?'

'Yes, I did rather,' Torrance mused, 'when I'd got used to his accent. He was pretty handy when it came to chopping wood. I say, you don't think Gipsy's serious serious about him, do you?'

Fran seized her opportunity. 'Well, I would not be at all surprised. Gipsy will have to settle down sometime, and she might as well do so with someone ... handy, don't you think?'

Having sown the seeds, Fran repaired to her kitchen to begin preparations for the steak and kidney pudding.

Gipsy and Ian arrived together later that afternoon, looking sheepish. 'What's the temperature like?' Gipsy asked Fran as they slid into the hall.

'Promising at the moment,' Fran whisper-ed. 'Just tread carefully, that's all. Don't start laying down the law, for God's sake! No histrionics, no confrontation. Take my advice, eat your dinner first, then break the news to him. What *is* the news, by the way?'

'We've decided to get married,' Gipsy said blissfully, glancing up at Ian, 'haven't we, darling?'

Thank God for small mercies, Fran thought fervently, hurrying back to the kitchen as Bruce appeared from his study to welcome his beloved daughter and her boyfriend.

'Huh, strange,' Bruce said, 'I didn't hear the doorbell. Must be getting deaf in my old age.'

'Abby let us in.' Gipsy laughed. 'She hap-pened to be in the hall. Well, Daddy, how are you? Oh, it's so good to be home again. You do remember Ian, don't you?'

Oh no, Fran thought from the kitchen, no, Gipsy, not now! Not yet! Leave it! Now is not the right time!

But Gipsy was already spilling the beans. 'Daddy, darling, Ian and I are engaged to be married! I'm giving up my job and my flat and we're going to Edinburgh to live when we've tied the knot!'

'Over my dead body,' Bruce said grimly. 'Quin's in Paris, now you're talking nonsense about going to Scotland to live with a man you scarcely know from Adam. Well, it's not good enough! I won't have it! So just clear off, the pair of you! Do what the hell you like from now on, make a mess of your lives, just don't expect me to pick up the pieces. First Quin now you. Of all the thankless ungrateful offspring! You've been spoiled rotten, that's your trouble. Well, what are you waiting for? Get out and leave me alone.'

Entering the arena, Fran said diplomatically, 'Dinner's almost ready. It would seem a pity to waste it after all the time I've spent cooking it, so why not go through to the dining room? The wine is on the sideboard. Would you mind opening it for me? I have never had the knack, somehow.' She placed a gentle hand on Torrance's sleeve. 'Please sir.' She glanced up at him appealingly.

'Oh, very well then,' he replied gruffly. 'Sorry, got a bit carried away. Missing Quin, you know. That's the trouble. Can't get used to his absence.'

'It's all right, Daddy. I'm sorry, too. I shouldn't have blurted out my news the way I did. I was just so excited,' Gipsy apolo gized, kissing his cheek. 'Am I forgiven?'

When Fran brought the pudding into the dining room, peace had been restored, the wine had been uncorked and Torrance was smiling at his daughter and her fiancé. Rising to his feet, Ian asked courteously, 'Shall I bring in the tureens for you, Miss Abbot?'

'Yes, thank you, that would be a great help,' Fran said, 'then, if you'll excuse me, I'll bid you goodnight. It's been a long day, and I am rather tired.'

'Abby darling,' Gipsy cried out concerned-ly, hurrying towards her, hands outstretched,

'I'm so sorry. All this is my fault, selfish pig that I am. I should have realized how tired you were. What can *I* do to help?'

'Just sit down and eat your dinner, then make the coffee. Above all, stop fussing! All I want is a good night's sleep and a bit of peace and quiet.'

Going upstairs to her room, Fran decided that discretion was the better part of valour. Best leave the lot of them to their own devices for the time being. She was tired of emotional upheavals, of pouring oil on troubled water. She was a cook-housekeeper, for God's sake, not a punchbag. Much more of this and she'd pack her bags, hand in her notice and shake the dust of Kingfisher Cottage from her shoes once and for all.

She knew, of course, that she would do no such thing, but it would do Torrance a world of good to think so. Another battle of wills between the pair of them, she thought, getting into bed, which she fully intended to win, even if it meant resorting to a touch of emotional blackmail to bring her temperamental employer to a more reasonable frame of mind.

Sooner or later, he would have to accept that his offspring were not prisoners but grown-up individuals free to choose their own paths through life, as he would have to accept that she, also, had a right to spiritual liberty. A wage earner she may well be, a wage slave she was not, and never would be.

If, as she suspected, she was to remain

254

committed to Kingfisher for some time to come, it would have to be on her terms. Realistically, she would need help with the housework, someone to relieve her of the washing and ironing. Her recent illness had, she knew deep down, weakened her constitution to some extent, robbing her of her former energy and initiative, leaving her prey to sudden bouts of physical and mental exhaustion, both enervating and frightening. And this was the silent battle she must fight alone if she was to fulfil her promise to Quin to look after his father.

At Bruce's insistence, Gipsy's wedding took place at Kingfisher. The month was June, the weather was glorious. Gipsy wore a simple white chiffon dress, a wide-brimmed hat, and carried a nosegay of pink rosebuds. The wedding ceremony took place in the village church, and Quin had come home from Paris to play the organ.

Recalling her days at Greystones Hotel in Scarborough, Fran had ordered fresh and smoked Scottish salmon, Melton Mowbray veal and ham pies, plump chickens from a local farmer and fresh fruit and vegetables from a market garden near Truro. The three-tier wedding cake she baked and iced herself, at the request of the bride, who said she couldn't care less about the icing as long as the cake was home-made.

The house was filled with flowers, wedding presents and people. Members of Ian's family had been invited to stay from Friday till Monday. Torrance had hired extra staff to help Fran with the housework – two capable village women and a couple of schoolgirls, who made beds, hoovered, dusted and polished, set tables and helped with the washing-up. Not the cooking, Fran had a plan of action so far as this was concerned, working methodically to make certain that nothing had been overlooked, writing shopping lists on a thick notepad on the kitchen dresser, reminders to order milk, cream, sugar, bread, butter, tackling the job with the precision of a quartermaster in charge of a field kitchen.

Menus had been worked out well in advance to cater to the requirements of the house-party guests, seven in all, plus the domestics, herself included, the family, Bruce, Quin and Gipsy, all of whom would want breakfast, lunch and dinner, snacks and cuppas. She added porridge oats to her shopping list; the Scottish contingent would expect porridge for breakfast, Fran reckoned, enjoying the challenge as she had done when she'd taken charge of the staff kitchen at Greystones. Being prepared was the key to success, and she wanted Gipsy's wedding to go without a hitch. Nothing left to chance.

She was tired, but so what? She worked happily with one thought uppermost in her mind. Quin was coming home.

Sixteen

It had been a day to remember. One of those perfect midsummer days, to look back on with joy when winter comes.

The bridegroom, his father and his two brothers had worn kilts, sporrans and glengarries, his mother and sisters simple summer dresses in varying shades of purple embellished with tartan shoulder sashes in honour of the Gordon Clan, to which they belonged. Bruce Torrance had been in his element, playing host, dispensing liberal quantities of malt whisky and champagne to his guests before the ceremony, to the consternation of Gipsy, who told him in no uncertain terms that if he took a nosedive on their walk down the aisle she'd never forgive him.

'My dear child, I'm as sober as a judge,' Bruce assured her, 'and I shall remain so until you are safely off my hands. Afterwards, I shall please myself. Fair enough?'

'All right, Daddy, you win! But do remember your blood pressure.'

'Why should I?' he riposted gaily. 'I doubt if it ever remembers me!'

Quin, who had heard the conversation, said, 'Don't worry, sis, I'll keep an eye on Dad.'

257

'Oh, Quin darling, you're such a comfort! I wish we'd had more time together. Are you really happy living abroad?'

'Blissfully so,' he laughed. 'I've just been telling Abby about it – about Paris, my apartment, my job. Dear Abby, she must have worked like a horse to see to all the food. The buffet is a work of art, and the flowers are magnificent.'

'She's been taking lessons,' Gipsy confided, 'and not just flower arranging. I talked her into taking driving lessons. She's had two so far, and she's thinking of buying a car if things work out all right. Just a second-hand jalopy, I imagine, unless—'

'Unless what? Come on, sis, what's going on in that scheming brain of yours?'

'Wouldn't you like to know?' Glancing at her watch, she exclaimed, 'Gosh, is that the time? I've heard of being late for one's own funeral, but if I don't get a move on, I'll be late for my wedding!'

Fran had taken a final look at the dining table before setting off for the church, to make absolutely sure that everything was in order, ready for the guests, who, on their return from the ceremony, would soon put paid to the food she had arranged with so much care and attention to detail.

Not that she minded about that. Food was meant to be eaten and enjoyed, and she had derived infinite satisfaction from the hours she had spent in the kitchen to ensure the success of Gipsy's wedding reception.

Happy the bride the sun shines on, she thought wistfully. The sun was certainly shining today, and although she had harboured certain misgivings that Gipsy was about to marry the wrong man, her fears seemed groundless when she saw the tender expression in Gipsy's eyes as she looked up at her bridegroom, and the adoring expression in Ian's as he promised to love and to cherish her all the days of his life. O, Perfect Love...

Singing the hymn, Fran thought that she also had experienced a perfect love. However fleetingly, she had known what it felt like to be loved, to be wanted, to surrender to the power, the passion and the pain of love. So what had possessed her to turn her back on love? She still loved Quin. She believed he still loved her. If so, why not...?

For one shining moment she'd envisaged a new beginning with the man she loved. A pipe dream, she knew that now. How could she have believed otherwise? What kind of a future was possible between herself, a mature woman, and an emotionally immature, man, years younger than her? How long would it be before he became resentful of her age, she of his youth? Far better to remember their brief liaison with no regrets than to attempt its resurrection.

The weeks following the wedding were well nigh unendurable. The house, robbed of the ebullient presence of the Gordon clan, of

Quin, who had returned to Paris, and of Gipsy and her bridegroom, who had left Kingfisher after the reception to spend their honeymoon in the Lake District, seemed deadly dull. It was as quiet as a graveyard now that Fran and Torrance were alone together, for all the world like Darby and Joan, Fran thought, scarcely knowing how to pass the time now that the party was over.

Torrance, she knew, had just begun to realize that his children – around whom his days had once revolved, on whom he had relied to add point and piquancy to his existence – had finally flown the nest; that, from henceforth, they would not be an intregral part of his life, popping home for weekends at frequent intervals as they used to. Now he appeared to Fran as a sad and lonely old man unable to come to terms with the loss of his loved ones from his hitherto busy, purposeful life as a successful, best-selling author of the many brilliantly crafted psychological thrillers that had ensured his fame and fortune during the past decades,

Worried by his physical and mental state. Fran did her utmost to stimulate him to a more positive frame of mind – encouraging him to continue sailing as a hobby, making certain that his favourite foods appeared at table – to little or no avail. Torrance had, seemingly, lost interest in sailing, food and writing.

In desperation, one day she had sent for his friend and physician, Doctor Franklyn, explaining that she had done so without her employer's knowledge. 'He'll probably sack me when he finds out,' she said nervously, 'but Quin's in France and Gipsy's in Edinburgh, so it was a decision I had to take off my own bat.'

Franklyn regarded Fran keenly, approvingly. 'You did quite right,' he assured her briskly. 'I've known Bruce Torrance for some considerable time now. Not an easy person to understand, as stubborn as a mule at times. But no need to tell you that, I daresay. Tell me, is he still hitting the bottle pretty hard? Come, now, you can tell me. I need to know what I'm up against.'

'Yes, I'm afraid so. Harder than ever since the wedding. I can't seem to get through to him these days.' Fran bit her lip. 'He seems to have lost all interest in everyday life. He spends hours alone in his study, but I know he's not working. I used to hear the clatter of his typewriter. And he's not eating properly, just picking at his food. That's why I rang you. I'm worried sick about him.'

Franklyn could see that. The woman looked tired, pale and strained. Not a happy state of affairs, he considered shrewdly, a comparatively young woman wasting her life in service to a curmudgeonly old devil who probably took her for granted. How long had she been with him now? Ten years? High time she was thinking of moving on, in his opinion, seeing a bit of the world. But then, strictly speaking, that was none of his business.

He said kindly, 'Don't worry, Miss Abbot, I'll pretend I've popped in on the off-chance. I shan't tell him you sent for me.'

The news was worse than expected. Franklyn said grimly, 'Thank God you sent for me when you did. His blood pressure's sky high, he has a heart murmur and there may be liver damage. May I use the phone? I'm sending for an ambulance.'

Awaiting its arrival, Fran hurriedly packed an overnight case with Bruce's dressing gown, pyjamas, slippers and shaving gear. He seemed dazed, uncertain what was happening, where he was going, or why.

Fran went with him in the ambulance. The Cottage Hospital was all too familiar. She would wait there until he was settled in a small private room, then return to Kingfisher with his top clothing. Franklyn would drive her back in his car. She also felt disorientated; everything had happened so fast. The doctor explained that Bruce would be given a morphine injection to ensure a restful night's sleep prior to the visit of a consultant the following morning to carry out a full-scale examination to determine the extent of the liver damage and decide on the necessary treatment.

Franklyn said, on their arrival at Kingfisher, 'I'm not entirely happy about your being alone in the house. Is there anyone who would stay with you? A friend or acquaintance?'

'No, thank you, I shall be quite all right. I don't mind being alone. In any case, there'll be plenty to do.' She smiled faintly. 'Besides, I have the animals to keep me company. The one thing I really dread is telling Gipsy. She'll be terribly upset, and I'm not at all sure... What I mean is, what shall I say if she asks how serious it is? I can't answer that question because I don't know myself.' She paused, 'How serious *is* her father's condition?'

'That is up to the consultant to ascertain,' Franklyn reminded her. 'If I were you, I'd simply say that her father is in hospital, resting comfortably for the time being. Say that his blood pressure was giving cause for concern on my part, and I advocated a spell in hospital to bring it under control.' He sighed deeply. 'Sufficient unto the day is the evil thereof. No need to frighten the girl. Just break it to her gently, is my advice. After all, my diagnosis of liver damage could well be wrong.'

'And the heart murmur?' Fran asked.

'Hmm, well, I was right about that, but it is just a murmur, a condition linked to hypertension triggered by abnormally high blood pressure, in my experience.'

'Thank you, Doctor,' Fran said gratefully, 'you've been more than kind.'

'Not at all, Miss Abbot. Please don't hesitate to call upon me if there's anything more I can do for you. And now, goodnight, sleep well.'

★   ★   ★

Gipsy hastened to Kingfisher when she heard of her father's illness. She'd tried to contact Quin, without success. 'I don't know where he is,' she said crossly, exhausted after her long journey from Edinburgh. 'How *is* Daddy? The truth, Abby! I had the feeling you were holding something back when you rang me the other night.'

'Not deliberately,' Fran said, filling the kettle for a cup of tea. 'I didn't know much to tell – then.'

'And *now*?' Gipsy's face turned deathly pale. 'Oh God, he's not going to die, is he?'

'Let's not go down that road,' Fran said firmly. 'An operation is on the cards, to remove a small tumour in the region of his liver. The consultant, Mr Berridge, is a first-class surgeon. He's confident that your father will come through it with flying colours. Now, sit down, drink your tea, and try not to look on the black side. Your father's a comparatively young man, and I'll be here to look after him when he leaves hospital.' She smiled encouragingly. 'I said *when*, not *if*!'

Gipsy burst into tears. 'I'm feeling a bit off-colour myself right now. You see, Abby darling, I'm two months pregnant! I was frightfully sick on the train.'

Fran had no idea what she would be in for when Torrance left hospital a month later. Impossibly tetchy and self-centred, nothing was right for him. 'What the hell do you mean no wine, no brandy or cigars? Now see here,

Frances, you're my housekeeper not my warder! As long as I'm paying your wages, you'll do as I tell you and like it. Is that clear?'

'Abundantly clear, sir. Your dinner's in the oven. It's a chicken casserole. Just help yourself when you're ready. The brandy and cigars are in the sideboard. Help yourself to them an' all while you're about it. As you so rightly said, I'm not your warder. You got it wrong about my being your housekeeper. I'm leaving!'

'Leaving? But you *can't*! What about *me*? What am *I* supposed to do?'

'What you have always done! Please yourself! I promised Quin I'd look after you when he went away. I've done my best, God knows, but enough's enough! You're on your own from now on. You don't need me, and I sure as hell don't need you!'

Torrance's face crumpled. He said hoarsely, 'But I *do* need you. I always have. I knew that the minute I clapped eyes on you. Please, Frances, don't go. Don't leave me. I'd be lost without you! This is your home. You belong here. Quin, Gipsy and I are your family! I'm begging you to stay! Not as my housekeeper but ... my wife!' He drew in a shuddering breath. 'I care deeply for you, Fran. I'm asking you to marry me!'

'Marry you?' Fran stared at him, wide eyed with surprise.

'If that's what it takes to keep you here with me, to keep my family intact, to dispel that foolish notion of yours that I regard you as nothing more than a housekeeper. Well, what is your answer?'

'My answer is no, Mr Torrance,' Fran said flatly. 'I'll stay on as your housekeeper, if that's "what it takes" to make you behave yourself. I have no desire to marry someone – anyone – as a matter of expedience, ta very much.'

'Have I said something to upset you?' Bruce frowned bemusedly. 'I thought you'd take my proposal as a compliment.'

'You thought wrong then, didn't you? If that's what it takes to keep me here with you, to keep your family intact, indeed! Well, sir, let's get something else clear, shall we? Since I've promised to stay on as your housekeeper, you'd best forget about brandy and cigars, stop playing the martyr and stop bellyaching and making a damn nuisance of yourself, otherwise I'll be off faster than a bullet from a gun. All right?'

The cut and thrust between the pair of them was as sharp and keen as ever, Fran thought, and this was one battle that she knew she had won hands down.

She'd had no idea at the time how much longer she would be called upon to cope with the demands of a tetchy employer. Certainly, Bruce's attitude towards her improved somewhat after their battle royal, and the news of Gipsy's pregnancy had given him something to think about apart from himself. But Fran had known that his state of euphoria at the prospect of becoming a grandfather, and the glad tidings that Quin's 'Sea Fever Symphony' had been performed, in Paris, to critical acclaim, would not last for very long, and she was right.

Soon he'd begun railing against the illness that had robbed him of his former joie de vivre, the pleasure he'd derived from alcohol and cigars and the necessity of frequent hospital check-ups to undergo X-rays and blood tests, which he dismissed as 'damned nonsense'. As if Fran was to blame for his indisposition.

'What you fail to realize, Frances,' he'd said bitterly, 'is that I *need* a drink now and then to lift my spirits. I'm a man, for God's sake, a force to be reckoned with, not a clapped-out bloody invalid!'

But Fran knew differently, having been warned by Doctor Franklyn that Torrance's life depended on his steering well clear of alcohol from now on.

'Believe me, Miss Abbot,' he'd said sympathetically, 'I know what you're up against, and I wouldn't blame you in the least if you decided to seek fresh fields and pastures new. It can't be easy for you fighting a running battle with a crusty character like Bruce Torrance. To be honest, I fail to understand the reason why you have stayed at Kingfisher Cottage so long.'

Fran replied simply, 'Because it's my home. Because I've been happy here. Oh, not all the time. But is anyone ever happy all the time? Because I promised Tarquin Torrance that I would take care of his father for as long as necessary. Does that answer your question?'

'Yes, Miss Abbot, it does,' Franklyn responded quietly, 'and your dedication to duty does you credit. I should warn you, however, that you have a dying man on your hands. With care and treatment, Torrance may well survive the next two years or so, during which time he will need the services of a qualified night nurse to take charge of him. I'm sorry, Frances, but that's the whole picture, I'm afraid.'

'I see,' Fran said hoarsely. 'Even so, I'll stay with him to the end. No matter how distressing that end may be.'

Up and doing early next morning, apparently in high spirits, donning his sailing gear, Wellingtons, a thick knit jersey and his yachting cap, worn at a jaunty angle, Torrance said briskly, 'High time I got a breath of sea air into my lungs. I've played the landlubber long enough! I'm taking the *Moth* for a trip down the Fowey to the coast. The old girl will be glad of a spin and so shall I! Not to worry, I'll be back in time for lunch. I fancy ham and eggs. Well, don't just stand there, Frances, looking like a wet weekend. Make yourself useful. After all, that's what you're paid for, isn't it?'

'If you say so, sir,' Fran riposted sharply tongue in cheek, but not nearly enough, in my view, to put up with the likes of you!'

Boarding the *Moth*, Torrance threw back at
268

her, 'I'm on my way now! Wish me God speed, Fran! A safe journey and a happy landing.'

And these were the words that would haunt Fran for the rest of her life when Torrance failed to return from his yachting trip down the Fowey. His lifeless body had been discovered in the cabin of the *Moth*, his death resulting from a sudden heart attack, which had, at least, spared him the horror and humiliation of a night nurse. At least he had quit the world on his own terms, with all flags flying, Fran thought, deeply regretting the loss of her old friend and protagonist, a man infinitely worthy of respect, remembrance – and love.

Torrance would have been both touched and gratified by the local newspaper headline: 'Tragic Death of a Legend in His Lifetime' above several columns recalling the flamboyant lifestyle of the well-known author Bruce Torrance, who had thrilled generations of readers, world wide, with his brilliantly crafted psychological crime novels set against the background of his beloved Cornwall.

National newspapers had picked up the story. There was even a mention of Bruce's demise on radio news bulletins. The 'Legend in His Lifetime' catchphrase had rung bells with the media, and also at the local telephone exchange, to Fran's distress, at a time when she could well have done without the constant interruption of answering the phone to well-meaning callers wanting to know the date and the time of the funeral. Eventually she left the phone off the hook to concentrate on her housekeeping duties: preparing rooms and food for Quin, Gipsy, Ian and members of his family who would be arriving at Kingfisher to attend the funeral.

As a matter of expedience, she had called in the women helpers from Gipsy's wedding to see to the bed-making, hoovering, dusting and polishing, aware that she could not possibly see to everything herself and desperately in need of Quin's presence to remove the responsibility of the funeral arrangements from her shoulders. He and he alone could decide on matters pertaining to the funeral service. All that she could possibly do was provide sustenance for all and sundry, as she had done at Gipsy's wedding, but this time without the heartwarming feeling of joy she had experienced on that occasion.

When Quin arrived, close to breaking point she had simply held out her hands to him and murmured, 'Thank God you're here!'

'I know, Abby, I know,' he said quietly, holding her hands tightly in his. 'My poor, dear girl, how dreadful all this has been for you. How selfish, how despicable of me to have burdened you with the responsibility for my father. I should never have gone abroad to live. I see that now. Can you ever forgive me?'

'There's nothing to forgive,' Fran said. 'You did what you had to do. So did I. No regrets. I cared deeply for your father, and I think, deep down, that he cared for me.' Close to tears, she continued, 'You mustn't blame yourself, Quin, neither of us knew, how could we, that he was living on borrowed time? I doubt he realized it himself – until...'

'Until *what*, Abby?'

'Until he set sail on the *Moth*, that last morning,' Fran said regretfully. 'I think he just wanted to sail on into oblivion, to the point of no return, and his wish was granted, God rest him. He must have known that sailing the *Moth* single-handed might prove too much for him, and so, being the man he was, he took a calculated risk on not sailing the *Moth* home again.'

In the days preceding the funeral, Fran's only respite from pain had lain in catering to the needs of those gathered beneath the roof of Kingfisher – no easy task, involving, as it did, an unfailing supply of food and drink from long hours spent in the kitchen, until, come nightfall, she would fall fast asleep the moment her head touched the pillows, waking in the early hours of the next morning to face the realization that her days in the place she thought of as home were number-ed.

Quin had told her sadly that once Bruce had been laid to rest in the village churchyard he would have no other option than to place his father's property in the hands of a reliable estate agent.

'Sell Kingfisher, you mean?' Fran had

asked, aghast. 'But *why*? It's your home, for heaven's sake!'

'It *was*,' Quin reminded her gently. 'No longer, I'm afraid. I'm so sorry, Abby, but I have a home of my own now, in Paris, and Gipsy has a place of her own in Edinburgh. I am truly sorry, I know how much Kingfisher Cottage means to you, but realistically, if I strained my resources to the limit and decided to hang on to the house, would you really want to stay on here alone?'

'No, I suppose not,' Fran admitted ruefully, 'but this is my home. I've been here nigh on twelve years now. Where would I go? What on earth should I do? Seek another job? Make another beginning in a a strange place, among strangers?' Her anger rose. 'Oh, I see! I've served my purpose, now you couldn't care tuppence what happens to me?'

'I *do* care, Abby,' Quin assured her. 'So did my father, which is why he made provision for you in his will. I happen to know that he has left you the sum of fifteen thousand pounds to ease your journey into a new future ahead of you. I quote, if memory serves me correctly, "To my housekeeper and friend, Frances Abbot, a lady who has gained my trust and admiration during the years she has spent in my service, I bequeath the sum of fifteen thousand pounds, in the fervent hope that when I am no longer in need of her kindness, wisdom and good advice, she will use my gift to her to set sail on a voyage of discovery to find the happiness and fulfilment

272

she so richly deserves.'"

Smiling mysteriously, her anger forgotten, eyes aglow, Fran said reflectively, 'I wonder what he'd have thought of me had he known that I was unworthy of his trust? You see, Quin, I never told him of our love affair, or you of my pregnancy, or the miscarriage of a child I wanted so much. *Your* child, Quin!

'Well, that's all in the past, isn't it? Now I have a whole new future ahead of me, thanks to a man who was, without a shadow of doubt, the best and dearest friend I've ever had. Your father, Bruce Torrance!'

She added, cutting through his astonishment, on her way to the kitchen door, 'I'll stay on till after the funeral, of course, then I'll be on my way. I really couldn't bear to see a For Sale notice in the garden. I've loved Kingfisher so much, as I've loved you and Gipsy, and always will. So let's not say goodbye, shall we? Just au revoir, until we meet again.'

'Abby,' Quin called after her. Too late. The door had closed behind her. Fran was already mentally on her way to her new future. Her voyage of discovery.

Part Four

Seventeen

She had treated herself to a second-hand Morris Minor, the wheels of which she had turned in the direction of Middleton, her birthplace and the scene of her earliest memories, wanting to rediscover her roots, to revisit the house in which her mother had cooked so many disastrous meals, forced by poverty to buy the cheapest cuts of meat and wizened vegetables, to rub a modicum of fat into flour to produce the rock hard pastry so despised by her sons.

The house seemed smaller than she remembered. Sitting in her car, she recalled the countless times she had let herself into the house after work, bringing with her the cracked eggs, broken biscuits and offcuts of salty bacon to supplement the weekend's food supply. How eagerly her mother had looked forward to her homecoming, how valiantly she had tried to provide a warm, welcoming atmosphere for her family, and how well she had succeeded despite the odds stacked against her: lack of money, increasing weakness and ill-health, her constant uphill struggle against debt, receiving little or no help, financially or otherwise, from her two hulking, layabout sons, the memory of whose callousness towards their mother still rankled. Time had done nothing to soften Fran's dislike of the pair of them.

Getting out of the car, she walked down a narrow ginnel and stared up at the back windows of the house, conjuring up memories of the rooms behind the blank, impersonal panes of glass, imagining the faded ghost of her mother flitting silently about those rooms, too weak almost to stand, let alone to cope with the cooking and cleaning, the washing and ironing, stricken by her sons' cavalier treatment of her, yet too loving, too loyal to admit to their faults, wanting peace at any price. Possibly, Fran thought, returning to her car, this was the reason why she had developed a rough edge to her own nature, as a means of survival against the slings and arrows of outrageous fortune.

By comparison with Scarborough and Cornwall, Middleton appeared dull and dreary, lacking in beauty and charm, with its rows of seam-straight streets and common-or-garden brick-built houses, and yet there was something about it, a kind of earthiness, which touched a chord of response in Fran's imagination. This, after all, was her birthplace, the town she had grown up in. Far from beautiful, but an integral part of her being.

Buying flowers, she drove to the cemetery to visit the graves of her parents and her Aunt Dorothy. Filling containers with water and arranging the flowers, she thought of Torrance's funeral, the packed church and crowds of mourners who had flocked to pay their last respects to a man who had been a well-known member of the community as far back as they could remember – quite a character: quirky, humorous, generous, moody, often irritable, difficult to please, clever and famous. Lovable despite his many faults and failings. In short, a human being whose death had left a hole in all their lives, especially Fran's.

Leaving Kingfisher had been one of the hardest things she had ever had to do. Gipsy had begged her to stay on until the cottage was sold, to show prospective buyers round the house, then, when the purchase was settled, to make her home in Edinburgh with her, Ian and the baby when it was born, an offer which Fran had gently but firmly declined to accept.

Quin had made no attempt to keep her, realizing she had meant what she'd said about leaving Kingfisher after the funeral, not wanting to see the For Sale notice posted in the garden. Still shaken by Fran's revelation that she had miscarried his child, Quin knew, deep down, that the death of his father had, in essence, ended her guardianship of Kingfisher, had freed her of her responsibility towards the Torrance family, himself above all.

It was he who had saddled her with the responsibility of caring for Bruce, and he knew that she would never have broken her promise to stay on at Kingfisher during his father's lifetime. Now Bruce was dead, and Fran was free to live her own life. And yet, when the time came to say goodbye, he had known how much he would miss her warm, comforting presence in his life.

Leaving the cemetery, Fran had booked herself a room for the night at a prestigious hotel in the town centre. Money was no object, and yet it went against the grain to squander it, realizing, as she did, the importance of financial security. On this occasion, though, she needed a comfortable bed and a decent dinner served in her room: a touch of luxury for a change. Room service with a smile, à la black and white Hollywood movies seen in her youth: glorious make-believe, depicting the lives of the very rich, who for once in her life, she wished to emulate for the sheer fun of it. Bruce Torrance, she felt sure, would relish the joke.

Freedom was a novelty to Fran after the vicissitudes of the past years, and especially the last weeks, when Bruce's illness had necessitated daily visits to the Cottage Hospital during and after his operation, until his return home, when she'd been called upon to act as a part-time nurse, and nothing she had done appeared to please him.

Finally, after his death, she had been faced with the responsibility of cooking for a houseful of mourners at a time when her resources were at a low ebb. Never had she shirked those responsibilities, and yet they had taken their toll on her. Food had appeared as if by magic. No one would ever know, none had suspected the effort required to cook and provide that food.

Now, here she was, as free as a bird, comparatively well off, the owner of a second-hand but serviceable Morris Minor, with nothing better to do than return to her birthplace to conjure up ghosts. Considering the many blind alleys of her life, how would she create a new life for herself until ghosts of the past had been lain to rest?

Little or nothing remained of the Frances Abbot who had spent her formative years in a dreary industrial town that had ceased to hold any real meaning for her after the loss of her mother. The passage of time had done nothing to soften the bitterness of that loss at the impressionable age of eighteen, when she had been poorly educated yet possessed of a burning ambition to make something of herself, to make up for her lack of formal education. Leaving school at fourteen, taking a job as a grocery shop assistant, knowing that her wages, however meagre, would come as a godsend to her mother, she had, nevertheless, developed a fondness for reading – poetry in particular – to her brothers' scornful amusement. Their cruel and insensitive teasing had reduced her to tears on more than one occasion, destroying her pleasure in reading the works of Shelley, Keats, Tennyson and Wordsworth, but never her remembrance of them.

A voyage of discovery, Fran thought, quitting her luxury hotel after breakfast the next morning. So where to begin? Why not Scarborough? The weather was fine for September, her favourite month of the year, with its colourful autumn flowers, shorn fields, stooked corn sheaves and its memories of harvest festival in a grey-stone church in Cornwall.

Greystones! Strange how scattered memories linked together to form a composite whole. She had been happy at Greystones for a short space of time. Catching sight of her reflection in the driving mirror, she doubted if John Hammond would recognize her as his former receptionist. She was older now, thinner, with a tanned complexion, her hair longer, drawn back from her face and worn in a loose bun at the nape of her neck.

Fran smiled reflectively at the clothes she had worn then, the tailored suits and neat blouses suggested by her dear old friend Charles Bessacre, the news of whose death, two years ago, had come as a shock to her when she had called to see him on a recent visit to Middleton. Would he have approved of her present apparel, slacks, a casual cashmere sweater, a paisley shoulder scarf and open-toed sandals, she wondered? Yes, she'd thought, almost certainly he would have, because that's the kind of man he was: 'With it', in present-day parlance. A joyous, lovable man who had been a tower of strength to her during his lifetime. God rest him.

Memories stirred strongly as she drove along the promenade to Greystones, the reasons why she had felt it expedient to leave Scarborough as she had done: unpleasant memories of Muriel Hammond's jealousy, her jibes of favouritism and accusations of setting her cap at her son. But there had been more to it than that: there was the realization that she had been on the verge of falling in love with John Hammond, a married man haunted by memories of his wife, Irene, to whom she, Fran, could never have held the proverbial candle, just as she had never held a candle to Pearl Drysdale in Peter's estimation. She knew that now.

Possibly she'd be wiser not to revisit the scene of so many memories. But she had come here to take stock of the past, to face it head on. Even so, she parked her car and entered the hotel with a feeling of trepidation, the way she had done a long time ago, when she'd the temerity to apply for a job for which she'd been totally unqualified.

Approaching the reception desk, she came face to face with a tall, elegantly dressed middle-aged woman, who said charmingly, 'Good morning, madam. How may I help you?'

'I'm not quite sure,' Fran demurred, not having thought that far ahead. 'Coffee, perhaps, or lunch? I'm just passing through.'

'Then coffee and sandwiches would seem an ideal solution,' the receptionist said helpfully. 'If you'd care to go through to the Seaview Lounge over yonder, I'll send a waitress through with the menu. The dining room isn't open yet, but we do offer a splendid selection of sandwiches: ham, roast beef, and so on, unless you'd prefer a ploughman's lunch?'

'Thank you,' Fran murmured, then, drawing in a deep breath, taking the bull by the horns, she said, 'I'm familiar with the Seaview Lounge. I've been here before. I once worked here, as a matter of fact, for a Mr John Hammond.'

The receptionist regarded Fran curiously, frowning slightly. 'Did you really?' she asked reservedly. Well, my husband's not here at the moment, but he shouldn't be long. I am Irene Hammond, by the way. And you are...?'

Fran drew in a sharp breath at this unexpected revelation. Then she replied, 'Frances Abbot, though I daresay my name won't ring a bell. It was a long time ago, and I didn't stay here for very long.'

Irene Hammond said bitterly, 'Long enough to hear the saga of the missing wife, I daresay. To come up against that poisonous mother of his. She was the reason why I left him in the first place. God, how that woman hated me! What happened afterwards was a nightmare. I went abroad with a friend of mine to think things over; next thing I knew, I was trapped in a farmhouse in the south of France at the time of the German occupation, with no means of escape.

'My friend, Anton Lefèvre, a French citizen by birth, had every right to be there, and so, when we had agreed to a marriage of convenience, had I. And that's all it was, a marriage of convenience. I loved Johnny Hammond, but I was married, in the eyes of the Germans, to a French husband, with no way of letting John know what had become of me. When Anton became ill, I stayed with him until he died. 'My greatest fear was that Johnny, believing me dead, would some day fall in love with another woman! Someone like you!'

Understanding the woman's jealousy and frustration, Fran said simply. 'No. The boot was on the other foot. I thought that I was in love with your husband, and perhaps I was at the time, but I knew all along that he was not in love with me. It was *you* he loved, *you* he longed for, and I couldn't be happier knowing that you and he are together again.'

Turning away, she added quietly, 'I'd best be on my way now. Just one thing, before I go. What became of his mother?'

Irene Hammond sighed deeply. 'She died last year, in a nursing home. What one might call a happy release.'

'I see. Thank you for telling me. And by the way, no need to tell your husband of my visit. As I told you, I'm just passing through.'

And then she was gone, her head held high, as it had been that day long ago when, shaking the dust of Greystones from her feet, she had travelled to Cornwall to become cook-housekeeper to Bruce Torrance.

Discovering Ernest's address had not proved too difficult since Alan had told her their brother's whereabouts. Her knock at the door of a pre-fab on a council estate in the Sandy-bed area of town had been answered by a stringy young woman holding a crying baby in her arms, who demanded, hostilely, 'Yeah, who are you and what do you want? If it's that no good brother-in-law of mine you're after, I haven't a clue where he is, an' quite frankly, I couldn't care less! I've told your lot before, so push off an' leave me alone!'

'My lot?' Fran queried.

'The perlice!'

'I'm not from the police.'

'The Town Hall, then! If it's the rent you're after, I ain't got it! He took it with him when I gave him his marching orders! An' that's not all he took! He stole me engagement ring, me Christmas Club card, me new shoes an' our Alfie's last week's dinner money! I just hopes that when they catch him they'll put him behind bars an' throw away the key!'

'What's your name?' Fran asked quietly.

'Ingrid Abbot, as if you didn't know,' the girl said warily. 'What's yours?'

'Frances Abbot. I'm your sister-in-law. May I come in? I'd like to talk to you. Is Ernest here?'

'No, he ain't. He's at work. He's a good lad,

is my Ernie, a good 'usband an' father. So if you're here to cause trouble, shove off! Why *now*, is what I wants to know! Where've you bin hiding all these years? A stuck up bitch, Alan called you, Miss High an' Mighty, a "holier-than thou mean bugger" who made his an' Ernie's lives a misery!'

'I see. And did he tell you about the fifteen hundred pounds he stole from me? Did he tell you that it was he who made mine and our mother's lives a misery? I thought not.' Fran paused momentarily, realizing that she was up against a brick wall of resistance in the shape of a hostile young mother brain-washed into believing the worst of her. She continued heavily, 'I'm sorry, I didn't come here to cause trouble, but to build bridges if at all possible. I can see now that I was wasting my time, so goodbye, Ingrid, and good luck. Oh, and by the way, this might come in handy.'

Delving into her shoulder bag, Fran handed the girl ten five-pound notes. 'To buy yourself a new pair of shoes,' she said, 'and to help with the rent. Or to buy your kids presents, come Christmas. Little Alfie, and this young man here. They are, after all, my nephews, aren't they?'

'I suppose,' Ingrid agreed awkwardly. 'This un's name is Jack, by the way. Called after his grandfather. If he'd been a girl, Ernie wanted him called Mary, after his mother.' She added grudgingly, 'You can come in now, if you want to. I'll put the kettle on for a cup of tea.'

And so Fran, entering the pre-fab, knew that this stage of her voyage of discovery had not been a waste of time after all, that her efforts towards bridge-building had not been in vain. Holding Jack in her arms while Ingrid made the tea, and later, when Alfie came home from school and Ernie came in from work, she knew, with a singing feeling of relief, that the former enmity between herself and Ernest no longer existed when, 'Hello, sis,' he'd said, holding out his hands to her. 'I'm real pleased to see you. Know what? I'd almost given up hope of ever seeing you again. It's been a long time. Far too long.'

Fran had known then that Ernest had never been the villain of the piece. He had simply followed in his brother's footsteps until, taking his life in his own hands, he had married, settled down, found himself a decent job and become a good husband and father. It was Alan who had been the troublemaker all along. Poor Alan. Where was he now? Fran wondered. Hiding in alleyways? Dodging the long arm of the law? Wherever he was, he was still her brother, her own flesh and blood, and worthy of her pity and forgiveness. Bidding her new-found family farewell, with promises to keep in touch, after a meagre supper of baked beans on toast, Fran headed her car along the coast road to Filey, where she booked in for the night at a hotel overlooking the sea.

She had been given a pleasant room with an unrivalled view of a bay necklaced with shore

288

lights and silvered by a full moon – a harvest moon. Strange how harvest time kept on invading her thoughts, linked to the many happy years she had spent at Kingfisher, memories of Gipsy, labradors, the *Moth*, her ups and downs with her touchy employer, which had added zest to her life, and finally her brief abortive love affair with Tarquin Torrance. All in the past. Kingfisher was more than likely empty and deserted now, awaiting new owners. Would they ever catch the ghostly clatter of typewriter keys from the study, the sound of voices and laughter from the drawing room, the chink of china and cutlery from the dining room, the aroma of freshly baked bread from the kitchen?

Up early next morning, Fran went down to breakfast. Enjoying a second cup of coffee, she considered the day ahead and the next stage of her voyage of discovery: Gloucester-shire.

Life appeared to be her oyster on this fine and fair September morning. Fran knew that she was on her way to discover the pearl within that oyster, had known all along that her journey would lead her inevitably to the quiet country graveyard where her friend Pearl Drysdale was buried. Pearl, whose memory remained fresh and fragrant.

Leaving Filey, Fran drove inland towards York, wanting to visit the Minster, to walk round the city walls and wander through the medieval streets that they encompassed.

Consulting her guide book, she headed for the Station Hotel, a spectacular Victorian edifice within walking distance of the city.

At a gift shop in the Minster precincts, Fran bought postcards to send to Gipsy and Ian, to Ingrid and Ernie and their offspring. Then, seeking refreshment, she walked down Stonegate to Betty's Café, where she treated herself to a cup of coffee and a sinfully delicious jam doughnut.

This was a fascinating city with a cosmopolitan air about it. Not that Fran had first-hand experience of cosmopolitanism, but she liked the free and easy atmosphere of York.

Some day she might return here, find herself a job and settle down, she thought, walking back to the Station Hotel to unpack her belongings, bathe and get ready for dinner. She had had a memorable day, and tomorrow, first thing, she'd be on her way towards Gloucester, stopping en route to visit Lincoln and Nottingham, where she would pay her respects to the memory of the 'mad, bad and dangerous to know' Lord Byron, a childhood hero of hers. Was he really as bad as he'd been painted? In any case, weren't most men dangerous to know to some degree or another?

Relishing her new-born feeling of freedom, Fran dawdled her way south, enjoying the fine weather, relaxing in the warmth of an Indian summer, thanking God that she had learned how to drive at Gipsy's instigation. Dear Gipsy, whose baby was due any day now, and with whom she intended to get in touch very soon.

Had she done wrong in refusing Gipsy's offer of a home with her and Ian? Fran didn't think so. A young married couple needed to be alone together to live their own lives in their own way, not saddled with a third person, however close that third person may be. Gipsy had finally understood and accepted Fran's point of view. 'But you will come to visit us, won't you?' she'd begged tearfully. 'You won't just disappear and forget all about me?'

'As if I could!' She held the girl in her arms. 'I love you. Gipsy. I always have and I always will. I just need my own space at the moment, as you and Ian need yours. All right?'

'Yes, all right, Abby. Sorry to be such a selfish little beast! Forgive me?'

'Gipsy darling, there's nothing to forgive. And I'll always keep faith with you, I promise!'

Remembering that conversation, and what lay ahead of her, Fran knew the time had come to keep faith with another beloved being – once an integral part of her life, for ever to remain a shining memory in the hearts of those who had loved Pearl Drysdale.

Eighteen

The scenery was familiar, unforgettable so far as Fran was concerned: the village where she and Pearl had shopped that spring afternoon long ago. There was the chemist's with its bottle-pane windows, the Bluebird Café, where they'd had afternoon tea, the thatched cottages, the church with its lych-gate and spreading cedars.

Fran had brought flowers for Pearl, dahlias, Michaelmas daisies and golden chrysanthemums. 'I'm here, darling,' she whispered. Tears filled her eyes and ran down her cheeks unchecked and unheeded. 'Remember me?'

A faint breeze stirred the branches of the cedars and ruffled the neatly mown grass of the churchyard. September sunlight slanted between overhanging branches. Autumn leaves drifted down from the hornbeams bordering the grey-stone walls. A robin fluttered down to perch momentarily on Pearl's headstone.

Arranging the flowers, Fran remembered the weekend Pearl had invited her to stay at the Grange during the war. Memories of that weekend invaded Fran's mind. Memories of The Grange with its massive front door, pillared portico, broad stairs, mullioned windows and richly furnished reception rooms. The drawing room in particular with its grand piano on which Pearl had played, by candlelight, Beethoven's Moonlight Sonata.

Leaving the churchyard, Fran remembered the village inn where she had stayed after the funeral. the Flag and Compass, that was the name of it, a small, unpretentious hostelry, she recalled, getting into her car but in no hurry to leave this picturesque corner of England where she had known both happiness and heartbreak, needing to come to terms with her memories. That was why she had come here in the first place, to get her life into perspective.

The inn had been caught in a time warp, Fran thought. Nothing had changed outwardly, so far as she could see. Yet everything *had* changed. Glancing about her, she remembered that Mr Bates had escorted her from The Grange when she'd finished helping his wife with the cooking and washing-up on the day of Pearl's funeral. Then she had bumped into Peter Drysdale, who had asked her to meet his parents, who were also staying at the inn – a request to which she had reluctantly agreed, in no mood to converse with strangers, to talk about Pearl or the funeral.

Peter's mother, Fran recalled, had made a great fuss of her and had gone so far as to write her a letter inviting her to spend her next leave with herself and her husband, an invitation which she had politely refused.

Now, entering the Flag and Compass in search of accommodation she was asked how long she'd be staying. 'Two nights, possibly three,' Fran told the girl who had appeared breathlessly behind the reception desk at the press of the buzzer on the desk top.

'Sorry, miss,' the girl apologized, 'but we ain't got a proper receptionist. No need, really. I work behind the bar, answer the buzzer when it sounds.' She smiled engagingly. 'You could stay from now till Christmas if you like. All our rooms are empty for the time being.' She added appealingly, 'There's a nice un vacant on the first floor, with an en suite bathroom, a comfy bed an' all mod cons. Would that suit?'

'Admirably,' Fran replied. 'Just show me the way.'

The room was pleasant, well furnished, with a view of the main street. The barmaid-cum-receptionist, whose name was Daisy, had taken quite a shine to her, Fran realized. She seemed reluctant to return to her pint-pulling duties. 'Excuse me for asking,' Daisy blurted, 'but are you famous?'

'Good grief no! Whatever gave you that idea?'

'Dunno really.' Daisy blushed becomingly. 'It's just that you seem kind of mysterious somehow. What I mean is, most of the folk who stay here are mainly old fogeys – begging their pardon, I'm sure – but you're not. You're

294

glamorous, kind of self-contained an, well, mysterious.' She sighed deeply. 'I'd give anything to look like you. to *be* like you!'

Fran said quietly, 'Take my advice, Daisy. Be careful what you wish for, in case your wish comes true.' She smiled wistfully. 'Self-containment, in my experience, is simply a disguise for loneliness.'

Venturing forth from her hotel room, in need of refreshment, Fran entered the Bluebird Café, now under new management, as she had suspected that it would be; it was scarcely likely that its former owners would still be baking scones and cakes in their dotage. Yet the Bluebird's air of slightly faded gentility remained intact, and the woman who came to take Fran's order was by no means young, but middle-aged and plump.

Drawing a bow at a venture, Fran said, 'I've been here before, during the war. What became of its previous owners, I wonder?'

'Oh, you mean the Misses Tucker? Well, thankfully they are still alive. In care now, of course, but The Grange is a wonderful nursing home, and they are being well looked after, thank goodness.'

'The Grange? But I thought that it belonged to the Galsworthy family. Sir Henry Galsworthy and his wife, Lady Eleanor?' Fran frowned disbelievingly.

'So it did,' the woman said, speaking discreetly yet warmly. 'The scandal came as a great shock to all of us, when it happened.'

'Scandal? What scandal?'

'Why, Sir Henry quitting The Grange the way he did! Going off with another woman, his secretary by all accounts, to live abroad somewhere or other, and putting his ancestral home up for sale! No one has seen hide nor hair of him since, nor that lady wife of his, though I've heard tell she's living in the London area with her brother and his wife. Making a damn nuisance of herself, I daresay. Huh, in my opinion, Sir Henry did right to get rid of her when he did. A nasty piece of work, I've heard tell, who made his life a misery. Well, she's got her comeuppance now, right enough!'

'Now, dear,' the woman continued, 'what can I get you? Coffee? A sandwich, or something on toast?'

'Nothing, thank you. Sorry, I've changed my mind!'

Leaving the café abruptly, sick at heart, Fran hurried back to the Flag and Compass to seek the refuge of solitude, her thoughts centred on Pearl, knowing how deeply she would have regretted the loss of her home.

Sir Henry's defection was scarcely surprising. Pearl had known all along of her father's penchant for other women. The poor man must have reached the end of his tether to have parted with his ancestral home, Fran realized. Curiously, the thought of Lady Galsworthy receiving her comeuppance awarded Fran no feeling of satisfaction. As much as she disliked the woman, the loss of her home and her husband must have come as bitter blows to a person of Lady Eleanor's temperament, whose raison d'être had lain in being the wife of a baronet, a well-known public figure, a former Cabinet minister no less, whose wealth, power and good name she had misused to bolster her own ego. How must she be feeling now? Fran wondered, a woman scorned and rejected, an object of pity and gossip, worse still, of ridicule.

Fran had quitted the Bluebird Café so abruptly from a sense of loyalty to Pearl, not wanting to indulge in idle gossip with its present owner. The very thought of it had appalled her. Having learned the salient facts of the scandal that had rocked the village to its core, she'd had no desire to pursue the matter further.

Gazing from her bedroom window at the street below, watching street lamps blossoming against the dusk of an early September evening, Fran knew that her mission here had been accomplished, that it was time to move on. Tomorrow she would revisit the churchyard to bid Pearl farewell, after which she would head southwards to Devizes to determine the whereabouts of Peter Drysdale. Possibly even to pay a flying visit to Wisteria Cottage to renew her acquaintance with Alex Condermine. It was all part and parcel of her voyage of self-discovery.

The weather had changed overnight. Rain and leaden skies heralded the demise of the

Indian summer days of warmth and sunlight. Daisy had seemed upset when she knew that her 'mystery lady' was leaving. 'Is it the weather, miss?' she asked mournfully. 'Yes,' Fran replied kindly, 'but I'll be back some day.'

She drove to Devizes via Stroud and Chippenham, stopping en route for refreshment, aware of a chewing feeling of nervousness as she neared her destination, the Bear Hotel, filled with a need for a place to call home, a sense of belonging. Tired of journeying, of packing and unpacking her belongings in hotel bedrooms, her voyage of discovery was beginning to wear thin at the seams.

So where did she really belong? In Yorkshire, Gloucestershire, Wiltshire or Cornwall? If only she knew where. Perhaps the answer lay here, in Wiltshire. How could she be sure? But who was she kidding? She knew where she belonged, right enough, but a return to Cornwall, to Kingfisher, was out of the question, since the people she had known and loved were no longer there, and her world would never be the same without them. Without Bruce Torrance, Tarquin and Gipsy.

Devizes had not changed, the street market was in full swing, the stone fountain in the square still splashed water into its ornamental basin. The Bear Hotel, on the far side of the square, was just as she remembered it, solid, imposing, as if it had taken root there, a kind of focal point of the community, patronized by the gentry, farmers, shoppers and house-

298

wives alike in need of refreshment, liquid or otherwise. Yet Fran hung back, not quite ready to face ... what exactly? The trouble was, she didn't know what, and felt reluctant to find out.

Instead, she walked along a crowded pavement to a café she remembered, above a baker's shop, a small café with crowded-together tables, smelling divinely of coffee and freshly baked bread, in no way as grand or intimidating as the Bear Hotel dining area with its hot-food smells, bustling waitresses and beer fumes from the bar.

Finding herself a window table overlooking the busy square below, ordering coffee and a toasted cheese sandwich, Fran considered her present situation. Chances were that Peter was no longer at the Bear. If not, this would prove to be a fruitless journey. If so, what would she say to him? 'Hello, Peter. Remember me?' And what if he didn't remember her? She had, after all, changed a great deal since their last meeting. Presumably, so had he? But how to find out?

Should she walk into the hotel, book overnight accommodation and ask point blank if Peter Drysdale still worked there? No, she didn't think so. So how to approach the situation more subtly? It was then she remembered Alex Condermine and the Bargee pub overlooking the Kennet and Avon Canal – Condermine's watering hole, which, she vaguely recalled, took in guests, as a sideline during the summer season. She could but try, and if Alex was still in the land of the living, he above all people would know the whereabouts of his favourite nephew.

The proprietor of the Bargee seemed nonplussed by the appearance of an attractive woman seeking accommodation at this time of the year. Visitors were normally thin on the ground come September, but why quibble? Extra income was always welcome come spring, summer, autumn or winter. He said jovially, 'Yes, of course. Happy to oblige, I'm sure. There's a nice room vacant on the first floor. You'll be wanting dinner and breakfast, I daresay?'

'Yes, I daresay I shall.' Fran nodded her agreement. 'Is there a private dining room, by the way?'

'Yes, ma'am, behind the bar parlour, next door to the kitchen. Handy for my wife, who does the cooking. We do a full English breakfast, and there's home-made steak and kidney pie on tonight's menu. And if you require lunch, we can offer you soup, sandwiches, or summat on toast, if you prefer.'

'Sounds fine to me,' Fran said. 'Now, if you will show me to my room, I'd like to freshen up a little.'

'Yes, of course, ma'am. This way. I'll carry your luggage. Mind the stairs, they're a bit steep.' He added engagingly, 'On holiday, are you?'

'Yes,' Fran replied. 'A touring holiday. The weather has been so lovely of late.' Attempting not to explain the inexplicable, she wanted to appear as dull and ordinary as possible so as not to arouse undue curiosity here as she had done at the Flag and Compass.

'Have you been hereabouts before?' the proprietor asked, switching on the electric blanket.

'Yes, once, a long time ago,' Fran said, taking a calculated risk. 'I worked for a man called Alex Condermine as a temporary housekeeper. I daresay he's long gone now.'

'Who? Alex?' The man chuckled deeply. 'Not likely! Comes in every lunchtime, he does, as regular as clockwork. You missed him by inches. He left not ten minutes before you arrived. It's a wonder you didn't bump into him on the towpath.'

'But I didn't come via the towpath, I came by road,' Fran reminded him. Then, changing the subject adroitly, 'Oh, the rain has stopped at last! Hopefully it will be a fine day tomorrow. I've been lucky with the weather so far.'

'That you have, ma'am. So where are you from?'

'Middleton, in Yorkshire,' Fran enlightened him. 'Have you heard of it?'

'No, ma'am, can't say as I have. But they do say as home is where the heart is, an' I daresay you'll be glad to get back there when your holiday is over.'

'I daresay you're right,' Fran replied, keeping her own counsel.

★ ★ ★

301

Later, she walked along the towpath to Wisteria Cottage, wearing a mackintosh, Wellingtons and a black tam-o'-shanter. Knocking on the door, she received no immediate reply, and guessed why not. Alex would be sleeping off his lunchtime drinking session at the Bargee. Finally, he called out gruffly, 'All right, all right, I'm coming,' the thickness of his voice betraying the level of his intoxication. He opened the door a crack. 'Well, who are you and what do you want?' he demanded hostilely. 'If you're here after money, you can bugger off. Got it?'

'Well, that's for me to know and you to find out, isn't it?' she laughed. 'Come on, Alex, don't tell me you've stopped fleecing people left right and centre to earn a dishonest living? I wouldn't believe you if you did! Now, open the door and let me in. What you need is a strong cup of coffee, or my name's not Frances Abbot!'

'Frances Abbot? *Fran?* Ye gods! Where have you sprung from, and what the hell have you done to yourself? You look marvellous! What happened to the puppy fat, the clumpy hairstyle and your old jumper and skirt?'

'Time happened,' Fran said wryly. 'What happened to *your* hair, by the way?'

'Oh stop asking damn silly questions! Come in and make yourself useful! Put the kettle on, do the ironing, mend the fire, clean the bath, polish the silver!' He was laughing now, holding her at arm's length, obviously delighted to see her again. 'Well, wonders will never cease. So tell me, why are you here? In need of a job, are you? If so, how soon can you start? Have you seen Peter, by the way?'

'No. No, I haven't. Is he still at the Bear Hotel?'

'My dear, he *is* the Bear Hotel! The general manager no less. He's done well. Working all hours, but he appears to thrive on it. He has a self-contained flat at the hotel and a bolt hole in Lockersleigh. A two up, two down cottage. He lived here for a while, but it didn't work out very well. He wanted a place of his own where he could sleep all day if he felt like it.'

'I see.' Fran had taken off her outdoor clothes and put the kettle on to boil. 'And what's new with you? Still living the life of Riley?'

'I'm finally divorced now,' he said matter of factly. Can't say I'm sorry. We never quite saw eye to eye. But what about you? Are you married? If not, you should be. You look shen – sorry – sensational. Shall I make you an offer you can't refuse? You could do a lot worse, you know. Think about it, a nice little home all ready and waiting for you, a devoted husband. Why not make an honest man of me?'

'No thanks, Alex! I'm fine as I am. Here, drink this coffee and sit down before you fall down.'

'You always had a sharp edge to your tongue,' he said ruefully. 'A pity really. I always fancied you, you know?' He chuckled mischievously, 'Almost swept you off your

303

feet at one time, didn't I? That day at King's Cross Station, remember?'

'Shall I ever forget?' Fran looked at him concernedly, noticing the pouched eyelids, the network of thread veins on his cheeks, his slackened lips and receding hairline, slightly stooped shoulders and trembling hands. He was a far cry from the man he used to be: smartly dressed, upright and self- confident. Far too self-confident at times, to her way of thinking. But it grieved her to see the man he had become through self-neglect and an over-fondness for alcohol.

She said, 'Who looks after you, Alex? Have you a home help, a housekeeper? Who sees to your food? Who does your washing and ironing?'

'Oh, I manage well enough,' he replied. 'A woman comes in twice a week to "muck me out". I have lunch at the Bargee. A local shopkeeper delivers groceries once a week. I make my own breakfast and supper, and Peter drops in occasionally to spend time with me, to sort out my finances, see to the garden and so on. Even so,' his lips trembled, 'I can't help feeling lonely at times, as if life has passed me by since I left the RAF. I really enjoyed the war, you see? I was somebody then. Group Captain Alex Condermine. Now I'm a clapped-out nobody.'

Glancing at her watch Fran said reluctantly, 'I must be going now,' donning her outdoor apparel, glad that she had brought with her a torch to light her way along the towpath back to the Bargee. 'I'll come again tomorrow, if that's all right.'

Alex said perceptively, 'But it's not me you came here to see, is it? It's Peter you really want to see, isn't it? Oh, I may be clapped-out, but I'm not stupid. Well, take my advice, for what it's worth. I happen to know he'll be at home tomorrow, at Thrush Cottage, so visit *him*, not me.'

'Thanks, Alex, I'll take your advice,' Fran said gratefully. 'But I'll visit you, too, Group Captain Condermine!'

Making her way back to the Bargee, alone in the dining room, Fran congratulated the proprietor's wife on the excellence of her steak and kidney pie. Then, tired and replete, she went upstairs to a warm bed to enjoy a good night's sleep, thinking that tomorrow would bring about her longed-for reunion with Peter Drysdale.

Looking up at the stars from her bedroom window, Fran prayed that tomorrow might bring about a closer understanding between herself and Peter. Now she had accepted that housekeeping, including cooking, ensured a decent income, and having overcome her initial detestation of the preparation and cooking of food, she envisaged finding herself a job, here in Wiltshire, staying close to Peter, inhabiting a small corner of his life if not the whole of it.

The new day dawned fair and clear. Alert and eager, Fran walked along the canal bank before breakfast, then returned to the Bargee to enjoy grilled Wiltshire bacon, scrambled eggs and toast and tea, served by Mrs Fell, the proprietor's wife, who asked if she'd slept well the night before and if she'd be wanting dinner this evening: roast saddle of mutton, mint sauce and all the trimmings.

'Why yes, I imagine so,' Fran assured her. 'Otherwise, I'll let you know well in advance. I'm not entirely sure of my plans at the moment.' Chances were that she'd be dining with Peter tonight, at Thrush Cottage, she thought, imagining a warm, firelit room, an intimate atmosphere conducive to quiet, meaningful conversation, a sharing of memories. So many memories of the war years – of Pearl. Above all, of Pearl.

Fran spent the time before her arrival at Thrush Cottage having her car checked at a local garage, buying postcards and stamps at the Lockersleigh village post office, glancing anxiously at her watch, then discovering the whereabouts of Peter's 'bolt hole', a modest dwelling set back from the road, with a neatly kept garden ablaze with autumn flowers, an iron gate and a narrow path leading to the front door.

Nervously, she opened the gate and walked up the path. Raising the iron knocker, she awaited the appearance of Peter Drysale on the threshold, in answer to her summons.

The door opened. A woman appeared on the threshold. The woman was Rachel Langtree.

306

Nineteen

Rachel regarded Fran curiously, wrinkling her forehead, uncertain of her identity. Fran would have known Langtree anywhere. She had scarcely changed at all. 'Ex-Wren Abbot,' Fran reminded her primly.

'Oh yes, of course,' Langtree said warmly. 'But what on earth are *you* doing here?'

More to the point, what was ex-First Officer Langtree doing here? Fran wondered. 'I'm on holiday,' she replied coolly. 'I came to see Peter. Alex Condermine gave me his address.'

'I see. Then do please come in. Peter's not up yet, but he shouldn't be long. He often sleeps late. Come through to the kitchen. I'll make some coffee, unless you'd prefer tea, and you can tell me what you've been up to since we last met. I must say that you are looking remarkably well, Frances. That is your name, isn't it? And you must call me Rachel.'

'Coffee will be fine,' Fran said dully, following Rachel to the kitchen, mistrustful of her motives, her hail-fellow-well-met attitude in the face of her presence here at Thrush Cottage, her close proximity to Peter Drysdale.

307

So why was she living here, beneath his roof? What precisely was going on between them?

Obviously Rachel knew Thrush Cottage like the back of her hand; her proprietorial attitude spoke volumes. Fran's heart sank to her shoes, realizing, as she did, that the tête-à-tête dinner of her imagination, being alone with Peter this evening, had been just that, a figment of her imagination.

Seated at the kitchen table, watching Rachel making the coffee, Fran asked bluntly, 'How long have you been living here?'

Rachel replied imperturbably, 'Ever since my sister-in-law, Lady Galsworthy, arrived on my doorstep to take up residence with myself and my husband. A state of affairs which I was not prepared to tolerate. Of course Ralph, my husband, felt duty-bound to offer his sister a home from home. We quarreled rather violently I'm afraid. When Peter heard of my dilemma, that I had left Ralph and had nowhere to go to for the time being, he offered me sanctuary here, at Thrush Cottage, which I was delighted to accept.'

She continued prosaically, 'Peter and I have always been close. You may recall that I was his wife's aunt by marriage.'

'I hadn't forgotten,' Fran said quietly.

'Of course not. How stupid of me. You and Pearl were best friends, weren't you? You must forgive me. Time has a way of blurring certain events, especially those too painful to remember.' She shuddered slightly. 'The night of the accident, for instance, and the

308

day of the funeral.' She handed Fran a mug of coffee. 'Thankfully, life goes on, as it must, so no use clinging to old, unhappy memories. What do you think?'

'That memories, happy or otherwise, have a way of clinging to us, not the reverse,' Fran said reflectively. 'Seldom, if ever, has a day passed, since those wartime years at Tanglewood, when I haven't thought of Pearl: her happiness on her wedding day, the horror of her death, the ghastliness of her funeral. She meant more to me than a friend, you see. She was the sister I'd never had and always longed for.' Tears sprang to her eyes. 'She was kind to me. So were you. I daresay you've forgotten that you granted me leave to stay on at the Grange after the funeral, to help the Bateses with the house-party guests that Lady Galsworthy had invited that weekend.' She smiled ruefully. 'You even left me an overnight case of your personal belongings, remember?'

'Did I really? Yes, I had forgotten,' Rachel admitted. 'All I clearly remember is my disgust over that house-party nonsense, quarrelling quite violently with my sister-in-law on that occasion and making up my mind that I never wanted to see or speak to her ever again. So you can imagine how I felt when she inveigled my husband into living with us, and why I accepted Peter's offer of ... shelter.'

'Yes.' Suddenly Fran *did* understand. Rising to her feet, leaving her coffee untasted, she said, 'I'm sorry, I shouldn't have come. I'd best be leaving now. I have things to do, promises to keep, a long journey ahead of me.'

'But Peter will be down any minute now,' Rachel demurred. 'Surely you don't intend leaving without seeing him? Wasn't that the reason for your visit?'

Fran said huskily, 'He may not even remember me. After all, you didn't, not until I'd reminded you.'

Realizing the futility of remaining at the cottage to meet the man she had once been in love with, dreading that first glimpse of non-recognition in his eyes, she knew the time had come to move on. Where to, she hadn't the faintest idea, but she'd think of somewhere. Somewhere.

She walked back the way she had come, picking up her car at the garage, then driving to the Bargee to pack her belongings, pay her bill and inform Mrs Fell that she wouldn't be wanting dinner after all. Then she kept her promise to visit Alex Condermine, about to set off for his lunchtime drinking session at the pub.

'You might have waited till after lunch,' he said grumpily, pulling on his Wellingtons preparatory to a walk along the towpath.

'I shan't be here after lunch,' Fran said flatly. 'You might at least have told me!'

'Told you *what*?' He grinned mischievously. 'Oh, about Peter's lodger, is that it? Huh, high time, in my opinion, that he committed to someone other than himself. Damn it all, any man worth his salt should be capable of more than one love affair in a lifetime! So you found out the hard way? Sorry about that, but you were barking up the wrong tree so far as that nephew of mine is concerned. Putting your money on the wrong horse, so to speak.'

He added contritely, 'I really am sorry, Fran, but you and Peter would never have been happy together, I knew that all along. You are a much stronger personality, a ... go-getter, in present day parlance. Peter, bless him, has always betrayed signs of weakness in his choice of women, following the death of his beloved Pearl. Can't say I blame him, she was a delightful creature, beautiful, kind and submissive, as different from you as chalk is from cheese. Well, why not admit it?'

'So what are you saying, Alex? That Peter is in love with Rachel Langtree?'

'How the hell should I know?' Alex muttered crossly. 'Your guess is as good as mine. They're probably sleeping together, but sex isn't love, is it?'

'No, I guess not,' Fran complied quietly, remembering her abortive affair with Quin Torrance, in which love, not sex, had been uppermost. She asked, 'Is that the way you see me? As a go-getter?'

'Sure! Why, what's wrong with that? You're decisive, strong minded as a rule, and I should know. You've given me more than one dressing down, as I recall. And you're not exactly a wilting flower now, are you? In fact, you look blooming. Another thing, if Peter and his "lodger" *are* making hay between the

311

blankets, he'll never commit to her. What's more, knowing Peter, he'll be feeling as guilty as hell. What did he find to say to you, by the way?'

'I didn't see him. I took the coward's way out – via the front door.'

Alex burst out laughing. 'Good for you! The action of a strong-minded woman! So what's next on your agenda? Where are you going to from here?'

Fran said simply, 'I'm going home.'

She spent that night in Marlborough at the Castle and Ball Hotel. Needing to replenish her wardrobe, to buy new underwear, shoes and an anorak, she had remembered Marlborough as a good shopping centre.

But first of all she rang Edinburgh for news of Gipsy. Ian answered her call. Fairly bursting with pride and excitement, he announced that Gipsy had given birth to a daughter in the early hours of that morning, and both mother and child were doing well.

'Oh, that's marvellous news,' Fran enthused, sharing Ian's excitement as he described his daughter's looks, her fuzz of dark hair and beautifully modelled face, blue eyes and rosebud mouth, her resemblance to her mother, and the way he had felt holding her in his arms for the first time.

Making a note of the address of the hospital, out shopping, Fran ordered flowers for Gipsy, not common-or-garden autumn flowers but roses and carnations. Not that

312

there was anything wrong with chrysanthemums or dahlias, but she wanted something special, to mark a very special occasion.

In due course, she would go to Edinburgh to visit Gipsy, Ian and the baby, Fran decided, but not until she had come to decisions about her own future role in life. Above all, she needed time to think about what that future might entail. At this moment in time she was too close to the past to think clearly about the future – her voyage of discovery having led to a reappraisal of herself and her former lifestyle – and possibly an impersonal hotel room, however comfortable and convenient it may be, was not conducive to deep, prolonged thought about the future ahead of her.

On a sudden impulse, entering an estate agent's office she requested a cottage to rent for a week or so, in the vicinity of Marlborough, no matter how remote, as long as it was well furnished, with all mod cons, a decent bathroom, hot and cold running water, an electricity supply and a telephone.

The receptionist said, 'Well, there's the Doll's House at Clatford. But you'd best have a word with our Mr Hastings, who has all the details. If you'd care to go through to his office, he's free at the moment. Hang on just a sec, I'll give him a buzz.'

Mr Hastings, a thin earnest young man, well mannered and with the air of a public schoolboy about him, said charmingly, 'How may I help you, ma'am?'

The bizarrely named Doll's House stood in a densely wooded area a few miles south of Marlborough, and it did somewhat resemble a child's toy, with its red-brick walls, tall chimneys, flat windows and an ornamental porch framing a blue front door with a brass knocker and letterbox.

The narrow path was flanked by neatly mown grass, flowerbeds and privet hedges. 'It's secluded but not isolated,' Hastings said. 'There's a village round the next bend, with a dozen or so cottages and a small general store. A butcher's roundsman calls three times a week, also a baker's van and a dairyman. Now, allow me to show you inside the house. It's small but well furnished, with a modern bathroom and a well-appointed kitchen.'

Fran liked what she saw. The layout was similar to that of her childhood home in Middleton, with four ground-floor rooms and a narrow staircase at the far end of the hallway. All the rooms were comfortably furnished, the front sitting room and the parlour with deep armchairs, bookshelves, side-tables, lined velvet curtains and good quality carpets.

Deciding to take the house for a fortnight, she wrote a cheque and drove back to Marlborough with the estate agent to pick up groceries, tinned food and so on, with a view to taking up residence early next morning, relieved at the prospect of staying put for a while, of drawing together the frayed edges of her life. How had Shakespeare put it? To knit up the ravelled sleeves of care? Was that it?

Apart from groceries, Fran treated herself to an anthology of wartime poems, two novels, a notepad and envelopes and a book of stamps. She would enjoy renewing her acquaintance with poetry, sleeping late if she felt like it, eating as and when she wanted, cooking her own meals, doing the housework, exploring the area, visiting the village store and writing letters to her friends and family.

Settling in had been a joyous experience: unpacking her belongings, finding out where things were kept and how they worked, discovering the whereabouts of electric sockets, cutlery and linen, cleaning materials and so forth. The owner of the Doll's House, a Mrs Priam, presently on holiday in Switzerland – so Mr Hastings had told her – obviously believed in labour-saving devices and creature comforts.

There were electric fires galore, table lamps, a bedside telephone on a carved oak chest adjacent to a luxuriously appointed double bed with a quilted oyster satin spread and a matching headboard, a television set opposite the bed, and a print of Degas ballet dancers above the white-painted fireplace.

And perhaps this was what she should aim for, Fran thought, a place of her own, however small, when she reached her final destination. Knowing she must earn a living, she toyed with the idea of opening a tea shop-cum-café, of building up a reputation for home-baked cakes and scones and offering lunchtime snacks: prawn sandwiches with homemade mayonnaise, creamy scrambled eggs on toast, quiches and vol-au-vents, individual shepherd's pies crowned with crispy mashed potato. But she was jumping ahead of herself, letting her imagination run riot. She must think sensibly, weigh up the pros and cons; that was the reason why she had come here, to bring common sense to bear on her future.

Might it not be better to find herself another live-in housekeeping job? To walk before she could run? There were so many imponderables standing in the way at the moment. The rising cost of property for one thing, of furniture and fittings. Scarcely likely that she would be able to buy and furnish a cottage and to splash out on a business venture at the same time. But she knew, deep down, that she would never be truly happy or fulfilled living in someone else's house, cooking other people's food, not after her long affiliation with the Torrance family and Kingfisher Cottage.

But nothing in earth or heaven comes as it came before, and she must cut her coat according to her cloth, not bite off more than she could chew, not rush in where angels might fear to tread, she told herself severely. She simply had this burning desire for independence at the core of her being. How

316

strange, she thought, that until now she had never fully understood or come to terms with that streak of independence, yet it had always been there, as a driving force, ever since the day she had gone behind her Aunt Dorothy's back to join the Women's Royal Naval Service.

Tired out after a long day, Fran slept well that night in Mrs Priam's lavender-scented, lavender-sheeted, plump-pillowed bed, awaking to the rat-tat of a brass knocker on a blue front door.

Scrambling out of bed, she called out, 'I'm coming,' putting on her dressing gown and slippers and hurrying downstairs to discover the butcher's van parked near the garden gate. 'Sorry,' she said, 'I wasn't expecting you.'

The van driver smiled broadly. 'That's all right, miss. No need to worry. I can wait if you wants to get dressed proper like.'

'Yes, thank you. Hang on just a sec.' Racing back to her room, Fran hastily donned slacks and a sweater, bundled back her hair, thrust her bare feet into sandals, picked up her purse and hastened to the gate to choose a fillet of sirloin, two lamb chops and half a dozen eggs. The transaction completed, she went back indoors to put the meat and eggs into the refrigerator. Then she plugged in the kettle, made herself a cup of coffee and sat down at the kitchen table to drink it, amused by her encounter with the pleasant young butcher's assistant, wishing she'd thought to buy a few rashers of bacon for her breakfast. *Breakfast*, she thought, glancing at the kitchen clock. Lunch more like. The time was eleven thirty. She'd slept solidly for nigh on twelve hours!

Later, properly dressed, she crossed the road to the woods, feeling the gentle rustle of fallen leaves beneath her feet, brown and gold autumn leaves, as she ventured deeper into the closely massed trees ablaze with the changing tints of late September.

Refreshed by her long sleep, her thought processes seemed clearer today. In the peace and solitude of the wood, she retraced her voyage of discovery from the day she had left Kingfisher to visit her childhood home in Middleton. It had been a necessary but distressing visit. Necessary to pay homage to her parents and Aunt Dorothy, distressing to realize that the first chapter in her life was over and done with for ever, except in memory. Her mother would always retain a special, unassailable place in her heart and mind, but there could be no going back to the old days, and perhaps it was better so. Her loved ones were at peace now, their destinies on earth fulfilled. Fran knew that now, and drew comfort from the thought of rest eternal for her beloved Mary Abbot.

Strange, Fran reflected, returning to the Doll's House, that the few men she had cared for had all been lost to her. Due to her own cowardice? she wondered. John Hammond, for instance. Why had she left Greystones so abruptly without seeing him? The answer to that came clear cut and simple. Because of Irene. In the circumstances of his wife's watchful presence, what would she have found to say to him? Remember this, that or the other? Remember when I took over in the kitchen that Christmas when the cook went down with flu? Remember that Christmas Eve service in St Mary's Church, when you stopped the car to kiss me? Remember the way we used to stand on the promenade together, looking out to sea? No fear! In the long run, why rake over the embers of a love affair that had never reached fruition.

By the same token, she had left Thrush Cottage without seeing Peter because of Rachel Langtree. Sensing a sexual liaison between them, she could not have borne the humiliation of seeing them together and attempting trite, meaningless conversation over a mug of coffee. An embarrassing situation best avoided.

She had liked Rachel in the Tanglewood days. She had been a fair-minded officer, both just and compassionate, imbued with common sense and dignity. What had happened to change that? Fran wondered. What had become of her good judgement, her common sense and her loyalty towards Pearl? How long had her affair with Peter been going on? Had her dislike of Lady Galsworthy been the excuse she needed to leave her husband and move in with Peter? And was Peter in love with her?

Alex had said that Peter would never commit to Rachel. But hadn't he already done so? Possibly Alex had meant that Peter would never marry Rachel? But she was already married. Or was that part of the attraction so far as Peter was concerned? Fran recalled that he had told her, a long time ago, that he would never remarry. She hadn't wanted to believe him at the time.

Sick at heart, Fran deeply regretted the romantic feelings she had once harboured for Peter Drysdale, making a complete fool of herself by wearing her heart on her sleeve. Not that he had appeared to notice. She knew now that she had meant little or nothing to him apart from a shoulder to cry on and occasionally to lean on. Well, so be it. Her voyage of discovery had at least put that chapter of her life into perspective.

Finally she thought of Quin, who, in all likelihood, she would never see again. Her role in the Torrance family had been unique, that of a friend not a servant; as an integral part of their lives she had been a mother figure to Gipsy, a person worthy of respect and love. Yes, love, but not the kind that crossed the boundary of decent human behaviour. So thinking, she had let love slip through her fingers. Too late now for regrets, but she still believed that she had done the right thing for all the right reasons, and she would always love and remember the man in whose arms she had discovered the true meaning of fulfilment.

The future remained uncertain, but at least, Fran thought wistfully, she had come to terms with the past. Her voyage of discovery had not been in vain.

Twenty

Preparing to leaving the Doll's House, glancing about her to make certain that everything was in apple-pie order, Fran thanked her lucky stars for the peace and solitude the place had afforded her during her brief stay there.

Closing and locking the blue door behind her for the last time, she thought how lovely the woods looked on this crisp October morning, how much joy and happiness she had derived from her solitary walks among those autumn-tinted trees, treading softly so as not to disturb the wildlife therein: the birds, the rabbits, the fallow deer and the voles and badgers busy about their own affairs, in search of food and safety from the dark days of winter ahead of them.

What lay ahead of her, Fran was not yet entirely certain. All she knew, beyond a shadow of doubt, was that she was going home – back to Cornwall, the place on earth where she truly belonged. Oh, not to the Fowey estuary or its environs, but loving

Cornwall as she did, its rugged coastline, magnificent scenery, picturesque villages, tracts of moorland, its folklore and the friendliness of its inhabitants, she knew instinctively that sooner or later she would find somewhere to settle, a place to call home.

Bidding a mental farewell to the Doll's House, Fran drove to Marlborough to return the keys to the estate agent's office, after which she crossed the wide main street to purchase a road map of Cornwall from the bookshop where she had bought her war poets anthology, writing paper and envelopes and the novel *Rebecca* by Daphne Du Maurier, the celebrated Cornish author – a book which, during the past fortnight, she had read more than once, enthralled by its evocation of Cornwall, its mystery and magic, penned by a woman who, by all accounts, had owned a house overlooking the Fowey estuary on the east coast near Truro.

Studying the map intently, Fran decided to head for the west coast, towards Padstow, Newquay and St Ives, stopping en route to consider the lie of the land and hopefully to discover a place that 'felt right', putting behind her all thoughts of ever finding another Kingfisher Cottage. A sheer impossibility she realized all too clearly. There would never be another Kingfisher, another Bruce Torrance, another Gipsy – another Quin.

Leaving Marlborough, she drove towards Taunton. Another one-night stand, she thought, booking into a wayside hotel for dinner, bed and breakfast, feeling suddenly lonely, in need of companionship, love and laughter to break the monotony of eating alone, of making what she thought of as 'top soil' conversation with waitresses and chambermaids who didn't know her from Adam and couldn't care less.

At bedtime, switching on the wireless, she listened to a concert of classical music from the Albert Hall, and thought about Eddie Musgrove and that Pouishnoff concert in a Methodist church hall what seemed like a lifetime ago. How strange that music had now become important to her, because of a young sailor she had half forgotten about until now, because of Pearl Drysdale and Quin Torrance.

Memories came flooding back to her. Memories of Tanglewood, the war years, those interminably long hours spent hammering out coded messages at a teleprinter keyboard. More importantly, a feeling of camaraderie with her fellow Wrens when night watches ended and they repaired to their cabins to climb thankfully into their bunks, tired but optimistic, to talk of this and that, mainly their current love affairs, until silence reigned supreme as one by one they fell fast asleep.

If only sleep would come to her now as easily as it had done then, Fran wished, tossing and turning restlessly in her hotel bedroom, aware of the comings and goings of other guests, the whirring of the lift, the clang

323

of its metal gates, bursts of laughter in the corridor outside her room, the faint beat of dance music from the ballroom below.

Still wide awake at one in the morning, switching on her wireless again, she heard the lilting voice of an Irishman bidding a warm welcome to his programme all those who, for whatever reasons, unable to sleep, might wish to share his vigil in the dark watches of the night. 'My name is Tom Evans,' he announced quietly, beginning his broadcast with a recording of Beethoven's Moonlight Sonata.

Inadvertently, Fran had switched to Radio Hilversum, otherwise she would never have heard a broadcast destined to enrich her life. She experienced an instant rapport with the voice on the wireless, that of a mature man, well educated, possessed of a bubbling sense of humour and a fund of compassion towards his fellow human beings.

Enthralled, she listened to the many and varied topics he raised regarding the plight of the homeless, those caring for elderly relatives to the point of exhaustion, latch-key children left to fend for themselves when their mothers were at work to earn a living in the absence of menfolk killed in action during the war. Children who had never seen the sea or the countryside, had never run barefoot along the sands, never paddled in rock pools, never picked clover and buttercups in sunlit meadows, had never read a book or entered a church, who, more than likely, had never eaten a decent meal in the whole of their lives. 'And so,' he concluded, 'if anyone listening in right now has a few shillings or pence to spare, please send them to me, Tom Evans, Radio Hilversum, and I'll make certain they are put to the best possible use.'

Up and doing early next morning, Fran penned a letter to Tom Evans. 'Dear Mr Evans,' she wrote, 'I am a lonely, middle-aged spinster, presently homeless. Listening to your broadcast last night, I have decided to donate the enclosed cheque for fifty pounds towards your latch-key children appeal. Yours sincerely, Frances Abbot.'

She posted the letter after breakfast, before continuing her journey to her next port of call, Padstow, via Okehampton and Launceston. A long drive with another one-night stand at the end of it, not that she minded, with her 'Voice in the Night' to look forward to.

She put up for the night at an hotel on the outskirts of Launceston. Sick and tired of unpacking her overnight case yet again, she completed the task and went down to the dining room to eat a solitary meal, before returning to her room to await the witching hour of midnight and Tom Evans's broadcast on Radio Hilversum.

Tonight he was stressing the importance of education as a means of advancement to the underprivileged. Young people who had never had recourse to universities, he maintained, might nevertheless educate themselves by means of joining public libraries, reading all the books they could lay hands on, attending lectures, learning a worthwhile trade on leaving the classroom. They could set their own goals of achievement, thus becoming valued members of the community. He spoke not dogmatically, but quietly and sincerely, finally admitting to his own efforts towards self-education after leaving school at fourteen, the pleasure he'd derived from his weekly visits to his local library to borrow and to read the works of Shakespeare and Charles Dickens, ending with the words, 'If I could do it, so could you.' Then, with that bubbling sense of humour of his, 'So endeth the first lesson! Now let's have some music, shall we? How about that old music hall favourite, "Hold your hand out, Naughty Boy"?'

Was it possible, Fran wondered, to fall in love with a voice belonging to a man she had never met and was unlikely ever to meet in the course of her life? No, of course not. Even so, in her present state of loneliness, she felt compelled to write to thank him for the renewed hope his words, his voice, had imbued in her, sparking a burning desire to learn more about music, literature and world events, to realize her full potential as a human being.

'You see, Mr Evans,' she wrote,

'I also left school at fourteen. Later, I joined the Women's Royal Naval Service during the war. Lately I've been drifting

326

from pillar to post trying to make sense of my life, planning to settle in Cornwall, perhaps in Padstow or Newquay. I once lived near Fowey, but the people I worked for are gone now, my employer Bruce Torrance, the writer, died recently. He was a great character, difficult at times, but we understood one another and I miss him.

What you said about self-education made sense to me. I've always loved poetry and I'm learning to appreciate music, but I know nothing about art and little or nothing about world events, history, geography or literature, come to think of it. I've never read Dickens, or the works of Shakespeare to any extent, though, like most people, I've picked up the odd quotation here and there. I'm what you might call 'a collector of unconsidered trifles', and I only know that because I heard it somewhere and the saying stuck in my mind.

I have never been abroad, never been to the theatre to see a play. Looking back, I daresay I was 'educated' in the stalls of the cinema, watching old black and white films: Wuthering Heights, Goodbye, Mr Chips, Great Expectations, David Copperfield, and so on. I often wished I could sing like Deanna Durbin, dance like Ginger Rogers, act like Katharine Hepburn or Greta Garbo, look like Vivien Leigh in Gone With the Wind. Some fine chance of that! I was just a plain plump little Wren, as ignorant as sin. Now I'm an ignorant-as-sin middle-aged woman, wanting to better herself, because of you.'

She signed the letter, 'Yours gratefully, Frances Abbot'.

Weary of journeying, Fran chose St Ives as her final destination, a charming fishing village-cum-seaside resort overlooking St Ives Bay, a haven for artists, quiet at this time of year, yet possessed of an underlying energy and purpose which she found both attractive and exciting. First she needed somewhere to stay until she had made certain that this was to be her future home. A rented cottage would suffice for the time being. And so, parking her car, she entered an estate agent's office to make enquiries.

The cottage she finally chose was perched on a hilltop overlooking the bay.

'Thanks, this will suit me just fine,' she told the agent, an earnest bespectacled young man who had conducted a guided tour of the property, pointing out its assets as he did so: the Rayburn cooker in the kitchen, for instance, which would also provide a plentiful supply of domestic hot water once it was lit and fed with coke from the fuel shed in the cobbled back yard, if she was sure she could cope with it.

'Not to worry, Mr Trevelyan,' Fran assured him, 'I cut my eye teeth on Rayburn and Aga cookers. I'm a cook by profession, you see. More precisely, a cook-housekeeper. At the moment I'm far more interested in the state of the plumbing, the electricity supply and the comfort of the beds than anything else.'

Young Trevelyan smiled broadly, liking this new unorthodox client of his. 'All I can possibly say is that to the best of my knowledge and belief, everything here in Bay Cottage is in mint condition, including the mattresses, the plumbing and the electricity. Any further questions?'

'Just one. How would you feel about lighting the Rayburn for me?'

'I'll be delighted.' He flushed slightly with pleasure. 'How long do you intend to stay in St Ives, Miss Abbot?'

'Permanently, I hope, if I can find a house I can afford to buy and providing there's a good public library.'

'What kind of house?'

'Not too small, ancient rather than modern. Near the sea. A house with character. I shall need to earn a living, so I may decide to take in visitors or open a tea-room. At the moment I'm considering possibilities, weighing up the pros and cons. I have a small amount of capital and that's about all. I have no furniture apart from a few pictures and ornaments which I keep in the boot of my car, and I fear that furnishing and buying a house at one and the same time might well leave me in a hole, financially speaking.'

Trevelyan said eagerly, 'Not necessarily, if –

supposing you found a suitable property – you applied for a mortage and bought second-hand furniture, not new – my firm would be willing to help out in that respect. We hold monthly auctions of good quality second-hand furniture. Carpets, dining-room, bedroom and lounge furniture, kitchen equipment and so on, often sold at ridiculously low prices on behalf of folk wanting more modern stuff.' He added appealingly, 'At least think about it, Miss Abbot, and let me know, if and when you discover a property that appeals to you.'

'Thanks, Mr Trevelyan,' Fran said gratefully, 'I shall certainly do so.'

Next morning, setting forth to explore St Ives more fully, wanting to make certain that she had found the right place to settle down in, taking note of the amenities, the architecture, and breathing in the atmosphere of the place, a feeling of peace laced with a tingle of excitement invaded her, to do with an aura of liveliness, of expectation, Fran imagined, with steep sunlit streets, flower beds, the sound of the sea in the distance, the raucous cries of wheeling gulls in the clear air of a bright October sky.

Shops were many and varied, looking as if they meant business. There were supermarkets, of course, the inevitable Woolworths, Marks and Spencer, the usual Boots the Chemist and WH Smith the newsagent, as there were in towns the length and breadth of the British Isles nowadays, she reckoned. There were also florists, tobacconists, boutiques, cafés, bookshops, art galleries, milliners, small confectioners and sweet shops, hotels, a cinema and, glory be, a public library. Yes, Fran thought, she could be happy here in St Ives. Not bored or lonely, but uplifted.

Then, making her way downhill to the harbour, her optimism was confirmed when she came across an artists' colony seemingly ensconced in an enclave of fishermen's cottages grouped on a cobbled quay overlooking the harbour with tethered fishing boats, at anchor, awaiting the swell of the incoming tide to refloat them. It was a colourful scene, lively and invigorating, warm and friendly, as artists, seated at their easels, looked up to pass the time of day with her against a background of screens on which were hung original works of art, for sale, to tempt end of season visitors into taking home with them reminders of their visit to Cornwall.

Pausing to admire the exhibition, one painting in particular, that of an old man, seated on a bollard, gazing out to sea, caught her attention. Uncertain whether or not to buy it – after all, where would she hang it if she did? – suddenly what seemed akin to a miracle occurred. Never would Fran forget the question, spoken by an American to one of the artists: 'Say, miss, is there anywhere my wife and I could get a cup of coffee and a bite to eat?' And the artist's reply: 'No, sir. Sorry, I'm afraid not. Not since the Ivy House Café closed a few weeks ago. The owner was taken ill, you see, an' there was no one to take over from her.'

Clasping her hands together, as if in prayer, Fran thought mistily, there is now. There *is* now. God willing, there is *now*!

Young David Trevelyan looked up in surprise as Fran entered his office; not that she had burst in unannounced, she was far too well bred for that. Even so, he was surprised, not to say pleased, to see her again so soon, unless, of course, she had come to complain about the Rayburn. Perhaps he hadn't lit it properly after all.

But she hadn't come about the Rayburn. She had heard of a café whose owner had been taken ill recently, leaving the business unattended. Would the owner consider renting it? she wondered. And did he, David, know anything about it? 'Hope you don't mind my calling you David, by the way,' she said, 'Mr Trevelyan is a bit of a mouthful, and I *am* nearly old enough to be your mother.'

'Are you clairvoyant by any chance?' he asked in amazement. 'I've just received a letter from the owner's son, a Mr Morgan, asking me to put his mother's property on the market. Apparently Mrs Morgan has suffered a stroke, which has left her severely handicapped and unable to live alone any longer, let alone to continue in business.' He added thoughtfully, 'Mrs Morgan, known locally as "Old Meg", was quite a character in her heyday, as tough as leather, of Romany stock, I believe. Everyone hereabouts knew and respected her. It seems a crying shame that she will have to part company with her home. She loved Ivy House, though I daresay it's in a poor state of repair nowadays, and will sell for the proverbial song, if someone even considered buying it.'

Reading David like a book, Fran asked, 'Someone like *me*, you mean?'

'Well yes,' David conceded, 'supposing that you would be prepared to purchase the property as it stands, fully furnished; to lumber yourself with a white elephant, a mortgage, repair bills and so on, not to mention broken-down furniture, threadbare carpets, a dodgy café in a lean-to conservatory with more cracked panes of glass than whole ones? So please, Miss Abbot, take my advice, think carefully about what you'd be letting yourself in for before going in at the deep end!'

'When may I view the property?' Fran asked, undeterred by his advice, however practical and well meant it may be, imbued with a gut feeling that Ivy House was destined to play an important role in her life from henceforth. And for once in her life she was absolutely right.

It had been a case of love at first sight. A spacious fan-shaped hall with doors to left and right revealed a curving staircase of Georgian design, and tall Georgian windows let in a maximum of light and sunshine.

Even grubby paintwork, carpet and curtains could not detract from the symmetry of the rooms or the loveliness of the Georgian fireplaces, even though they were cluttered from end to end with gimcrack ornaments, just as the floor space was jam-packed with old furniture, tables, chairs, sofas, sideboards, whatnots and domed cases of stuffed birds and desiccated butterflies. There was tarnished silverware on the dining room sideboard, a gadrooned tray, teapots and an assortment of cutlery cheek-by-jowl with Britannia metal milk jugs and sugar basins.

There was even a Victorian upright piano in one corner of the room, with brass candle-holders and a piano stool covered with faded red velvet. Opening the lid of the piano, Fran saw that the ivories were yellow with age and neglect. Pressing one of the keys, a tinny sound emerged.

David Trevelyan pulled a face. 'Do you play the piano?' he asked, glancing at the instrument with distaste.

'No, not yet, but I intend to take lessons,' Fran assured him.

'Not on that pile of junk, I hope?' he said sourly. 'It's only fit for a scrapyard, along with the rest of this rubbish!'

'Oh, come on David. It isn't all rubbish! It doesn't seem like you to be so pessimistic. What's wrong?'

'This house is wrong,' he burst forth. 'Oh, I can see you're smitten with it, but you'd be a fool – begging your pardon – to even think of buying it. And you *are* thinking of buying it, aren't you?'

'No, David. Not *thinking* of buying it, intending to buy it. It's a lovely house, spacious and charming. A bit run down, of course, but just wait till I've had a go at it!'

'You haven't seen all of it yet,' David said darkly. 'Wait till you've seen the kitchen and the conservatory.'

'Then lead on, "Plum Duff",' she said merrily, 'and do cheer up. For heaven's sake, man, you should be rubbing your hands in glee, having sold a white elephant to a fool like me without really trying, on the contrary, doing your darndest to persuade me not to buy it. But I love this house. Impossible to explain, I just know that I shall be happy here. Flat broke, perhaps, but happy.'

The kitchen was far better equipped than she had anticipated, the adjoining café in need of not repair, but demolition. Thinking quickly, decisively. Fran reached the obvious conclusion that the dining room would seat far more diners than a lean-to conservatory had ever done. That if she worked hard to provide a more extensive menu than coffee and sandwiches, and opened the doors of Ivy House to visitors in search of bed and breakfast accommodation, she might well earn a decent living in the long run.

Finally latching on to her enthusiasm,

Trevelyan agreed to present a firm offer of six thousand pounds for the house and its contents to old Meg Morgan's son and heir, which the man, relieved to be rid of the property, gladly accepted on his mother's behalf.

And so, when the contract had been signed, sealed and delivered, when Fran had parted with a sizeable amount of her inheritance from Bruce Torrance, not one whit perturbed by the state of the house, she rolled up her sleeves and, armed with buckets full of scalding hot water laced with soda crystals, she set about cleaning Ivy House from top to bottom, having first consigned Meg's less presentable items of furniture, old bedding and threadbare rugs to a rag and bone merchant's cart.

Wondering what to do about the dun-coloured carpet in the hall, which gave a bad impression, she made a thrilling discovery. The hall was tessellated in lovely colours of blue and grey with touches of coral. Ripping up the old carpet, she felt that the house – her house – had given her a kind of welcome-home present.

Dusty and dishevelled, she hurried down to share her delight with her newly acquired artist friends, a gregarious lot who trooped back to the house with her to view the mosaics. One couple, Roger and Mavis Garbutt – Roger tall and beefy, his wife stockily built and eager to lend a helping hand with rolling up the carpet – congratulated Fran warmly on her discovery. Roger said, 'I'd pick up that blue-grey colour if I were you, when you begin redecorating.'

'*Redecorating?*' Fran hadn't thought that far ahead.

'Not to worry, love,' Mavis assured her, 'Roger's a dab hand with a paintbrush. He'll slap on a couple of coats of emulsion before you can say knife! Business ain't exactly brisk at the moment, not at this time of year, so we'll all be pleased to help you get started with your caff, won't we?'

'Yeah, of course,' everyone agreed spontaneously. 'Just tell us what you want done, and we'll do it!'

'Well, what are friends for?' Mavis said mistily. 'We all thought the world of old Meg. It's just so nice to know that you love Ivy House as much as she did.'

It was then Fran realized that she really had come home at last.

Twenty-One

Early next spring, wandering from room to room, Fran could scarcely credit the changes that a winter of hard work had brought about.

The old conservatory had been demolished, the kitchen was now spick and span and the dining room was ready to accommodate visitors in need of refreshment. Not just coffee and sandwiches, but a whole new range of dishes of the kind she had dreamed up long ago, and which she had been up since the crack of dawn to prepare. Individual steak pies, shepherd's and cottage pies, homemade scones and sausage rolls, chicken and mushroom vol-au-vents, prawn cocktails, freshly baked fruit pies served with clotted cream. And now, at long last, her efforts had begun to reap financial rewards.

Visitors were now requesting overnight accommodation, dinner, bed and breakfast, seemingly enchanted by the new look Ivy House Hotel, with its mosaic-patterned hall, blue-grey walls, white-painted shutters and elegant staircase, the treads of which were now covered with coral-coloured stair carpet.

In short, the Ivy House Hotel had arisen

like a phoenix from the ashes, with more than a little help from her friends, and a sizeable bank loan to boot, underwritten by young David Trevelyan, which had made possible the purchase of new beds and mattresses, new carpets and curtains to replace those bequeathed to her by old Meg Morgan of blessed memory, who had died recently from a second stroke.

How strange, Fran thought, that a woman she had never met had exerted so great an influence on her own life, just as a man she had never met had exerted an equally important influence when it came to broadening her horizons. For the sake of a voice in the night, Fran had now joined evening classes to learn French and art appreciation. Moreover she was learning to play the piano, and she had taken the trouble to tell him so. Not that she had received so much as a word of reply from Tom Evans. But of course, how stupid of her. She hadn't given him an address!

There were times when she had wondered if he really existed? Was he a flesh and blood human being or just a voice? Had he received her letters? She supposed he must have done, as that cheque she'd sent him towards his latch-key children appeal had been cashed. She hadn't forgotten about that, and, now that she was settled in her new home, she would derive the keenest pleasure from inviting a few underprivileged youngsters to spend a few days beneath her roof, to introduce them to the simple pleasures of a seaside holiday: rock pools, paddling and donkey riding, Cornish ice-cream, warm beds, with plenty of good wholesome food to tuck into.

Pie in the sky? A pipedream? More than likely, but she could at least try to share a little of her own good fortune with others less fortunate than herself. Never had she ceased to mourn the loss of her own and Quin's child, and even becoming godmother to Gipsy's baby had not lessened her grief over the loss of her own, or the loss of her child's father either. But she preferred not to think of it too often. After all, why cloud a promising future with unhappy memories of the past?

Quin, Gipsy had told her when she had gone to Edinburgh to attend the christening, was now romantically involved with a girl of his own age, a French girl named Manon Dupré, with whom he was sharing an apartment in the Rue de la Paix – news which Fran had accepted fatalistically, knowing that Quin was bound to have fallen in love with a woman much younger and more desirable than herself sooner or later. Someone more suited to him than she had ever been or could ever hope to have been.

'I'm so sorry, Abby,' Gipsy had uttered bleakly. 'Perhaps I shouldn't have told you.'

'Why ever not? If Quin is happy, then so am I! No regrets! What happened between Quin and myself was a mistake. I knew it at the time and I still cling to the belief that I was right in ending the affair when I did. So let's not spoil this celebration by raking over old embers, shall we?'

'No, I guess not,' Gipsy conceded quietly. 'Just thank you for being here, the best and dearest friend I've ever had!'

Returning home after the christening, Fran thought of a promising future. She must cling to that belief, making the best of what she had; a home of her own, friends, new interests in life. She loved the cool simplicity of Ivy House, the blue-grey walls and gleaming white paintwork, the uncluttered rooms and the feeling of space now that they had been cleared of Meg's surplus furniture. Not that she had parted with the old woman's belongings wantonly, but bearing in mind how much they had meant to the old lady. And the furniture hadn't all been past redemption; the sideboards, for instance, and some of the bedroom furniture, tallboys and maplewood wardrobes, had emerged glowingly from liberal applications of beeswax polish and elbow grease, as had the circular mahogany table that had taken pride of place in the dining room, and would continue to do so. It was such a generously large, friendly table, Fran decided, placing on it a shallow crystal bowl filled with golden roses as a centrepiece.

Old shabby carpets and curtains had, perforce, ended up in the back of the rag and bone merchant's horse-drawn vehicle. She'd had no compunction whatever in getting rid of rags and tatters. Then, to her amazement she'd discovered that the boards beneath the threadbare floor coverings were as sound as a bell, honey coloured, requiring only waxing and polishing to restore them to their former glory. So why cover them at all apart from a scattering of colourful Persian rugs, which would cost far less than new wall-to-wall carpets?

Discussing the matter with Roger and Mavis Garbutt, Roger nodded sagely and said that what she needed was a sander to buff up the boards prior to the waxing process, which he'd be happy to tackle, on one condition.

'Which is?' Fran asked timidly,

Mavis burst out laughing. 'That you'll accept the portrait of the fisherman gazing out to sea as a gift from my hubby an' me. It's called "The Dreamer", by the way, an' we think it would look just fine hanging over your drawing room mantelpiece.'

Deeply touched, then imbued with a flash of inspiration, Fran said, close to tears of happiness, 'Thank you both so much. I adore that painting. But why stop at just one painting? Now that my café is up and running, why not cover the walls with your paintings? Blue-grey will make a perfect background! Ivy House could become a kind of art gallery! Oh, wouldn't that be wonderful?'

'It certainly would,' Mavis said eagerly. 'But are you sure you wouldn't mind? After all, your customers will be wanting food, not pictures!'

'That's up to them to decide, isn't it?' Fran

reminded her. 'I'll provide the grub, you and your pals provide the paintings.' She added mistily, 'After all that you and they have done for me, it's the least I can do to express my gratitude in return for all your help and support since I came to Ivy House to live. I know what! Let's christen my café "Meg Morgan's Gallery".'

There had been a celebration party to mark the opening of the gallery, the name of which Roger had painted above the dining-room door. The artists' colony had been busy all day hanging their pictures, doing so artistically so as not to overcrowd the walls. The effect was stunning. The vibrancy of the paintings had added colour and importance to the room.

That evening they had trooped back to enjoy the food Fran had set out on the circular table for them. There had been ohs and ahs of satisfaction as they tucked into the buffet. Wine bottles were opened, toasts raised to the memory of Meg Morgan, and to their hostess, whose kindness had made the event possible.

Roger, a self-appointed master of ceremonies, had called upon the deeply embarrassed hostess to say a few words on this momentous occasion. Fran, who had never made a speech in her life, said simply, 'Thank you all for being here, for your friendship, which has made this one of the happiest days of my life.' Then, inspirationally, she began to sing, in her pure, clear soprano, the words of 'Auld Lang Syne'. Everyone joined in. Hugs and kisses were exchanged, a few tears were shed, and then the party was over.

Later that night, alone in the dark, unable to sleep, staring up at the ceiling, aware of the faint sound of the sea washing in on the shore of St Ives Bay, the time had come, she thought, to settle for friendship, not love, as she remembered the many times she had given her heart, to no avail. Her recent voyage of discovery had convinced her of that.

Now even her 'Voice in the Night' appeared to have deserted her. A new presenter had taken his place.

The story of her life so far, Fran conjectured. Possibly she was just one of a host of women, world wide, destined never to find happiness or fulfilment in love, marriage and motherhood. An eternal spinster? If so, far better to settle for friendship, which was far more easily available than love.

She had, after all, succeeded in creating a new life for herself here in St Ives. Against all the odds stacked against her, she had established a role in life as an hotelier, a respected member of a worthwhile community. She had a home to feel proud of, a reasonably secure financial future ahead of her, so why not be content with that?

Fran knew why not. Because what she really wanted was ... love.

The man was middle-aged, not outstandingly

344

tall but broad shouldered and possessed of what could best be described as a kind of presence, an aura, which set him apart from the crowd, Mavis thought, as he came along the promenade towards her and paused to admire the picture she was painting – a view of the harbour with its tethered fishing boats, white-winged sea birds and a group of fishermen gathered together on the quay.

Mavis noticed that he was wearing slacks and a black polo- neck sweater and carrying an overnight bag. Glancing up at him from her easel, she thought that he reminded her of someone, an actor, though she couldn't for the life of her think who. Humphrey Bogart? Dirk Bogarde? John Gregson? No – Ronald Colman. But he was dead, wasn't he? And this man was very much alive, and he was clean shaven, not a sign of a pencil moustache, besides which he spoke with an Irish accent. Not a pronounced Irish accent, not as thick as Irish stew, but Irish nevertheless, as he admired her painting and asked if she happened to know the whereabouts of a Miss Frances Abbot.

'Fran? Yes. She owns the Ivy House Hotel, not a stone's throw away from here. Just go back the way you came, turn left, and Ivy House is well nigh on the corner. Why? Are you a friend of hers?'

The man smiled. 'I'd like to think so, but I can't be sure. You see, the lady and I are strangers. We've never actually met!'

'Oh, I see,' Mavis responded. 'Well, if it's

accommodation you're after, you'll be well looked after at Ivy House, though she may well be fully booked. You really should have booked in advance, you know.'

Tom Evans sighed deeply. 'I would have done so, of course, had I known her address. Now, if you'll excuse me, I'd best find out, hadn't I?'

At last, he thought, he had found his 'Lady of the Night', as he had christened her mentally. But she had taken some finding, and for all he knew she might well be some crusty, middle-aged spinster, as ugly as sin. Even so, he wished to thank her for her generous contribution to his latch-key children's fund, and to establish whether or not she was prepared to take in a dozen or so deprived kids during the summer vacation.

He rang the doorbell of the Ivy House Hotel, and awaited a response to his summons. When the door opened to reveal an attractive woman wearing a pinafore and dusting flour from her hands, he asked, disbelievingly, 'Are you Frances Abbot?'

'Well, yes. At least I was when I woke up this morning. If it's coffee you're wanting, the café isn't open yet, but you're welcome to a cup in the kitchen, if you don't mind watching me work.'

Was she mad inviting a strange man into her kitchen? Perhaps, but he had a kind face, besides which she had the strangest feeling they had met before.

He said, 'That's very kind of you, Miss

346

Abbot. May I leave my valise in the hall? I'd like to stay a while, if you have room for me.'

'Yes, I—' She stopped speaking abruptly.

'Is anything the matter?' he asked concernedly. 'I could come back later if this isn't a convenient time for you.'

Fran was standing stock still, her eyes closed, listening intently. 'Would you mind repeating that?' she asked.

'I said I could come back later if this isn't a convenient time for you.'

'I heard what you said. It was the way you said it.'

'I'm sorry, I don't understand,' he replied in that familiar voice of his, laced with the quiet but unmistakable Irish accent she had heard so often before in the dark watches of many a long, lonely night.

Opening her eyes, Fran asked breathlessly, 'Are you, by any chance, Tom Evans?'

He laughed. 'Well, I was when I woke up this morning!'

Fran said, 'I'd begun to think that you were a figment of my imagination. I was in transit at the time I wrote to you. On a kind of voyage of discovery, not thinking very clearly, I'm afraid, otherwise I'd have known that you couldn't possibly have replied to my letters. So how did you find me?' Not daring to ask *why* he had wanted to find her.

He said, 'Remember you once mentioned having worked for Bruce Torrance at his home near Fowey? Well, I made that my first port of call: talked to the local inhabitants, most of whom remembered you well, not that any of them knew your present whereabouts.

'Then I met up with the pub landlord, who gave me the name and address of Bruce Torrance's daughter, who knew exactly where I might find you. So here I am! You see, Frances, I'd so long wanted to meet you face to face, to thank you for your generous response to my latch-key children appeal.'

'Oh? How is it going on?' Fran asked eagerly. 'Please, do sit down Mr Evans, while I make the coffee. The table's a bit cluttered, as you can see.' Plugging in the kettle, she said 'I do all the cooking myself, though I do have two young girls from the village to help out in the café, to clean the bedrooms and so on. They should be here any minute.'

'The appeal's going remarkably well,' he said, 'thanks to people like yourself. And my name is Tom, by the way.' He smiled. 'Allow me to make the coffee while you get on with your cooking. I'm quite domesticated. Living alone, I've had to be. I'm a dab hand at bangers and mash and bacon and eggs.'

'Oh well, if you wouldn't mind. I am a bit busy in the mornings, but everything's under control – more or less.' She blushed becomingly, aware that she was babbling slightly, reacting strangely to the presence of Tom Evans in her kitchen, by no means a figment of her imagination, but a very real and attractive human being.

'I find that preparing food well in advance, seeing to the vegetables and so on for the evening meal, I can usually take time off in the afternoons, take a walk along the sands, recharge my batteries, so to speak,' she explained, pausing to remove a tray of scones from the oven. 'I start supper around six; we dine at seven, then, when the tables have been cleared and the washing-up's done, I have the rest of the evening to myself. That's when a friend of mine comes in to answer the phone and serve snacks to the guests.' She added apologetically, 'Sorry, I must be boring the pants off you!'

'Far from,' Tom assured her, handing her a cup of coffee. 'The wonder is that you make such good use of your time. I congratulate you, Frances. I only wish that I had my own life so well organized. The trouble with me is that, in my line of work, writing, broadcasting, being sent from pillar to post at a moment's notice, I've never known the joy of a real home, a settled existence. You see, Frances, I've always been a kind of latch-key kid myself.'

Fran's heart went out to him. But it really didn't have all that far to go.

Tom elected to stay on for a few days, and they spent afternoons together walking along the sands, making plans for the children that Fran envisaged taking in during the summer school holidays.

Tom said hesitantly, 'But are you quite sure you'll be able to cope with them at what will be a busy time for you?'

'I've thought about that,' Fran said, 'and decided not to take in visitors while they're here. Meg's Gallery will remain open of course. No problem there. I'll see to the cooking beforehand, give the kids their breakfasts then spend the rest of the day with them. My artist friends will take it in turn to look after the café.'

Eyes sparkling, cheeks aglow, she continued, 'I'll make sure those children have the time of their lives. And it won't be a one-way thing. I'll be having the time of my life, too, watching them enjoying themselves: making sandcastles, donkey riding, paddling in rock pools, devouring ice-cream cornets. Well worth closing the hotel for a few days, don't you agree?'

Tom said quietly, 'You're a remarkable woman, Frances. You do realize that, don't you? I sensed as much from your letters. Until we met, I couldn't begin to guess just how remarkable.'

'Who? Me?' She frowned slightly, then laughed. 'But I'm not in the least bit remarkable. If I give that impression, I can't think why. I'm just an ordinary hard-working woman making the best of my life: counting my lucky stars for the home I'd always longed for and never had, until now, for good friends and neighbours. It's thanks to you, Tom, for the help and encouragement you've given me in making more of my life in so many ways.' She had stopped walking to face him. 'If it hadn't been for you, I would never have taken music lessons or joined night classes to learn about art and world affairs. Above all, would not have been given the opportunity to help those latch-key kids of yours. I really am grateful.'

He asked perceptively, 'Tell me, Frances, when you spoke of a voyage of discovery, what were you searching for?'

She said, 'It's hard to explain. A rather long involved story, I'm afraid. I felt I'd made a mess of my life, taken so many wrong turnings. I thought that retracing my steps, going back in time, would help me to find out why I'd gone wrong. I needed to stop chasing impossible dreams and ask myself what I really wanted from life.'

'And did you find the answer?'

'Well yes, I suppose so.'

Taking her hands in his, Tom asked, 'Those ... impossible dreams of yours? Had they to do with ... love?'

He paused, then said, 'We have a great deal in common, you and I. You see, my dear, life-long, I too have been in search of an impossible dream. A dream of one day finding someone to love who would love me in return. A lovely, caring, generous-hearted woman who would love me unreservedly, as much I loved her.'

Cupping Fran's face in his hands, he said gently, 'I believe that I have found the right person at last. No, don't look away, darling, all I'm asking is that you will think over what I've said and tell me if there's room in your heart for me.

'I know you have your own life to live, a lovely home in a place you so obviously adore, and I wouldn't want to change that. What I can't bear is the thought of losing you, of never seeing you again. Having found you, I'd be lost without you.' Uncupping her face, he said, 'I'm sorry, perhaps I shouldn't have told you all this. I didn't mean to upset or distress you in any way. I'll leave now, if you'd rather.'

Fran said slowly, 'But I was hoping that you would be here to help me look after the children. I was planning to ask you tonight, after supper. I just didn't know how you'd feel about it. I mean, if you'd want to or not!'

'Not *want* to? My dear girl!'

They walked on together, hand-in-hand, totally at ease with one another, two happy people whose disparate voyages of discovery had brought them, at last, to a homecoming of the heart.

Epilogue

Never had Fran forgotten that magical summer when the first of Tom's latch-key children had come to stay at Ivy House. And to think she had once told Bruce Torrance that she knew nothing about 'nannying'. True enough, she hadn't a clue about babies, nappies or feeding bottles, and it had come as a relief when Torrance had told her that his offspring were in need not of nappies, but, in essence, a steadying influence in their lives.

The same had applied to Tom's latch-key children, scraps of humanity who had never, hitherto, felt sand beneath their shoes, seen the sea, a donkey, tasted ice-cream or eaten three square meals a day. Fran's heart had gone out to them, to a pair of recently orphaned children, in particular, Billy Petch and his sister Polly. Billy, a stalwart ten-year-old with a manly, couldn't care less attitude to life, and pretty little Polly, who had sobbed her heart out, at bedtime, over the loss of their mother.

Towards the end of that summer, she and Tom had been married in a simple ceremony at St Ives Parish Church, followed by a celebration party held in Meg Morgan's Gallery, an occasion attended by family and friends, including Gipsy and Ian, Ingrid, Ernie and their offspring, the entire artists' community, Tom's colleagues and, surprisingly, Alex Condermine. Fran had not expected him to accept her wedding invitation, sent as a gesture of goodwill, believing that he might not be up to a journey from Wiltshire to Cornwall. Even so, she'd been pleased to see him, and had greeted him warmly on this, the happiest day of her life.

'So you've made it at last, have you?' he'd said mischievously, holding her hands. 'About time, too, in my opinion. You'd never have been happy with that precious nephew of mine. He and that ex-Wren officer girlfriend of his are still living together, by the way, as snug as bugs in a rug, getting nowhere fast. And here you are, as pretty as a picture, as happy as a lark. Well, good luck to you, m'dear.' He grinned amiably. 'You'll never find a better kisser than me, that's for sure!'

Smiling mysteriously, Fran said, 'Wanna bet?'

Gipsy, pregnant once more, had confided that Quin and his girlfriend were in America. 'A concert tour,' she'd explained. 'That brother of mine is making quite a name for himself. Does Tom know about Quin, by the way?'

'Yes, I told him.'

'About ... the baby?'

'Of course. He had a right to know. How

354

could I have possibly married him otherwise?'

'Even knowing you risked losing him?' Gipsy asked.

'Rather that than a marriage based on subterfuge, half-truths, lies,' Fran said quietly. 'I trusted implicitly in Tom's understanding and forgiveness, and my faith in him was justified, as I knew it would be. Now, let's forget about the past, shall we, and concentrate on the future?'

But the past had a way of invading the present, and the next item of news, vouchsafed by Fran's brother Ernie, was something she wanted to hear, concerning Alan.

Speaking sotto voce, not wanting to be overheard by the other guests, Ernie said, 'I've heard tell that Alan's in South America. Argentina, by the postmark. No address, an' the letter wasn't signed, but I knew his handwriting. All it said was, "Not to worry, our mutual friend is doing fine, working as a ranch hand, so lots of freedom and fresh air. Plenty of grub, booze and women, and earning good money. He said to tell you he's sorry for the trouble he's caused you, and seeks your forgiveness." Well, that's it in a nutshell.'

'Thanks, Ernie,' Fran said huskily, 'that's my best wedding present of all.'

In the fullness of time, Fran and Tom had decided, if possible, to legally adopt Billy and Polly Petch as their own ready-made family. Not a straightforward proceeding, they had discovered; it entailed lengthy court appearances and in-depth questioning to establish their suitability as parents. Normally, younger couples were given preference in such cases. On the other hand, the Evanses had done sterling work on behalf of deprived youngsters, and Tom's latch-key children's appeal had weighed heavily in their favour.

They had won out in the long run, and Fran remembered, with infinite joy, the day that Billy and his sister had crossed the threshold of their new home.

It was then Fran had decided to close Ivy House as a hotel and café, to concentrate on motherhood. And yet, in his wisdom, Tom had understood her need for self-expression, hence his suggestion that she should open a café-cum-art gallery in the town centre of St Ives. In essence, a rebirth of Meg Morgan's Gallery and a venture to provide an outlet for her creative energies. Planning menus, arranging the paintings and meeting people would be good for her, Tom considered thoughtfully, especially since his own career often entailed long periods of absence from home. Roving reporters were meant to rove, to cover news stories and events abroad. Fascinating work, but tiring, involving seemingly endless hours of travel, overnight stays in foreign hotels, the burning of midnight oil writing reports, researching the next assignment, genning up on interviewees, making certain one had one's facts right.

All too often, Fran's letters had been

delayed, sent on to him in a bundle – letters filling in details of the children's progress, their exam results, visits to the dentist to have their teeth checked, Polly's interest in cookery, Billy's decision to become a reporter when he was old enough – just like his dad. Tom had seized on those letters as manna from heaven, those potent reminders of the home, children and wife he loved so much.

Whenever possible, he had rung Ivy House to speak to Fran, just to hear her voice across the miles of their separation, often through crackling atmospherics, to tell her he loved her, to hear her reply, 'I love you too, my darling.'

Now, in the twilight years of their marriage, in the quietude of Ivy House, getting up from her chair and crossing to the window to look up at the stars, Fran thanked God for the happiness and fulfilment the years of her marriage to Tom Evans had given her. True, they were growing old physically, but what matter? Deep down, Fran felt as young at heart as she had done on her wedding day, twenty-four years ago.

The stars were very bright tonight. Fran remembered the night, long ago, when she had first become aware of this treasure-trove of heaven. Hearing the familiar sound of the sea in the distance, she thought about the many roads she had travelled, through life, to achieve this homecoming of the heart.

Listening intently, she imagined she heard

the sound of voices, the laughter of friends, the tinkling of Meg Morgan's old joanna in the other room, the closing of the front door when the children came home from school, as hungry as hunters, calling out to her, 'Mummy, Mummy, where are you? What's for tea? We're starving!'

Thankfully, she had always been there for them, and so had Tom whenever he'd been given leave of absence from his globe-trotting. Times long over and done with now that Polly and Bill were grown up with families of their own to bring up and care for.

Occasionally, before Tom's retirement as a news correspondent, Fran had accompanied him on trips to Ireland, New York, Paris and Rome when the children were at university. But no matter how much she'd enjoyed her glimpses of cities far more glamorous than her own natural environment, she had always longed for her return to St Ives, to Ivy House. To her beloved Cornwall.

Now, here she was, a happy, fulfilled wife and mother, looking forward to her husbands return home – tomorrow.

Now, tomorrow was here! Getting out of Bill's car, Tom stood at the garden gate for a while, looking up at Ivy House, filled with the joyous anticipation of holding Fran in his arms once more.

Now, there she was, standing on the door-step to greet him, then hurrying down the path towards him, smiling, hands out-

358

stretched, her face aglow with the joy of seeing him safely back home again. Home, he thought: four walls encompassing the people he loved best on earth.

Gathering Fran into his arms, he whispered, 'I love you, mavourneen, I always have and I always will.'

'As I shall always love you, my darling,' she murmured contentedly, leading him indoors to continue their love story together.

Mrs Southgate

MB.

DES   JK.

इT

JP